Claudie's Kinfolks

By Dillon Anderson

I AND CLAUDIE
CLAUDIE'S KINFOLKS

DILLON ANDERSON

Claudie's Kinfolks

An Atlantic Monthly Press Book
Little, Brown and Company · Boston · Toronto

The author wishes to thank the following
magazines for their kind permission
to reprint material which previously
appeared in their pages: *The Atlantic
Monthly; Collier's; The Southwest Review.*

89B1887

ATLANTIC—LITTLE, BROWN BOOKS
ARE PUBLISHED BY
LITTLE, BROWN AND COMPANY
IN ASSOCIATION WITH
THE ATLANTIC MONTHLY PRESS

*Published simultaneously in Canada
by Little, Brown & Company (Canada) Limited*

PRINTED IN THE UNITED STATES OF AMERICA

*To the denizens of Bug Hill near
Independence, Texas; also to its
habitués and mortgagees*

Acknowledgments

Andrew Jackson Wray, Major Raymond Dickson, Birdsall Briscoe, Wheeler Nazro, Louis Letzerich the Dingbat, Eleanor Stierhem, Knox Burger, Joe Hutcheson, Henry Holland, Gerster Brown, Dutch Hohn, Frank Michaux, R. A. Cutter, Max Felix, Joe Johnston, John Wisdom and Mrs John, Mrs. Wirt Davis, Bobby Cutler, Roger Branigan, Bob Bowie, Joe Anderson, Mac Farrell, Ted Weeks, Dudley Cloud, Allen Maxwell, "Rattail" Foster, Phil Kidd, Richard Burns, Maude Tomlinson, George Fuermann and the various oil companies doing business in Texas have each, wittingly or unwittingly, contributed to the material in this book. In the case of the individuals named the contribution has been witting — in the form of encouragement, suggestions, and sometimes a willingness to read the material in its raw and first-draft form. The oil companies give away in filling stations excellent road maps of Texas — very valuable research material for such a volume as this.

D. A.

Contents

Claudie's Kinfolks

I

Thicker Than Water

PERSONALLY, I want to be fair. I never claimed that
Claudie didn't have his good points. The big lug — all
six and a half feet of him — grew up strong as an ox,
and just as clumsy. Also the Lord settled a stout musical
voice on Claudie. I'll admit that he always did sing a
fine brand of country bass, and some of the close places
he didn't work us out of he sang us out of — but he'd
sometimes forget the words of the song.

Another thing, Claudie always depended on me
plenty, and at times he was an awful burden to my
mind — active as it is. I mean over a lot of things he
just couldn't understand — even in Alabama where he
grew up.

Take relatives, as simple a thing as that. A lot of
Claudie's tribe had moved to Texas and done well, everybody said, and he had it in his mind that if he went
and visited them, some of this prosperity might rub
off on him. Why, all the years I and Claudie spent
chowsing around from pillar to post, never latching
onto a real good thing, these well-heeled Texas kin of
his were like a jack for his model-T mind.

"Claudie," I used to explain to him, over and over,

"when you get right down to it there ain't but two kinds of relatives you'd turn up — the ones you'd be ashamed of and the ones that would be ashamed of you. Don't you see? If you've done better than they have, you wouldn't want them hanging around mooching on you; now would you?"

"I don't 'spect I've done better than none of my kin, Clint," he'd answer with the same stubborn look that always skimmed his burly bran-colored face when he was losing an argument with me.

"But s'pose they've done better than you have? Why would they want you around?"

"Blood, they say, is thicker —"

"Yes, I know; I've heard that before. Blood is thicker than water — but not much."

This would always bring it up about Lafe Brim, Claudie's cousin that was so well off somewheres over in deep East Texas; Claudie claimed he had used to take Lafe fishing when they were little kids, and Lafe would be sure to remember him. And he would mention one he called Loblolly that was prominent in politics down in the Mexican border country, but Claudie didn't know the town Loblolly lived in either. Then he'd fall back on his Aunt Minnie Gastrick that didn't even live in Texas. She lived up in Oklahoma. She was the widow of a dead Osage Indian, and Claudie claimed she had more durn money than you could run and jump over. He'd admit, though, that she hadn't even seen him since he was in knee britches back in the potlicker belt of Alabama. Also, there was one that was a real sport Claudie always said — the one they called Windy. He'd grown up in Boggy Slough. That was the closest town to where Claudie's folks lived, and, according to Claudie, Windy had been in on several good things in the State of Texas. He never said, though, what they were. Why, he'd even bring it up, when I'd nearly argued him down, about his Cousin Eph that Claudie used to play hookey from school with — Eph that had gone to Texas on his uppers and got right rich selling junk in Port Arthur. But when Eph's name would come up, I'd always have to remind Claudie that Eph was dead.

I swear I never put any stock at all in any of these rich-kin rumors until that spring in Beaumont when our friend Jules Rabinowitz, the Persian Prophet from New Orleans, gave me and Claudie a free reading on our future.

Jules had put us up the night before in the back end of his Salon of the Persian Prophet that had been a barber shop before that, since the striped pole was still up in the front. But it had a bedroom in the rear with some extra cots. Also, Jules had lent us some hair oil, a little corn medicine for Claudie's feet, a fill of kerosene for our lantern, a cotter key that fitted our trailer house coupling, and enough coffee to last us two or three days. I and Claudie needed these things and a lot more, too, since we'd hit Beaumont pretty low the day before, and I don't know what we'd have done if I hadn't learned Jules was in town. Jules bought us a big hamburger apiece that night and cold beer, but that was only after we'd agreed to move along the next morning.

Well, the next morning came, and while we were having breakfast with Jules in the back part of the salon, it came out that he would have to stake us to about a five-dollar loan for gas and oil, a fresh spark plug and a few other things for the car and trailer house. "Otherwise," I'd pointed out to Jules, "how can I and Claudie make good on our deal to leave?"

Jules claimed he trusted Claudie and all that, and me too, he said; but just the same, he went along with us to see that we spent the five on nothing but what would make us ready to roll.

Then, just before we drove off, I had to tell Jules that I and Claudie were not headed for any place in particular and might not go very far after all. At this Jules's already little eyes narrowed and his plump lips puckered and tightened; then all of a sudden a fine, generous look loosened the skin all over his face, and he offered to give me and Claudie a reading on the house. "Won't cost you a cent," he said as he studied a map of Texas on a calendar hanging there in the kitchen. "I'll give you gents a full-dress rundown on your future. Will you have it with tea leaves or the crystal ball?"

"I like the ball better," I told him, and Claudie nodded.

We followed Jules into the parlor part of the salon where it was all hung heavy with dark curtains, and we studied the green glass chandelier while Jules got into his purple Persian robes. He sat down on his side of a table covered with blue velvet and put us on the other side where the regular customers sat to get their futures read.

Claudie said he wanted to know what all his rich Texas kin would be apt to do for him, and I told Jules I was interested in my fortune generally and the hell with mooching on any kinfolks.

Jules slid a shiny red satin cover off a big glass ball that had some kind of a light under it, and for a long time he sat there staring way deep down into it. I looked at Jules with his bald head shiny and slick like a peeled onion while his fluffy white hair fringed it all around. His green pea-sized eyes caught the light from the bottom of the crystal ball, and at certain angles they shone like a cat's eyes in a bright light at night.

"From the astral regions of occult infinity the stars yield their mysteries to me through the crystal ball," Jules began in a new voice. He talked slow and solemn, like a man in a pulpit reading from the Good Book itself.

"You wayfarers have wandered far and wide; you have gone to the uttermost parts of the South. You are on the threshold of the bountiful destiny that is due unto you by your providential and infinitesi-

mal rights. One of you, called Claudie Hughes, is a
sturdy worker in the vineyard. Manual labor is his
forte, if not his fortissimo, and his melodious bass
voice is like that of Taurus the bull . . ."

On Claudie, Jules had gone about as far as he could
go, and he paused for breath.

"The other — Clinton Hightower by name — pos-
sesses much wit and charm. He is blessed with executive ability, a very useful talent for conserving the
sweat of the brow. You two thus have abilities which,
properly combined, will lead on to victory and success.
But in recent times your harvest of the Lord's boun-
ties has been lean indeed. In fact, you sorry dead-beats
both landed in Beaumont yesterday flat broke."

"You can say that again, Jules," I spoke up, but he
didn't; he was really in a steep trance by this time,
and I doubt if he heard me at all. He didn't even slack
up before he went on. "Your entire horoscopes are
cast in double image before me now. Clint's future is
bright, too, and in the same firmament with Claudie's
blood relations. I figure if you'll set still I can handle
both your fortunes at one reading."

"Howzat?" Claudie asked.

"Shut up, Claudie, and leave him alone," I scolded.
"Can't you see Jules is only on the near edge of our
fortune. This is going to be a double-header."

"Claudie's kinsmen," Jules lectured right ahead,
"have prospered indeed in the great Texas empire.
And these opulent kinsmen are kind people, as I see

the crystal; generous to a fault also. At the hands of these blood relations you will be well received. I see them scattered to the four corners of the state, and for every one who will be kindly disposed I see a bright star in the crystal ball where all is spread before me.

"Ah, there is special brightness. Let me see. It comes through now clearer than before, in luminous splendor, and the city appears to be El Paso. Claudie's kinsmen there have prospered mightily. Now let us look further in the western portion of the state."

Then Jules threw his hand up before his eyes and ducked like he'd been swung on. "The vibrations! They're dazzling," he said. "There's a light that just flashed with the brightness of the noonday sun. And every last one of the vibrations I'm feeling is a pure thousand-watter — cosmic as hell too, men. This is sensational! There's something terrific in store for you both in the west."

Jules shaded his eyes and tried to look again into the crystal, but it was too bright for him. It plain blinded him.

"Truly, gents," he said, "in all my years as a seer I've never come across anything like this. My crystal is a new model, guaranteed to handle all fortunes except kings, dukes, presidents and the Grand Exalted Rulers of certain lodges, but what I'm seeing puts an awful strain on its capacity. It's really not built to handle a future as bright as I see for you here. You men are destined for something colossal. The spot is Amarillo or its environs. The light is so bright I cannot place it in the city exactly."

"Could you draw a little finer bead there, Jules?" I asked. "I mean like a name or a street address in El Paso or Amarillo. A little more work right now might save us a lot of time later on out there where there's so much space."

"The stars," he said, coming out of his trance fast, "do not reveal matters of pure detail. Surely you don't have to be spoon-fed your fortunes. Get high behind. Get a move on and use your wits. Be aggressive in dealing with this well-heeled kin. Step right up and stand up for your rights!"

Even after he'd switched off the light under the crystal ball, shucked out of his Persian robes, and opened the windows, Jules said the air in the room was still so full of cosmic vibrations that he could hardly get his breath. We went outside so Jules could breathe some fresh air, and I borrowed his road map to study the way to Amarillo before we left. I noticed one thing here that bothered me some. The only place in Texas farther away from Beaumont than El Paso, where the light was awful bright, turned out to be Amarillo where it had damn near blinded Jules. But it was Amarillo we left for.

We had trouble with both trailer house tires north of Liberty, and it was after dark when we got to Cleveland. We parked behind a filling station and put up for the night there.

"What's cosmic vibrations, Clint?" Claudie wanted to know just before we turned in.

"Cosmic vibrations are about the most important ones of all. Understand?"

He said he was beginning to, so I explained I was a little tired and would tell him the rest next morning.

2

There is a big brindle depot in Cleveland where two railroads cross, the B. & W. and the H. E. & W. T. The first stands for Beaumont and Western, and the second for Houston, East and West Texas, but in Cleveland they call one the Boll Weevil and the other Hell Either Way Took.

I and Claudie used the public part of this depot early the next morning and took off for Amarillo, which, according to Jules's road map I'd kept, was not over a thousand miles from Cleveland.

It was a warm April day, and all the signs of spring were thick about us. Birds were singing, clean little flowers in several pale colors were growing alongside the road, and the dogwood blooms in the woods made the green leaves look greener.

As we drove along, Claudie kept throwing his shoulders back and sticking his chin forward like a man standing up for his rights. He was doing the part of his fortune that he'd understood all by himself. I found I was feeling pretty good, too, breathing scents of new buds and wild onions. We rode until, just as we were passing a side road marked by a sign that said "Burdenville 5 Miles," Claudie yelled. "That's it, Clint; that's the name of the town." He pulled the emergency, and we stopped in a cloud of dust.

"What's up?" I asked. "You know these tires won't stand that kind of a stop."

"Burdenville," Claudie went on. "It's the name of the town I've been tryin' to 'member ever since we come to Texas. It's where Cousin Lafe Brim lives. Let's go visit Lafe." As he said this he backed up fast, liked to broke the trailer coupling, and turned into the side road toward Burdenville. He didn't even wait for me to agree.

It was a very poor road, sandy, crooked, and rutted, but we made it. Just as the one o'clock whistle on the sawmill was blowing, we pulled into Burdenville and saw that it wasn't much of a town at that. Claudie wanted to rush right out and find Lafe. "No, Claudie," I said. "That is hardly the way to go about it."

"Why not?" he wanted to know, and I told him: "There is more to the art of visiting kinfolks than you'd think, Claudie. You don't just throw yourself at them. That's not what Jules meant by aggressive. That's the way poor relations would do, and poor relations are poison. You've got to make kinfolks wonder if you haven't maybe done better than they thought. Let them suspect you might die first and leave *them* something. Kinfolks in such a frame of mind will kill the fatted calf for you."

Claudie gave in on this, but said he was bothered some about the way our old car would look to Lafe. I told him to forget it. "It's exactly the kind of car that a stingy relative would be driving so he could hoard up his money," I explained. "Also, he can see no money's been wasted on this old trailer house of ours."

"I guess so," Claudie allowed. "But what do we do next?"

"In the first place," I told him, "you can't let Lafe see you with that hungry look on your face." Claudie always looks hungry except right after he's eaten.

"But we're down to less than two dollars, Clint," he argued. "We can't let ourselves run plumb out."

"O.K. But I think we can do a lot for about thirty cents. Look right there across the street," I said and pointed to a sign that read: "Steve Stewart's Café — Chili 15 Cents." We went in and asked for two chilis with crackers.

The noon hour was over, and we didn't see anybody in the café but the fellow behind the counter that took our order. He was a big, heavy-set citizen with a fat face and droopy eyes. He quit picking his teeth and yelled "Medium twice" as he started walking back toward the rear of the café. By the time he got there, a big hand stuck two bowls of chili through a hole in the wall, and Steve slid them down the counter toward us.

The crackers were in a round blue bowl in front of us, and we went to work on the chili. After we'd eaten about half our chilis and all the crackers, I asked Steve for more crackers and some tomato ketchup. "Please," I said. His face clouded up a little, but he dipped the cracker bowl into a barrel under the counter and set it out again, full. Then he went back and opened a ketchup bottle that he slid down the counter until it came to a stop right in front of us.

I filled my chili bowl with ketchup, and so did Claudie. It took the whole bottle, and I could see Steve watching us out of the corner of his eye. By this time he wasn't picking his teeth any more. He was gouging himself with the toothpick.

When our chili bowls were half empty again and the crackers were all gone, I spoke to Steve and asked for some more ketchup and crackers — in a nice way, too.

"Oh, no, you don't," Steve said. "Not today. You've done et a quarter's worth of crackers, and that ketchup costs me twenty-three cents a bottle wholesale. What the devil do you fellers expect with two fifteen-cent bowls of chili?"

"Crackers and ketchup," I answered. "Do you furnish them with chili or not?"

"Yes, but —" Steve started.

"All right, then," I went on; "please pass the crackers and ketchup."

By this time Steve was right across the counter from us, with his hands on his hips and his legs spread apart. He stood just like a man that was not going to pass us anything else.

"Kindly remember, Steve," I said, "we have not paid you yet. Please pass everything that goes with chili."

Steve said he'd see that we paid, all right, and I said we would stand up for our rights. This seemed to ring a bell with Claudie, and he stood up, threw his shoulders back, and stuck his chin out at Steve. But there was something about Claudie, with his face hanging there over the counter, that Steve couldn't stand, and he let Claudie have it on the point of his chin. That was about the worst thing Steve could have done, because it caught Claudie right in the middle of standing up for his rights, and it fretted him.

He reeled and staggered back from Steve's lick, then he reached for Steve's collar. It was loose enough for Claudie to get his left hand inside the front of it, so he pulled Steve forward and bent him clear over the counter. Then, with his right hand, Claudie slapped Steve's face five or six times until Steve sagged and yelled, "Sonny, Sonny, come here! Help!"

A big fat boy about eighteen or nineteen came running through a swinging door in the back of the café and made for us. Claudie turned Steve loose and got ready for Sonny. While Steve panted and rubbed his face, Claudie and Sonny squared off. Sonny put his fists up before his face and started to weave and shadowbox. I could see he'd fought before, but he didn't have time to go far into his act before Claudie grabbed him by the shoulders and started to shake him. He was very rough about it, like a terrier will shake a rat, and pretty soon Sonny's tongue was hanging out; his face turned fire-engine red, and he was down on his knees. It all happened before I had a chance to hit anybody.

Steve and Sonny were done; they'd had enough, I could tell, so I put fifteen cents on the counter.

"This is for half of two chilis," I said to Steve. "The other half of both chilis is there in the bowls." Then I and Claudie walked out and let the screen door to Steve's café slam hard.

"Come on now, Claudie," I said, "let's find the hotel before we go to see Lafe. A relative that is registered in a hotel looks a sight better than one with a wicker suitcase at the front gate."

Claudie was ready. Also, he was a little ruffled from the fight and in need of sprucing himself up before meeting any kinfolks. It cost us four bits apiece in advance for a room at the Ritz Hotel, a painted two-story affair across the street from the railroad freight station. The room clerk that was also the depot agent came over and took our money; he told us that Lafe Brim lived a mile or so out of town on the road we'd just come over. Then he went back across the street to his other job.

We washed up and shaved and got into the cleanest

clothes we had, but Claudie fussed some about the
dollar we'd spent.

"It's like bread, Claudie," I kept telling him, "that's
been cast upon the water. It'll come back in sandwiches, and maybe dessert with whipped cream."

Claudie laced his shoes all the way up and said he
was ready to go. In fact, he was in such a hurry that we
left our razor, hair oil, comb, some dirty clothes, and
about everything we owned in the world, except the
car and trailer, scattered around that room at the Ritz
Hotel.

3

Lafe Brim's house was painted yellow, and it had
two chimneys, one at each end. Several big cedar and
magnolia trees shaded the front porch. The fences
around the place were all up, the hay was stacked in
even ricks, and the stock in the pasture looked fat and
well-fed. From these signs and the big barn in the rear
I could tell that a visit with Lafe would be worth
while if we handled it right.

We waited outside the yard gate until a colored man
came from behind the house and called the dogs
off. Then Lafe came up from the barn and Claudie rec-
ognized him. "Hello, Lafe; it's me, your Cousin Claudie," he yelled.

"Hello, Claudie," he said. At first Lafe did not seem to be as joyful as Claudie was, but when I let it drop that we were staying at the Ritz Hotel in Burdenville, Lafe asked us if we wouldn't like to come in and have a bite to eat; he thought there would be some cheese and crackers for us. I told him no, thanks, we'd just eaten our fill and weren't much hungry. This made a big hit with Lafe, and he urged us to kindly come into the parlor so we could meet the missus.

As we went into the house I thought I did not know when I had seen such a scrawny-looking man as Claudie's Cousin Lafe — living there on a place, too, where the stock seemed so well-fed. Lafe wouldn't have weighed over one hundred fifteen pounds wringing wet, his face was thin and gaunt, and his eyes were both sunk way in.

Lafe's wife, Eunice, would have made three of him, anyhow. She was built like four pillows, and it seemed she was the one that owned the place where they lived. It had belonged to Enman, her first husband, Eunice let us know pretty soon; and after he'd wasted away and died, she'd married Lafe. She brought us some lemonade in the parlor and showed us several pictures of this first husband of hers. She went on to tell us the whole story of how she'd waited on Enman day and night for nearly five years while he was losing weight and getting weaker before he finally passed on to his reward. Then she pointed out that Lafe, himself, had lost twenty-two pounds in the three years he'd been married to her. Lafe nodded his head in very solemn agreement.

Eunice spoke next, with feeling and pride, I thought, about how sick one of the neighbors was that very afternoon. "She is very low," Eunice stated, "and if you ask me, she will not last through the night." Nobody asked anybody anything, but Eunice added that as soon as the milk was put away she was going down the road to sit at the sick bedside all night long.

It was about sundown when the colored man came up to the house with the night's milking — two big foamy pails. Eunice went back to strain the milk, and Lafe asked us if we could stay to supper. I agreed that we would stay to eat and keep him company; so when Eunice came in to tell us good-by, Lafe told her that I and Claudie would stay to have a bite of cheese and crackers with him. At this second mention of cheese and crackers, Claudie looked like a man that had lost his last coon dog. I knew his mind was wandering back to the dollar we'd wasted at the Ritz Hotel.

Now I have seen big changes come over people in my time, like when they get religion or snake-bit; but I never saw anything before to match what happened to Claudie's Cousin Lafe as soon as Eunice left for the night. Lafe's hospitality boiled over. First he brought out a brown jug full of strong red whiskey and gave us each a big swig. Then he took one himself, blew out a big breath, smacked his lips, and actually seemed to gain ten or fifteen pounds in weight. Lafe stated that his mention of cheese and crackers had been only for Eunice's ears. There was a cold roast in the oven, he told us, and we'd divide it three ways as soon as we gave the liquor a better chance to whet up our appetites. While Lafe was gone to get some water to wash the next drink down with, I spoke to Claudie. "See what I mean?" I said. "With your kinfolks we are now right in the groove. Jules really had the right dope."

"I'll say," Claudie answered.

Lafe had no sooner come back with the pitcher of water than the phone on the wall started ringing fast and fierce. It jangled out a short, a long and three shorts, and Lafe jumped for it. "That's our ring," he said.

After he'd said hello, Lafe listened for a long time and then said, "Well, I'll be durned. The Kommanding Kleagle himself." He listened some more and went on, "Why, the dirty jackasses! They must not have knowed that Steve was the Ku Klux Kleagle or that Sonny was Kleagle of the Ku Klux Kubs."

The rest of what Lafe said came in a blur until I heard him hang up. But his last words rang in my ears. "Sure; eight o'clock in front of the Ritz."

Lafe turned back to us and his eyes were all ablaze. He looked as if he'd gained another eight or ten pounds.

"I've got to go, men," he said. "I've got to be at the Ku Klux Klan meeting at eight," he went on. "Two tramps come to Burdenville today and beat up the

Kommanding Kleagle of the Klan, Steve Stewart. Right in his own place of business, too. Then they beat up his boy, Sonny. We're gonna tar and feather them both and ride them out of town on a rail."

As I watched Claudie's face go blinky, I found the mixed taste of chili and crackers and whiskey boil up in the back of my mouth; then I heard Lafe saying, "It'll be a lot of fun. You fellers want to come along?" Claudie sat there squirming like a catfish as Lafe went on: "I've got a spare hood here in the chifforobe, and there's another one upstairs. It used to belong to Enman. There are plenty of sheets around here, too."

"When do we suit up?" I asked, quick as lightning, and Lafe's answer was to run upstairs to get Enman's hood.

As soon as Lafe was gone, Claudie jumped out of his chair and said, "That's us they're after, Clint. Let's get out of here; let's beat it."

"Wait a minute, Claudie; hold it. I know it's us they're after, but you're way out of tune with your cosmic vibrations. Where could we be safer than in a hood?"

Before Claudie could think up an answer, Lafe was back with the dead man's hood. It was a nice fit for Claudie, but it took him a few minutes to get used to it. We found that Lafe's own spare hood was a perfect fit for me, and since sheets will fit anybody, we were soon macked out for the night. Then, just before we took off, I said, "Do you suppose we have time for one

more swig from that jug before we go, Lafe? I believe
Claudie needs it." Lafe looked at the clock on the
mantel and said we had just about enough time.

4

When we got to town, we could see the big fiery
cross in the middle of the street that ran between the
railroad station and the Ritz Hotel. Fifty or sixty
sheets were gathered there, and others were coming
up from all sides. As we joined the crowd we saw a
three-legged washpot there beside the fiery cross. It
was full of tar, and it had live coals of fire under it so
the tar wouldn't get too sticky. Alongside was a duckin
sack they said was full of goose and guinea feathers.

Pretty soon one of the sheets climbed up in the rear
end of a touring car and started talking. It was Steve
Stewart, the Kleagle, all right; I could tell his was the
same voice as the one that had lost the argument with
us about the tomato ketchup that afternoon. First he
was saying something about the sacred unfailing bond
of the Ku Klux Klan, and next he was saying some
very mean things about me and Claudie — but mainly
about Claudie. I nudged Claudie and started to ask
him to hold his temper, but it was not Claudie I
nudged. I stopped myself just in time, though; then I
looked everywhere for him. But they all looked big,
and they all looked so much alike that I knew I had

lost Claudie. Made me feel right lonesome for a minute.

"The tramps are in Room Number 3 on the second floor," I heard the Kleagle say, and I knew he had the room number right. "That brings us," he went on, "to the business part of the meeting." The time had come, the Kleagle pointed out, for somebody to go inside and bring the tramps out.

Everything got graveyard quiet at that statement, and I could hear the crackle of the flames on the fiery cross that the Kleagle was holding up above his head. A heavy voice from one of the sheets said, "Why don't you go in, Steve?" but Steve answered that that was no part of the job for the Kleagle himself. Then he called for silence and said, "Once more, in the sacred, unfailing bond, is there nobody who is going to step inside and bring them tramps out?"

About this time two sheets moved, one from way over to the left, and the other from somewhere in the center of the crowd. They came together below the fiery cross at about the same time, and the Kleagle picked out the biggest one to go on this mission for the Klan. He thanked the sheet he hadn't picked, while the other went in. I felt sure that I and Claudie were the only ones that night that knew what the report would be — I mean about the tramps being gone. And when the Kleagle got the report, he really lost his temper. He said, by God we'd wait until the tramps came back. So, while we waited I tried again to find Claudie, but still it was no use. One sheet that I thought was Claudie was not; it was a fellow that took me for his brother. He spoke of a Jersey cow he wanted bred to my registered bull. "Any time," I said and moved away as fast as a man in a sheet can move.

I don't know how long we'd have waited if the hotel clerk hadn't come across the street from his depot job and told the Kleagle that the tramps had left the Ritz that afternoon to go to Lafe Brim's place. Right away a lot of loud talk ripped and snorted through the crowd about running the tramps down at Lafe's place. Then the Kleagle spoke up and showed he was a real leader; he stated that we would run them down at Lafe's place. He pointed out there was a short cut; we could follow the railroad track and go through the back gate to Lafe's pasture if Lafe would go in the lead to show us how to get there. That way, the Kleagle said, we should slip up on the tramps from the rear. At this, the sheet with Lafe in it went forward and said, "O.K., Steve, let's go," so the Kleagle handed him the fiery cross and we took off.

As we marched single file down the railroad track, I turned my mind on Lafe. I figured he was bound to know by that time what I and Claudie knew. But whose side was Lafe on? Blood, I calculated, was a little thicker than water, but who knew how it would stack up against hot tar and feathers with the whole Burdenville Chapter of the Ku Klux Klan thrown in? I didn't know the answer to this, but one thing was clear: I belonged as close to the head of the line with Claudie's Cousin Lafe as I could get. The closer I got, the fewer sheets there'd be between me and Lafe's place where our car was. So I scrambled ahead along the rough, uneven ballast on the sides of the railroad track; and when we passed a siding where there was more room, I moved ahead until I was right behind Lafe. By this time the fiery cross had burned plumb out, and my eyes were getting used to the pitch-dark.

When we got to the turning-off place Lafe yelled back and started down the dump. I was right alongside him as he walked through the muddy burrow pit to the wire gap that led into his pasture. Ahead I could barely see the outline of a little clump of trees and, beyond, Lafe's big barn.

Lafe said he had the cross on his hands and needed some help with the barbed-wire gap. I tried it, but it was too tight a gap for a man of my weight, so, while the rest came toward us from the railroad track, another sheet came up and opened the gap fast. "Ouch! Durn that barbed wire," the other sheet said, and it was Claudie. It made me downright proud of him — a man that I'd seen baffled by many a loose, easy gap in broad-open daylight.

"Claudie," I said in a low voice, "it's me, Clint. Let's stay right behind Lafe and we might be able to make a break for the car."

"Not," Lafe cut in, "until after you fellers get beyond that elm mott there ahead of us. It's pretty thick.

Let me go first and show you the way through it." I thought I'd never heard even my own kinfolks sound so good as Lafe did.

Next we were in the pitch-dark of the narrow path that led through the trees, and the only noise was the clump, clump of all the sheets walking along behind us. The black muggy air was crammed and jammed with the heavy vibrations of something about to happen; then the still scary corner of the world in the elm mott blew up. It exploded!

I am sure that no lions and tigers fighting over a carcass in Africa ever raised a ruckus so fierce or furious as the one that boiled up in the mott. Roars and growls and screams cut through the night-quiet like a thousand dull saws on a knotty log, and the sheets shot out in all directions. People ran into trees, they ran into each other, and they ran right out of the sheets. But they all got away, and in a few minutes nothing was left but empty sheets on the trees and along the barbed wire around Lafe's pasture.

When I ran, I went toward Lafe's house where our car was parked. Claudie was there beside the car, and he was out of his sheet. Lafe was standing there, too, and he was about the calmest man in his talk I'd ever heard. He said, "I'd plumb forgot about Samantha, the old brood sow. She had a big litter down in the mott night before last, and you know how fractious a sow with a young litter can be. You fellers like a little drink?"

"No, Lafe, I believe not," I told him as I stepped on the starter. "I and Claudie better move along, I expect. It's getting a little late."

When we got to the Cleveland road where we'd turned off that morning I spoke to Claudie in a very serious way. "Claudie," I said, "we'd better travel as far tonight as our gasoline will take us. We haven't lost a thing in Burdenville. Except what we left at the Ritz." I added. "But we can't go back." Then I saw that Claudie had something in his hand. It was our razor. He dug around some more in his clothes, and I soon saw that he had on, or in his pockets, everything we'd left at the Ritz Hotel.

"Remember, Clint," Claudie spoke up, "Jules said, 'Be aggressive.' He said, 'Step right up,' and that's what I done when the Kleagle wanted somebody to go to our room."

"What I don't understand," I said, "is why the Kleagle picked you instead of the other sheet that stepped right up at the same time. Wonder who that was."

Claudie chuckled, "You can't fool me, Clint. I knowed you was the other one."

It made me almost sorry I hadn't been, but something big and fine rose up in me the way it always does in a pinch. I couldn't let him down, so I said, "You are a hard man to fool, Claudie."

I I

Lady Poetess

IT WAS BETWEEN his Texas relatives, you might put it, when love came to Claudie that same spring — between his Cousin Lafe Brim that had married the farm down below Burdenville, and Amarillo where Jules Rabinowitz's vibrations had spotted an awful good thing along the kinfolks line.

Where this love came to Claudie wasn't anywhere near Amarillo though; it wasn't even halfway. It was on a sandy creek bank in Denton County near the place where some gears in our car broke down. Also one of the trailer house tires had come plumb off the wheel in a deep sandy rut in the road that even the red ants wouldn't cross in dry weather.

Well, I'd been the one that had to find the Billingsley farm close by, and I'd been the one to work out the deal with Mr. Billingsley for us to fish on shares there in Little Ellum Creek alongside the Billingsley place.

Then, with spring blooming all around us, the fish getting better by the day, the birds singing more and prettier in the freshly green trees, there was a feeling in the air that, without the help of anybody's kinfolks, something really worth while might turn up any time. You know how it is in the spring of the year.

This was when Claudie had to go and fall for the lady poetess. I remember well the morning it happened. Claudie was sitting there on a willow stump looking at an old newspaper. I was watching the trotline we had strung out across the bluish-green hole in Billingsley's Bend, thinking some very confidential things about Lilly Lee, the oldest Billingsley girl, and the beautiful way her hips swayed when she walked; also, how everything was more so when she ran. And when Claudie spoke up I hardly heard him. "How's that?" I said.

"I said this shore is a pretty woman, Clint — here in the Denton newspaper. Says she's a lady poetess." And as he spoke I couldn't help noticing the mushy look that bridled Claudie's long, horse-type face.

Well, only so as to please Claudie, I went over and took a right close look at the slick, brown-and-white part of the newspaper that had the picture of the pretty woman in it. At that, it took me quite a few minutes to get my mind off of Lilly Lee Billingsley and onto the picture of the lady poetess there in the newspaper. She looked to me like an old-fashioned girl that hadn't been around a great deal, this lady poetess. She had big, sad-looking eyes, and they were cast down toward, say, the feet of the person taking the picture. Her hair was done up in a kind of a fluffy pile on top, and she was wearing a heart-shaped locket.

Still, in spite of the sad look in her eyes and all, damned if she wasn't actually smiling a little in the picture — like, maybe, a girl that was of a mind to break down and enjoy life, if she didn't have a tragic past or a bad liver or something like that. Below the picture it had her name in print, "Emma Rhodes Sylvester, Local Poetess."

The piece in the paper went on to tell how Emma, when she wasn't writing poetry or giving her poems at recitals, worked in a millinery store in Denton.

"Sure she's your type, Claudie?" I asked him.

"The Good Lord must've made somebody for everybody, and she looks like the one for me," he said.

"Claudie," I said to him, "I'm afraid it's only the time of the year that's got ahold of you, and —"

What changed the subject here was a yank on our trotline, so Claudie bailed out the skiff and paddled over to take a big, flapping, yellow catfish off; but when he came back from stringing him and rebaiting the hook with pork rind, Claudie still hadn't taken his mind off of Emma Rhodes Sylvester. He said the main thing he wanted to do was to go right in to Denton and see her.

"Claudie," I said, "you can farm and you can fish and you can sing bass, but I'm afraid you hardly belong to Emma's social set. She's very well known for her poetry and all, and that's pretty high society around here."

"Well," he said, "maybe you could get us into some

high Denton society." I knew then that Claudie was sure enough smitten, to be talking such a way as that.

"The only way you get into any society that is higher than what you are already in is if you are a social climber. Now you wouldn't want us to be any social climbers, would you?" I said "social climbers" in the same way that you say "rotten eggs," and Claudie said, "Oh, no. I shore wouldn't, Clint."

"Well, then," I said, "about the only deal I can think of for you is to write a little poetry your own self."

"And would that make me a social climber?" Claudie wanted to know right off.

"That, Claudie," I told him, "depends on what kind of stuff you turn out. If it's too fancy and hard to understand, you are getting pretty close."

About this time old man Billingsley came whistling along to weigh and gather up our day's catch, and Claudie helped him.

I looked at scrawny old Jonathan Billingsley, with his crooked nose and goose-foot skin, and as I watched him weigh the fish, I thought a lot of fine thoughts about the Good Lord and Mother Nature. I thought about how wonderful it was that that scrubby old crock and Mrs. Billingsley, as big around as a bale of cotton and blamed near as heavy, could ever have produced Lilly Lee, their oldest daughter. Lilly Lee had light green eyes, and shiny brown hair, and a swaying sweetness in her walk that a man, once he'd seen it, could never forget. I hadn't seen her that day, but I might as well have, since about everything I looked at — from turtles on the creek bank to bluebirds in the willow trees — reminded me of Lilly Lee.

"Mr. Billingsley," I said, when he'd finished, "I believe we'd like for you to leave that last little channel cat, so Claudie can fry him for our supper tonight. If you've already weighed him, just uncount that part, will you?"

"It's all the same to me," he said. "He weighed two and a half pounds. That knocks off twenty-five cents."

Then Jonathan Billingsley paid us three dollars and eighty cents for the thirty-eight pounds of catfish he had weighed up, and we gave him a nice gar we'd caught, for the old Billingsley tomcat's supper. Jonathan didn't have a child that he was any fonder of than that old, yellow tomcat — Bruce was his name — and when we handed the old man that fat gar for Bruce, he sat right down on a log for a little visit with us. He fired up an old black pipe that smelled like dead stovewood when it burned, and said, "You fellers figuring to stay here much longer?"

"We've got a big deal in Amarillo," I said, "but we like it here pretty well. And right now we're not quite ready to leave. Claudie's about got him a sweetheart in Denton."

"You don't say," Jonathan said. "Well, they's another feller wants to fish this hole too, but I told him you all had first call on it if you wanted to stay on. You have done pretty good so far, and the nickel a pound I make on these fish at Denton keeps my gasoline bill paid up."

"We'll stay," I said, my mind back on Lilly Lee again, "a while longer."

And about this time Lilly Lee herself, in a little old summery gingham dress, came running down the path. She said, "Hello, fellas," to me and Claudie both, and smiled big; then she sat on the log there by Jonathan, looking pretty as a big dish of strawberry shortcake.

"They's just one more thing, then," the old man went on. "I'd like for you to agree to stay on till the bees swarm. That ought to be sometime in June, and I'll need you then. Women and kids is no good with bees." Lilly Lee giggled at this and showed her pretty white teeth.

"Claudie here is a fair man with bees," I stated. "He'll be on hand if you need any help when they swarm."

After Lilly Lee and the old man had carried the fish up the steep sandy path that led away from our creek bank, Claudie spoke up. "Clint," he said, "why did you have to go and tell him I was a good hand with bees? I don't know ary thing about bees."

"I only told him you were fair," I said. "There's nothing to being fair. I'll tell you what to do when the time comes. Also we've got to stay here and save up some more money before we make the run for Amarillo. We don't want to land on our uppers in the hottest spot Jules found for us in the whole State of Texas."

I expect I'd have forgotten all about the picture of the lady poetess in the Denton paper if it hadn't been for the way Claudie acted next morning. Right off he shaved, and it wasn't his day to shave at all. The reason why, I soon found out; it was so he could skip over his upper lip. He said he believed he might look different with a mustache, and he hardly wanted the lady poetess to see him the way he'd always been. Also, he parted his hair away over on one side, to change some more the regular way he'd looked before he'd fallen for Emma Rhodes Sylvester. He was getting different all right, and one person that noticed it was Lilly Lee, when she came down to the trailer house that morning with old man Billingsley. "Claudie's getting to be a dude," she said and giggled, just before she ran back up the path ahead of the old man. She was always that way it seemed; never would settle down and talk; always wanting to run off.

Have I mentioned how fast Lilly Lee could run? As fast as a jack rabbit anyhow. She never wore enough clothes to slow her down, and when she'd run, round muscles seemed to spring up everywhere and all work together to make her go faster and look prettier.

"What's a ode, Clint?" Claudie asked me, a little while after Lilly Lee had run up the path.

"A what?" I said. "Can't you let a man sit and think?"

"It says here that Emma Rhodes Sylvester won a prize because she wrote up a ode."

"What kind of an ode?" I asked him. I really wasn't paying him a lot of mind, if you want to know the truth.

"A ode to a urn. Reckon that's the kind of poetry for me?"

"One to a churn would be more your speed, Claudie," I said.

"That wouldn't make me any social climber, would it, Clint?"

"No, come to think of it, I don't believe it would. But why don't you do one on Nature? After all, Mother Nature has rigged up a hell of a lot of beauty around here, and some of it must be worth sweating out a rhyme over. Just look around you, Claudie. Then think up some words that rhyme."

"Maybe I could do one about Lilly Lee."

"Listen, Claudie," I said, "aren't you getting a little mixed up with who it is you've fallen for? You wouldn't be untrue to the lady poetess, now, would you? I expect you'd better leave Lilly Lee to me."

"I guess you're right, Clint," he said.

That afternoon Lilly Lee came to the creek to fish for perch; and I would have had a real chance to settle down and talk some with her if she hadn't brought along that little wart, Luke, the youngest Billingsley kid. Luke was about seven or eight; he was snaggle-toothed, and I never saw him when he didn't have a terrible cold. He wanted to know right off whether fish could hear, and I told him sure they could, and to be quiet or they wouldn't bite. Then he wanted to know why mules didn't have colts, whether a policeman could arrest God, whether I had hair on my chest, why snakes didn't belch, and where Claudie was.

"Claudie," I said, "is in the trailer house. He's writing a poem, Luke, and you'd better be quiet or he'll come out here and eat your ears off. He's awful fractious when he's writing poetry."

Lilly Lee told Luke to shut up; she boxed his jaw a couple of times so he'd know she meant it; then she wanted to know what had come over Claudie that he was writing a poem. I rolled me a cigarette and one for her and told her all about Claudie and Emma Rhodes Sylvester. "He's got her picture from the Denton paper pinned up right there inside the trailer house," I told Lilly Lee and laughed. She did too, but not much; then her eyes got very narrow all of a sudden, and she seemed to be serious. I figured she wasn't believing me much in what I'd told her about Claudie.

Along about then Luke caught him a little perch the size of a bar of soap and said he wanted to take it up to the house so he could gut it and fry it. Lilly Lee said no, he'd better stay; but Luke started to cry, and I said, "Let him go, Lilly Lee. He's going to catch his death of cold if he stays on this damp creek bank any longer." She told him to go ahead; then she seemed a little shy to be there alone with me for the first time; but she stayed.

It was a nice warm afternoon — May by this time — and the crickets were chirping friendly in the grass, two scissortails were making their nest in a tree right up over us, and the wild verbena had our world there on the creek bank fixed up with a solid blue carpet. I watched a pert little green lizard turn brown on a chunk on the bank of the creek; then I threw a rock that scared him so he jumped onto a sycamore leaf and turned back green again — all before I even said another word to Lilly Lee. What I finally said was, "Have you been looking at that little lizard too, Lilly Lee?"

"Uh-huh," she answered, and smiled, but without looking at me.

"You're a mighty pretty girl, Lilly Lee," I told her. She looked me right in the eye for the first time and said, "I don't know what Claudie sees in that lady poetess."

Before I could tell her, I heard Claudie calling me from the trailer house. He yelled, "Clint, can you think of a word that rhymes with woolly worm?"

I believe this was when Lilly Lee really began to believe the whole story about Claudie and his poetry. We got up from the bank and walked to the trailer house, where Claudie was sitting on the floor beside the lantern with the stub of a broken pencil in his mouth. When he saw Lilly Lee with me he hung his head and grinned.

"Claudie," I said, "there ain't a word in the English language that will rhyme with woolly worm. Why did you have to pick one for your poem? Try something else."

"How about squirm?" he asked.

"O.K., Claudie, O.K. Let's see you work up some poetic thoughts that squirm."

"But I've done wrote it down," Claudie said, "and there he is, right there on tne lantern." I looked, and sure enough, there he was; and as woolly worms go, he wasn't a bad-looking one, with brown and black fuzz in even rows around him and a little orange streak that ran all the way down his back.

I noticed next that Lilly Lee was not looking at any woolly worm. She was standing with her hands on her hips, staring at Emma's picture pinned up there inside the trailer house. She looked almost mad or hurt, and it seemed for a minute that tears would come in her eyes. Then she turned and ran as hard as she could go up the path toward the house. After she'd passed the bend in the path, I turned back to Claudie and saw that he'd been watching Lilly Lee run, too.

"Remember, Claudie," I told him, "it's Emma Rhodes Sylvester you love."

The next day the Billingsley storm cellar caved in, and with the whole family digging for the food they'd stored there, the old man let me and Claudie take the

fish into Denton before they went bad. We went in
Jonathan's old pickup. This gave us our first chance to
find out whether he'd been gypping us on the fish we'd
been catching; and it made us both feel mighty good
to learn that, sure enough, fifteen cents a pound was
all that catfish brought in the Denton market.

While Claudie helped them patch up a leaky tube at
the garage, I went up to the courthouse square where
the stores were. I bought some corn medicine and got
a free almanac; then, on the way back to the garage,
I really got stunned — beauty stunned, I mean. It happened so quick — she came out of the Elite Millinery
store across the street from me and drove right off in
her car — that I didn't get things straight at first. But
when I added everything up, I knew why I thought I'd
seen her before. She was about Lilly Lee's age, but she
was some taller than Lilly Lee, and she had a sweet,
sad look in her big brown eyes, and she was wearing
a heart-shaped locket. I noticed a little smile flicker
across her face as she came out of the millinery store.
I watched her get into a red sedan there in front of the
store, and I hoped the self-starter wouldn't work; I'd
give her car a crank. But it did, and she drove off.

"Clint," I said to myself, as the red sedan went down
the street, "there goes Emma Rhodes Sylvester, but
she's got too much class for Claudie." So I went by the
racket store to buy me some stationery before going to
the garage.

I told Claudie about the corn medicine, and I

showed it and the almanac to him; but I wasn't about to tell him about the stationery I'd bought, or why. Instead, I hid it inside my shirt.

On the way back to Billingsley's Bend I thought about Emma Rhodes Sylvester. It just went to show, I figured, how much difference there was between Claudie and me. When you really fall in love, you've got to see her in person; you don't just cave in over a picture in a newspaper. But the way she stuck in my mind, so beautiful, so elegant, and so frail and all — why, hell, it was about the most romantic thing that ever happened to me; up to then, I mean. Also, I realized, as we drove home, that the time had come to speak to Claudie about Lilly Lee; so I said, "Claudie, Lilly Lee sure is a fine girl, isn't she?"

"Sure is," he said.

"She wouldn't mind whether a man was in high society or not, Claudie," I went on. "He wouldn't have to write any poetry for her."

I could see that Claudie thought about this a lot, and when I asked him when he was going to try his poem again, he said, "The last of the week, or maybe next week, Clint."

"Poetry, Claudie," I told him, "is a thing a man ought to take his time about." Claudie nodded his head and looked a little pitiful, I thought.

The next morning I discovered I'd been thinking about Emma Rhodes Sylvester some, off and on, all the night. I studied her picture there on the trailer house wall, and I knew for sure it was a case of true love at first sight; so I got out my stationery and wrote Emma a nice letter. I don't remember it all, but I know I told her I loved poetry about as much as anything in this world; then I stretched a point a little, I suppose, and told her it was mainly her poetry I was interested in, so how would it be if sometime I went into Denton and met her. Oh, yes, I told her I was sort of an inventor, spending a few days fishing at Billingsley's Bend. Then I hid the letter, along with the stationery, before Claudie came in with eight big catfish and a nice gar for Bruce.

"You might take that old gar up to the house right now," I said. "Bruce hasn't had one today." When Claudie'd gone, I hurried up to the Billingsley mailbox and put the letter to Emma in it.

The answer arrived three days later. Lilly Lee came running down the path with it, and Claudie was sitting right there on the willow stump all the time. Of course, he wanted to know what I was doing getting a letter and all, so I had to tell him it was from the government and about something he wouldn't understand. Lilly Lee hung around a while and kept teasing Claudie because he hadn't got any letter, and when she wouldn't quit he chased her back up the path toward the Billingsley house. She gained on him, though, every step of the way.

This gave me my chance to read Emma's letter. It was on purple stationery with ERS at the top in long looping curlicues, and it said, "Dear Mr. Hightower," and about how glad she was to hear from me. She'd always preferred men who loved poetry, and she would wish that I should come and hear her recite sometime; and then afterward wouldn't I care to come to her house for tea? I could just see the picture, too: Emma and me sitting on a plushy davenport in her parlor and both of us drinking tea with our little fingers sticking right out into the air. I would find out something, too, about that sad look in her big brown eyes.

Claudie stayed gone long enough for me to write Emma right back and say it would pleasure me plenty to go to Denton for a round of poetry and tea; such doings, I wrote, were my idea of the finer things in life. I also wrote her that my chauffeur named Claudie would drive me in for the next recital; when was the next one to be? I ended the letter, "Your fond admirer, Clint."

I beat Lilly Lee to the mailbox when Emma's answer came, but I don't mean I outran her; I just went first, that's all.

"Dear Clint," Emma's letter said. The next recital, it went on to say, would be a week from Thursday at the high-school auditorium, 3:00 P.M.; and afterwards wouldn't I care to have tea at her cottage? "Sincerely, Emma," it ended.

A couple of days later I noticed Claudie had shaved off his mustache and started parting his hair in the regular old way. He hadn't said anything more about trying to get up a poem, and I'd asked Lilly Lee to tear up all the newspapers before Claudie got ahold of them. I told her any dope that would fall for a picture in a paper should be saved from himself, and she'd agreed right off. . . .

But, somehow, on Wednesday, the day before the recital, Claudie got ahold of a paper up at the Billingsley house and brought it to me. "Look, Clint," he said, "Emma Rhodes Sylvester goes on tomorrow," and he had a trace of that same pitiful look on his face that I'd seen the day when he sat there on the willow stump and saw her picture for the first time. "Let's us go in and hear Emma," he said. He was pretty excited, all right.

I was ready for this, as you can see; I'd already written Emma that Claudie was my chauffeur. Still I didn't want to have to explain Claudie to her any more unless I had to. So I asked him, "Claudie, have you done your homework?"

"What's that?" he wanted to know.

"Your poem. You haven't written it yet, have you?"

But all that big, bullheaded lug would say was, "No, but I want to go anyhow."

"But you've shaved off your mustache."

"Uh-huh."

"You want me to go along, too?" I asked.

"Of course, Clint. You'll have to help me to meet Emma. You always do that part."

"What will Lilly Lee think about us going to Denton to see the lady poetess?" I asked. This was my trump, and Claudie was really baffled. I could almost see him wobbling inside as he stood there by the trailer house with the newspaper still in one hand.

"Clint," he finally said, "you can explain things better than I can. Could you tell Lilly Lee that both of us wants to see Emma? Would you do that for me, Clint?"

"Now, Claudie," I said. "Look at me — in the eye, I mean. Aren't you ashamed of yourself? Aren't you now?"

But he wouldn't look at me. He only scratched himself around the back of the neck and finally said, "Sure, I'm ashamed. I shouldn't've ast you to. But I still want to go see Emma." That's Claudie for you; contrary as a mule.

The next morning, early, I worked it out with Jonathan for us to take the fish to Denton in the Billingsley car; then I and Claudie spent the rest of the morning getting cleaned up and dressed. When Lilly Lee came down to the trailer house about noon, with Luke, she saw how dressed up we were, and I had to tell her why; we were going to Denton.

Big tears came into her eyes, and she seemed ready to run. "You all are going to see the lady poetess," she said, her lips trembling.

I wanted to deny it, but I saw right off it was no use. There was a way, though, to be noble about it for Claudie's benefit. "I'm the one, Lilly Lee," I told her, "that wants to go to Denton and see the lady poetess. Claudie's only going along to keep me company." But she boxed Luke's jaw and ran up the path anyway.

Claudie's voice actually shook when he said, "She knowed better, Clint, but you tried. You are a real friend."

"Think nothing of it, Claudie," I said. "I'd do it for you any day of the week. But see that you don't forget what I've done for you."

We were in the car with a tub full of fish in the back and about to pull out for Denton, when old Jonathan Billingsley came running around the corner of the house, yelling at the top of his voice and scaring and scattering the guineas, the chickens and the cats out of their shade.

"Hold it, hold it!" he was calling out. "The bees have swarmed. I've got to have some help."

"O.K., Mr. Billingsley," I said. "Claudie'll be ready in a jiffy."

Nobody that knew Claudie would have failed to admire the way he took it. He swallowed a couple of times and climbed out of the car. I went with him back to the trailer house, where he took off his clean clothes, folded them and put them all back in his wicker suitcase. Then he did a peculiar thing. He took Emma's picture down from where he'd pinned it on the wall, and he was about to tear it up when I said, "I wouldn't do that, Claudie. Let me keep it for you."

Claudie put on his old blue overalls and jumper —

but his hair was still combed nice — and as we walked back up the path he asked, "What do you do to bees, Clint?"

"Just do what Mr. Billingsley says, Claudie," I told him.

"But you said you could tell me."

"Bees vary, Claudie," I explained. "I don't know these particular bees, but listen to Mr. Billingsley. They're his bees; he knows how to handle them."

Up at the house Lilly Lee fixed Claudie up for the bees. She tied binder twine around his ankles so the bees couldn't get up his britches legs; she had some heavy leather gloves for him, and she tied them over his cuffs with binder twine too. Then she put a big red gingham bonnet on Claudie and stitched some screen wire across the front to keep the bees out of his face. And as I stood there watching Lilly Lee, so busy and careful about Claudie, and making such a to-do over him from head to toe, it was almost enough to make me wish that I was the one that was going after Mr. Billingsley's bees.

I left for Denton in plenty of time to sell the fish and then get to the high-school auditorium by three o'clock. I'd have made it, too, if I hadn't had a flat right on the edge of town; and then, later, I got the wrong directions for the high school from the filling-station man where I borrowed some stuff to fix the tire with. I don't know why people can't give simple

directions across a town they live in — one no bigger
than Denton, I mean.

Anyway, when I finally got there the program was
well under way, and from the folded card some starchy
little girls gave me at the door, I noticed that Emma
didn't go on until last. This was a break for me, I figured. I walked down toward the front — where, at a
poetry reading, like at a prayer meeting, a man can usually find some vacant seats — and waited for Emma
to go on.

I saw then what I'd have to sit through first, and
that was pretty bad; it was a heap of fancy talk being
put out by a badly wrinkled old lady with a quavery
voice and dressed within an inch of her life in pink and
purple crinoline. She was wearing a big red hat, too,
that was all littered up with imitation fruit and flowers — and with some kind of a green bird's wing too,
if I remember rightly.

When I went in she was talking — and enjoying it
as much as anybody, I figured — about birds flying all
by themselves away up in the sky, flying all night long,
some of them. Then she spoke about winding rivers;
rocks and rills; vales, trees and little flowers; about
blue skies, too, complete with stars and a new moon;
also she spoke of clouds floating up on high — and
whenever there were clouds they were, according to
this old lady, always fleecy; about sunsets and sunrises
and Nature's pristine uttermost, all macked out in

green mantles — such wonders to behold — and forsooth. Forsooth, she said several times.

Then she got on to love, and she was crazy about love, from all the fine things she said about it. Love, she allowed once, was like a set of eagle's wings to help her fly up over the tree tops and plumb away from wherever she'd been; also it was fire burning bright that couldn't be put out except by the right people, and so on.

Along toward the end she was telling about the ocean blue, and it was plain, before she'd finished, that seeing the ocean once had done something considerable to her; and she was boiling over with pretty words — so much so that if any of the words she used had rhymed with any of the others, I'd have been ready to claim this stuff she was putting out could have been classed as poetry, in a pinch.

By the time the old gal was winded and done, I was about pooped out myself and overly ready to get out of there, except for one thing. All this time I hadn't been listening too close; I'd been saving myself for Emma Rhodes Sylvester and her poetry. But the damnedest thing happened, right after the old lady quit. The meeting started breaking up, and at first I thought it was sort of a seventh-inning deal to give people a chance to take a breather and get their feet back on the ground. But, no, they were through; it was all over.

I saw a little guy in a linen suit standing limp there in the aisle while his wife rushed up to the platform, and I buttonholed him. "I've come a long ways, mister — eleven or twelve miles over some pretty sandy roads — just to hear Emma Rhodes Sylvester," I told him.

"That's too far," he said.

"But, when does she go on?"

"She's been on," he answered. "That was Emma that just finished. Took her a long time, didn't it?"

"That old lady couldn't be Emma," I said. "I saw her picture in the paper."

"That picture," he said, "was taken more than forty years ago. But Emma's vain, and it's the only one she'll let them use in the newspaper."

"I see," I said and walked out with the little guy.

There in front of the auditorium was the red sedan I'd seen in front of the millinery store and in it was the pretty girl I'd thought was Emma. I had to ask him who she was and all.

"She's Emma's niece come for her," he said. "Fine girl; married to the deputy sheriff."

I drove the eleven or twelve miles back to the Billingsley place as slow as the old car would go. When I turned in at the gate about sundown, I saw Mrs. Billingsley there on the front porch sitting on every bit of a rocker and over the edges too. She looked cool as a cucumber. The bees, she told me, were all back and settled, and nobody stung even once. Jonathan, she said, had gone down the road to borrow a wire stretcher. He had to fix the hole in the fence that Claudie made when the bees got after him.

"Where's Claudie now?" I asked her.

"I declare, I don't know," Mrs. Billingsley said. "He was out back a few minutes ago. I heard Lilly Lee teasin' him about the way he got all scratched up in the barbed wire when he ran through the fence. That Lilly Lee; she sure is a caution now, ain't she?"

"She's a caution all right," I told Mrs. Billingsley.

"Claudie threatened to spank her if he could ever catch her," she said.

"But nobody could catch Lilly Lee — not even a jack rabbit," I said.

"You're right there, Clint," she answered, happy the way she always was when anybody bragged on how fast Lilly Lee could run.

I went on down toward the creek bank where the trailer house was parked. I had passed the bend in the path when I saw them in the bluing dusk. Claudie had caught Lilly Lee, but he wasn't exactly spanking her. They were both sitting on Claudie's willow stump, watching the trotline. It was awful quiet, and I could hear Lilly Lee laughing and talking. The first thing I heard her say plain was, "You can't ever tell Pappy what I done."

"What d'ya mean?" Claudie asked.

Lilly Lee giggled a happy giggle and said, "I poured coal oil in the hive to make the bees swarm."

I I I
Eleven-way Elixir

IT WAS THE DAY after the Billingsley bees swarmed
— or the day after that — when the letter came from
Claudie's Aunt Minnie Gastrick, the rich one up in
Oklahoma that was the widow of a dead Osage Indian.

Lilly Lee Billingsley came running down the path
to our clearing on the bank of the creek yelling,
"Lookie, Claudie's done got a letter."

Lilly Lee ran right back, and after she'd turned the
bend in the path that led toward the Billingsley house,
Claudie opened the letter. He read on it for a
long time before a big catfish hit our trotline and
started whipping it back and forth across Billingsley's
Bend. Claudie bailed out the skiff to go get him and
said he'd finish the letter after he'd got the hook re-
baited and all.

"While you're at that, kindly let me see the letter,"
I said, and he handed it to me. It was all on one sheet,
and it read:

DEAR CLAUDIE —
Cousin Stella is visiting with me here, and she gave
me your address down there in Texas. You were al-

ways such a sweet little boy that I've often thought of you as my favorite nephew. You're the one born that awful dry year, aren't you? But since I married and moved to Oklahoma so long ago, I haven't heard much about you. Have you amounted to anything? Are you prominent? The reason why I am writing is because I am an old woman now, and I am not very well. I have no children, and I want to make out a will, but I am not going to leave my money to any shiftless relatives; would you? Please drop me a line and tell me how you are, Claudie. Your loving aunt,

MINNIE GASTRICK,
Pawhuska, Oklahoma

"Claudie," I said after he'd come back and finished reading the letter, "there's a touch of destiny in all this."

"Howzat?" he asked.

"I mean, Claudie, if there's anything to you, that letter ought to bring it out. Remember your fortune."

"But I haven't amounted to a hill of beans, Clint," he answered. "I ain't up to bein' prominent."

"Listen, Claudie," I said, "from the way the Bible speaks of an ox in the ditch, the big deal is to get him out — even on a Sunday and it wouldn't be any sin. Sometimes I think you are like an ox in the ditch that would just as lief stay there. What I think you mean is that you ain't prominent so far —"

Then, while he paddled out and took another walloping big catfish off, I read the letter again and found

that for his Aunt Minnie's sake I was almost ashamed
of all that Claudie had not amounted to in Texas.

"Tell me something about this aunt of yours, Claudie," I said. "What all do you remember about her?"

"She's very religious, and she's allus been a big pro-
hibitionist. I 'member that much. She put her Indian
money in some kind of company that made her rich,
they say."

"How prominent do you expect she'd want you to
be, Claudie?" I asked him.

"Damned if I know, Clint," he said. "Why?"

"Well, you know that if you are going to make the
grade for Aunt Minnie, I'll have to figure out a way,
and I was just trying to size up the job."

I looked at Claudie, sitting there on a willow
stump, good-natured and all, but dumb as a fence
post. I studied Claudie a while — heir to all that
Gastrick money if he could so much as look prominent
to his Aunt Minnie from a distance. I thought about
the guy that built the Panama Canal with yellow fever
raging all around; I thought about those Egyptian
kings that built the pyramids in Africa with wild animals roaming all around; I thought about Edison figuring out the way to make light globes when there
never had been anything better than lanterns before;
and then, when I thought of the job it would be to
make Claudie prominent, I found I was all worn out.

Along about noon Lilly Lee brought us a batch of

old Denton newspapers, so I rested and read them all afternoon while Claudie watched the trotline and waited for me to think up something that would put him solid into his Aunt Minnie's will.

The next morning I woke up with an idea bubbling up in my mind like clear water in a live spring. Claudie made us some coffee on the coal oil stove, and while I drank it I sat there watching the dew on the grass sparkling bright in the morning sun and figured the whole thing out.

"Bring me them newspapers, Claudie," I yelled. "Right now, before you run the trotline. Hurry up while my mind is in high gear."

He came running with the papers I'd read the afternoon before, and I found what I was looking for. It was a picture of a fine figure of a man that covered nearly a fourth of the page. It had his name there in big print, and below that it read:

PROMINENT WELDER AND LODGE OFFICIAL CURED

Samuel L. (Sam) Willis suffered with a kidney ailment eight years before he found relief in Eleven-way Elixir. "I had lost thirty pounds," he says, "and I was in a rundown condition for years without knowing why. No appetite; swelling of my feet; spots before my eyes and pains low in my back. Nothing seemed to help until I found Eleven-way Elixir. From the time I finished the first bottle I felt better. The back pains disappeared after the third bottle. My appetite is better than ever now, and I've gained back all my lost weight plus five pounds in the three months since

I went on Eleven-way Elixir. I wouldn't be without it
and neither would my wife now. It cured her gas pains
in no time."

THE ELEVEN-WAY ELIXIR COMPANY

Dr. Lafayette Sour
Denton, Texas
President and Chairman of the Board
(Adv.)

"Now, Claudie," I told him; "you've seen them
Eleven-way Elixir billboards all over the state. A very
well-known tonic. Think of it! All made right there in
Denton."

"Uh-huh," Claudie said, but he still couldn't see
where my mind was headed. "Aunt Minnie always
took Eleven-way Elixir. She usta have bad stomach
trouble that she took it for."

"That's perfect," I told him. "I can just see the sign
now, Claudie, under your picture in the paper. 'Prominent citizen of Little Ellum community cured.' That
ought to qualify you right into your Aunt Minnie's
will."

"But I'm all right, Clint," he answered. "Only thing
wrong with my appetite is I sometimes want more to
eat than I get."

"I've seen you when you didn't look so good," I told
him. "Plenty of times. Sort of peaked and sallow in
the face — watery-eyed, too. A sluggish liver could
cause that, or a gall bladder that needed toning up.
Or even a floating kidney."

"I feel all right though, Clint," he said, studying his hands inside and out.

"Hands a little numb?" I asked him.

"A little," he admitted. "But I feel pretty good."

"Well, if you ask me," I went on, "you don't *look* any too good right now. Let me feel your pulse."

He let me, and after I'd counted a while I shook my head and said, "Feels pretty sluggish to me. Say, wait a minute! Let me hold on some more and catch that little skip again."

"Little what?" and I saw his lower jaw sag.

"Little skip," I explained. "Ever so often it don't beat. It just skips. Oh, there it is; skipped two in a row. But I wouldn't bother, Claudie. So far it's always started up again." I let this soak in a while before I turned loose of his wrist; then I said, "How do you feel now?"

"I might be a little sick to my stomach if I'd had any breakfast," he answered.

"Well, you're liable to, anyhow," I said, "judging from the peaked way you look around the gills. You're just the color of damp things that live under rocks. Maybe you'd better lay down on this pallet in the shade of the trailer house where you can get some fresh air."

"I need fresh air, all right," Claudie said as he stretched out on the pallet and started holding his side.

"I sure am sorry," I told him, looking worried,

since I was by this time. "Is it your side now, too?"

"Hurts there more'n anywhere else," Claudie grunted and began to slobber some.

"Stay right where you are, Claudie," I said. "I'll run up to the Billingsley place and see if they haven't got some kind of strong medicine for you."

"Get some Eleven-way Elixir, Clint," he groaned as I left.

Old lady Billingsley had some all right — a nearly full bottle — and Lilly Lee came along with me so she could help me give it to Claudie.

"We'd better run, Lilly Lee," I said. "He's pretty bad off." I knew that Lilly Lee could run a lot faster than I could, so I didn't even try to beat her back to where Claudie was; I just ran right along behind her down the path to Little Ellum Creek, and by the time we got there — with Lilly Lee in a little old thin gingham dress running the whole way and all — I'd near about forgotten Claudie and what an awful shape I'd left him in.

He was worse off than that when Lilly Lee reached him. She held up his head that was bobbing around like a chicken's with the limber neck, and she poured all the Eleven-way Elixir that was in the bottle right down him.

In a few minutes Claudie came to a little, and I could tell he knew me again. He knew Lilly Lee too, because he asked for some more of what he'd had and grabbed her by the hand when he spoke, but she said

there wan't any more. Then he sat up and asked me to
roll him a cigarette, since he was still too nervous to
hold the makings. I rolled one for him, one for Lilly
Lee, and one for myself, and we all smoked until
Claudie spoke of being hungry. At this Lilly Lee
jumped to her feet and ran back up the path to get
Claudie something to eat.

After she'd passed the bend in the path, I looked
back at Claudie and saw that he'd been watching
her run too, and the color was beginning to come back
in his face. He was scratching himself around the ribs
the way he does any morning in the world and seemed
to be nearly normal again. I showed him the bottle
that had helped him so much, and when he saw that it
really was Eleven-way Elixir, he grinned big and said
he was cured.

But when he got up to walk around and try out how
well he was, he staggered down toward Little Ellum
Creek; then, with trying to keep from falling in, he
reeled back my way and went down on his hands and
knees in some bull nettles that were growing close by.

"Take it easy, Claudie," I said. "You ain't quite
well yet," but he got back up and went on weaving
around the clearing there, humming to himself and
snorting every so often like a mule colt. Then he
started to sing, and by the time Lilly Lee got back with
a plate of fried eggs and corn pone, Claudie had the
woods ringing with the song. It was an old religious
song called "Glory For Me," and I could tell by this

time that Claudie was drunk as a fiddler's bitch. He wouldn't do anything I asked him to, but for Lilly Lee he ate the breakfast she'd brought and then started singing again. This time it was "Beulah Land." He was singing so loud and so bassy, and looking at Lilly Lee in such a fond way that it scared her, and she ran back toward the house.

2

"Now, all we've got to do," I told Claudie about noon, "is go to Denton and report your cure to Dr. Lafayette Sour. You'll be all written up and —"

"Then we'll send the clipping to Aunt Minnie," he said. He looked plumb well and as happy as a pig in the warm sun.

"Claudie," I told him, "your mind is working like forked lightning this morning. Now go and see if we've got enough gasoline to drive into Denton. And pump up that left rear tire. It's got a slow leak."

I showed Claudie's letter to Jonathan Billingsley, and he said he was awful happy to learn we were about to be heirs; he'd be glad, he told me, to watch the trotline for us while we went in to Denton to see Dr. Sour and the Eleven-way Elixir headquarters. We left right after noon.

Now, after I'd seen those big billboards — dozens of them all over the state — with Eleven-way Elixir painted on them in six-foot letters; and after I'd seen all the things in the newspapers about the way it would cure just about anything that went wrong with a person's system, it was hard for me, at first, to get used to this place in Denton where they made the tonic itself. It was not a big factory at all; it was a little square brick building on an alley that led off from the jockey yard.

Just inside the Eleven-way Elixir place was a desk with papers knee-deep on it — bills of all kinds — and farther to the rear there was a big black pot, about twice the size of the pot they cooked that tar in down at Burdenville. Alongside the pot there were several ten-gallon tins marked "Grain Alcohol" and one big round bottle with a label that said "Dr. Lafayette Sour's Eleven-way Elixir Concentrate (Formula Secret)." It was about the color of wet hickory bark.

I and Claudie stood there looking over the layout until a fat colored man walked in the back door with a big case full of empty bottles on his back. He was naked to the waist and so shiny with sweat that he looked like patent leather.

"We want to see Dr. Lafayette Sour, the head man of the Eleven-way Elixir Company," I told him. "We want to report a cure."

"Dr. Sour's done gone to the drugstore, but he won't be gone long," the colored man said as he started opening the alcohol tins with a can opener. We watched him as he poured the alcohol out of four tins into the big black pot; next, he poured in the bottle of Dr. Sour's Eleven-way Elixir concentrate, and then when he threw a hose in and turned on the water, a cloud of yellow steam came off. It was really dense, and we watched it bounce against the ceiling before it went over in one corner and settled there above the desk.

"Tenth batch today," he said. "Since Dr. Sour done fired all the other help and moved down here, I'm near about workin' myself to death." Then he started filling Eleven-way Elixir bottles out of a little spigot there at the bottom of the pot, and after he'd filled a dozen or so, Dr. Sour himself came in by the front door.

He was a long, lean fellow with caved-in cheeks and a high voice, and he seemed at first not to want us around much; but when I told him about how Claudie had been cured the day before, it got us in good with him right away. He shook hands with us and said he believed it was the worst case he'd heard of to be cured so fast.

"When," I asked him, "do you wish to take Claudie's picture so you can write him up in the paper?"

"Oh, we're not doing any testimonials now," Dr. Sour stated. "We've got plenty already."

"But this one is pretty important to us, Doctor," I said. "We'll give it free."

"Nope. Sorry, boys. No more testimonials."

"Look, Doctor. You don't understand. We might even pay for having Claudie's picture taken," I said; and Claudie added, "If I can get wrote up pretty quick."

Now I don't often say the wrong thing, but this time I could tell I had, and so had Claudie. "Listen, fellows," Dr. Sour said, and all of a sudden he looked much taller. He was mad. "I will not be coerced, nor will I be bribed. You men are about to offend my ethics."

I could see he had us, but Claudie couldn't. He was only mad. His face looked like a bad storm coming up as he bellied up to Dr. Sour with his chin about even with the doctor's eyes. Then he said, "I've come to have my picture took."

"Today, we mean," I added as Dr. Sour looked Claudie up and down — all six and a half feet of him. He studied some more the stubborn look on Claudie's face; then he snickered at me and said, "That's a fine idea. We can use one more. The photographer is in the next block."

"We're ready," I told him, and over we went to the place where the picture was to be made. They had some nice clothes for Claudie to wear from the waist up, and that was all of him that would show in the picture — so the big blonde lady photographer told us. Then she said — and I could tell she meant it too — "We will take this picture when you pay your bill here, Lafayette; provided you pay in advance for this one."

"Now, Cynthia, be reasonable," Dr. Sour said. "I can take care of it by Saturday, I'm sure."

"Start taking off those clean clothes, brother," she said to Claudie; and her words came out through her teeth like a snake's tongue. Claudie didn't answer her, but he didn't start taking off any clothes either, and I knew things were on dead center unless I stepped in and took over, so I said, "Will you take Claudie's picture if we pay for it? But we don't want none of Dr. Sour's back bills."

"You mean you want to pay me?" she turned to me and asked.

"How much will it be, please, ma'am?"

"Six dollars for the negative and two prints — the regular price."

"Can you make it five for one print, Cynthia?" I asked her.

"It's a deal," she said. "Where's the five dollars?"

"Pay her, Claudie," I told him, and he paid her five of the only six dollars he had in this world.

She was down under that black curtain behind the camera in no time, lining the thing up and telling Claudie to lift his chin a little — no, not quite so much; turn some more to the right, and so on — just about as good a job, I figured, as the six-dollar deal would have been.

As we left the place Dr. Sour turned and spoke to

the lady photographer. "Thank you, Cynthia," was all he said, but you should have heard the haughty way he said it. Cynthia closed the door.

Back at the Eleven-way Elixir headquarters I spoke to Dr. Sour about when Claudie's testimonial would come out. I was glad to find that he was so reasonable and not speaking any more about ethics, but he wouldn't let us pin him down for sure about just when he would write Claudie up and run it in the newspaper.

"It might be too late if it ain't pretty soon," Claudie told him.

"What do you mean, too late? I don't get it," Dr. Sour said.

"For certain purposes, he means," I added, trying to stave the doctor off. But Claudie had already put his foot in it; the doctor could tell by now he had something we wanted.

"Gentlemen —" he said, pausing and spreading his legs there in the door of the headquarters as he rocked back and forth, "just why is it you are in such a hell of a hurry to get this testimonial run?"

"We have our reasons," I told him.

"And suppose I didn't run the testimonial until you told me about them," he said.

"Excuse me a minute, Doctor, while I speak with my associate alone," I said, and I took Claudie around to the back of the headquarters.

We talked it over and decided that the doctor had

us where the wool was short. Claudie was the nearest he'd ever get to being prominent, and right then that seemed pretty far. All we could do was make a clean breast of it and see if the doctor wouldn't pitch in and help. So we went back and told him about Claudie's aunt that was so rich and not feeling at all well, but of course we didn't tell her name. We hardly knew him well enough to.

We finally got Lafayette to agree to run Claudie's testimonial that same week, but it cost us a third of whatever Claudie was going to get when his Aunt Minnie passed on to her reward. At first the doctor wanted us to cut him in for a full half, but we talked him out of it by all agreeing first that I should have a third. Then, until the doctor agreed to cut his part down to a third, Claudie was standing there with less of his Aunt Minnie than either I or the doctor had. "After all, Lafayette," I said just before we clinched the three-way trade and shook on it, "who the hell's aunt is this, anyhow, that's going to pass away?"

After we finished the deal and wrote it up, I and Claudie both got on fine terms with Lafayette. He gave us five full bottles of Eleven-way Elixir fresh right out of the vat. We split one of them three ways then and there, and it seemed to help everybody's feelings a lot. The doctor agreed that when he wrote Claudie up he would do his best to make him prominent. "Religious, too, Lafayette," I told him, "if you find a way to ring it in."

Lafayette then got very confidential with us and told us enough that we could see he had his troubles too. The fact was, he pointed out, the Eleven-way Elixir Company had once been very prosperous and made all kinds of money, but ever since prohibition was done away with, the business had gone down and down. The company was just barely holding its own with sales in some of the dry counties in Texas and Oklahoma, and the bills of all kinds were piling up. Lafayette said that, as a matter of fact, for the past six months he'd been no more than one jump ahead of creditors all over. "You saw the nasty attitude Cynthia the photographer took," he said. "Well, she's about the nicest creditor Eleven-way Elixir has got left."

We split one more bottle of Elixir with Lafayette before we left, and that was enough. Claudie sang while he drove, all the way back to Billingsley's Bend.

3

The week passed, and Claudie's testimonial didn't come out. It was pitiful, too, the way he'd go every day to get yesterday's paper when the Billingsleys were through with it up at the house, and if they weren't through, he'd wait until they were. We saw pictures of other people that had got relief from spells of all kinds — and one Mexican that grew a new set of teeth at seventy-eight — but no Claudie.

Then the next week we noticed that no Eleven-way Elixir testimonials at all showed up for several days, and we both began to feel sorrier and sorrier for Dr. Lafayette Sour — and for ourselves somewhat also. The doctor was going broke, that was true; but there was no way that we were exactly prospering either, what with time passing, Claudie's Aunt Minnie getting older by the day up there in Oklahoma and wondering to her dying day, maybe, whether Claudie had ever amounted to anything in Texas. It was awful.

Then, on Friday of the second week, Lafayette, our Denton partner, came through for us. It was Lilly Lee that found Claudie's picture in the paper first, and she brought it down early in the morning.

"Look, Claudie's in the paper. He's all wrote up," she hollered as she came running toward the trailer house. "Says he's prominent." Her eyes were all lit up like people's at a fire.

That's what it said, "Prominent," when it told about Claudie. "Prominent Church Worker Gets Relief," the headline read, and the rest of it went about as far as the doctor could go with only Claudie to write up. The picture of Claudie was real good, and his name was right too. What he'd got relief from, in the way the doctor wrote him up, was a little balled up — asthmatic congestion and chronic catarrh — but nothing could take much away from the high and happy morning we had there on the banks of Little Ellum Creek the day that Claudie got prominent.

I don't know whose idea it was to open up a fresh bottle of Eleven-way Elixir, but it soon was everybody's — Jonathan Billingsley's too, since he came along after a while to find out what on earth must have happened to Lilly Lee that she wasn't back up to the house to help her mother with the things. This was the way we found out what was just about the right dose of Elixir, because when we'd split one bottle four ways that morning, and with Lilly Lee there too and Claudie's picture in the paper and all, I remember saying to myself, out loud, that I never felt better in all my life.

We cut the clipping out, and nothing would do with Claudie but we should go into Denton and mail it special delivery to Claudie's Aunt Minnie at Pawhuska. Afterwards, we went around to the newspaper office and bought a dozen copies of the paper. We cut Claudie out and sent clippings to a lot of his other relatives all over — picking the older ones, of course, just in case.

Then we went by the Eleven-way Elixir headquarters to speak to our friend Lafayette, but the sight we saw there would have broken the heart of a wooden Indian. The front door was closed and a big printed sign was nailed on it saying, "Notice to Creditors." Lafayette was sitting on the steps under the sign with his head in his hands, his bloodshot eyes half-closed and the circles under his eyes the color of fried liver.

"Buck up, Lafayette," I said. "It can't be that bad."

"The company is bankrupt," he said without so much as looking up, and I noticed his breath was strong with Eleven-way Elixir. Bankruptcy, it looked like, was about the only thing it wouldn't cure.

"This is the end," Lafayette went on; "I've got nothing left."

It was his life's work, he kept saying, and so on. Then he said what made him feel worse than he did about himself was thinking about his stockholders. "I've failed them, too," he groaned and began to look twice as bad as he had before.

"You must be forgetting about Aunt Minnie Gastrick," I said to cheer him up. "You know, Claudie's aunt. You've still got a third of her."

But Lafayette only groaned more when I said it. There wasn't a thing that I and Claudie could do but leave, and we drove back to Billingsley's Bend feeling so sorry for poor old Lafayette that it put a right smart damper on Claudie's new prominence.

4

When we didn't hear from Claudie's Aunt Minnie in a couple of weeks, it got us both to stewing and fretting some. "Just suppose," I said to Claudie one day, "that letter had got lost and never reached her." This thought began to bother me no little bit, so we took the one clipping Claudie'd saved for his own self and mailed it. We even went into Denton and had it registered at the post office. After that we both felt better about everything, and every day we still didn't hear from her we found we could pass it with more ease, since we figured she could be too sick up there in Pawhuska to drop Claudie even a post card.

It must have been a month or more before we got the letter postmarked Pawhuska, Oklahoma. Claudie almost tore it up opening the envelope. Sure enough, it was from Claudie's Cousin Stella, and she told him in it how his Aunt Minnie had passed away the Saturday before. "I'm writing you, Claudie," she went on, "because for some reason Minnie made you the main heir in her will. Nobody understands why. All she left me was the house and furniture here in Pawhuska. Everything else goes to you. So you'd better come on up here and take over your fortune."

Lilly Lee was hanging around when I read this part out loud to Claudie, and she flew up the path with her bare heels scattering the dew as she ran. In a jiffy the whole Billingsley tribe and some relatives that were staying with them turned up there with us in the clearing by Billingsley's Bend. They couldn't have been any nicer to us if we'd been European royalty of some kind. Some of the Billingsley kin seemed to take it pretty hard when I picked Jonathan Billingsley instead of them to borrow ten dollars from — I mean to buy gasoline and cylinder oil for the trip to Pawhuska. I figured it was best to leave the trailer house with him as security, but he didn't want me to.

We drove first into Denton to get our partner, Lafayette Sour. We found he was low sick, and Mrs. Sour looked pretty puny to me, too, when she came to the door and told us about Lafayette. She said he was asleep and she wasn't about to wake him up for us.

"We've got no time to wait," I told her. "But when he wakes up, tell him Claudie's aunt has passed away and we're all in the money."

"I'll tell him," she said in a flat voice and closed the door.

We had an awful lot of car trouble: bad connecting rods, bad spark plugs and five flats. We spent the ten dollars, and we had to sell at cut rates all of the Elixir we'd brought along in order to come out even on what it cost us to get our old car to Pawhuska. But we made it. We got there about noon the next day.

Aunt Minnie Gastrick's house was a big two-story white one with iron dogs and a bird bath in the yard, and inside it was all plushed out with heavy furniture and a lot of deep dark-colored rugs.

We went in and found Cousin Stella was there and so was the lawyer. He was a bushy-headed old codger with glasses pinched on his nose, and Cousin Stella told him through thin lips who Claudie was. She looked like a woman that had been singing in a choir all her life but was on the verge of swearing off.

Then, after everybody had said some fond things about Aunt Minnie that had passed away, and Cousin Stella had put on a little crying spell, the old lawyer pulled the will out of the big roll-top desk there in the parlor. I and Claudie were ready to see it, too, and I studied it over the lawyer's shoulder so I could be sure that it was legal and so on. It was signed all right, with witnesses and a red ribbon.

Cousin Stella dried her eyes with a lace handkerchief and said she wanted to quote a little scripture from Timothy, so we all bowed our heads and she quoted, "But they that will be rich fall into temptation and a snare, and into many foolish and hurtful lusts which drown men in destruction and perdition." Nobody said "Amen."

"Kindly sit down," the old lawyer spoke, "and I will read the last will and testament of Minnie Gastrick."

We sat, and he read some details about how Aunt Minnie was sound in her mind, possessed of a first-class memory and how she wished to be buried decently. I thought I'd bust, he was reading so slow. Claudie was hanging on the front edge of a straight chair with his face all lit up like the front end of a Dallas moving picture show.

Finally, after the part about Cousin Stella getting

the house and furniture, we got to the part of the will we'd been waiting for. It said:

"I have no children, but I have two fine nephews down in Texas that I want to remember in my will. There is Elton Pine, my sister's child, who lives in Laredo." ("That's Loblolly," Claudie whispered to me.) "But Elton writes me he has prospered greatly in a financial way, so I leave him my love. My other nephew seems to have gone more into church work instead of seeking a fortune. He lives near Denton, Texas. And so, to my religious nephew, Claudie Hughes, I give and bequeath all the rest and residue of my entire estate."

"What's that?" Claudie asked out loud, but the lawyer simply read on in a voice flat as a flitter: "It consists of twenty-three thousand shares of the capital stock of the Eleven-way Elixir Company."

Then he rolled up the top of the desk and showed us the piles of pretty green stock certificates. They were all decorated around the edges with fine little curlicues, like cigar coupons are, and when the old lawyer started handing the green certificates to Claudie, Cousin Stella went into another bad crying spell.

By the time we'd counted the certificates and piled them into the back of our car, the whole thing had sunk in on Claudie. He was about ready to go back and join Cousin Stella in a crying spell.

"But no, Claudie," I said. "There is one thing you

haven't noticed. Look what it says on every one of these certificates — right up at the top: 'Fully Paid and Non-assessable.' I suppose you know what that means."

I saw he didn't.

"That means it won't cost you a thing to be your Aunt Minnie's heir. Also she's left you a real lead on another well-heeled relative. Here's a name. That's more than we've got on the Amarillo deal."

Born to Pick Cotton

YOU SHOULD have seen Lilly Lee's eyes shine and
sparkle when she saw all that Eleven-way Elixir stock
— the whole rear end of our car full of it. She hugged
Claudie and she hugged me too, right there before
her pappy, Jonathan Billingsley. Old lady Billingsley
was extra happy too; she thought the certificates were
coupons you could get Eleven-way Elixir with.

I and Claudie tried to tell them the stock was no-
count, but they wouldn't believe a word we said, the
certificates were so pretty. But they had to believe us
when we told them we were due to go right away
to Laredo on business. So we traded the Billingsleys
every last one of the pretty certificates for all the watermelons the trailer house would hold. We got the
best and biggest ones in the patch.

We made it to San Antonio the next day   over
halfway to Laredo — so I and Claudie sold the watermelons at a road crossing in the edge of town. Then
we took out for the Mexican border.

In Laredo it turned out that Claudie's counsin Loblolly was more prominent than the railroad depot or
the Rio Grande River. His face was all over posters
on every telephone pole we saw for miles before we

got to Laredo, and the closer we got to town, the bigger and thicker the posters got. "Vote for Elton Pine for Sheriff," the signs all said below Loblolly's picture. Also the signs showed that the election was to be the very next day.

"I may have to take back what I said about relatives, Claudie," I told him as we drove into town. "Here's one that may pay off big. Maybe make you a deputy or something."

Claudie only pulled the throttle down another notch.

The next day was a big day. We didn't exactly meet Claudie's cousin Loblolly, but we talked to him on the phone. He claimed he couldn't remember Claudie and hadn't cared a damn about his Aunt Minnie Gastrick, but he told us how we could make the forty dollars we made on election day. The only thing we had to do, besides leave town after the election, was round up stray Mexican wetbacks and deliver them for two bits a head at the courthouse to be voted by Pancho Fox, the guy that was going to be Loblolly's deputy. We found we could haul as many as a dozen in the trailer at one time. And after the voters were turned loose, we'd take them back to where we'd found them for a nickel or a dime apiece — or for nothing at all if they were broke, since chances were they'd be ready then to make another trip to the courthouse to be voted again by Pancho Fox.

That night, across the Rio Grande in Nuevo Laredo,

I and Claudie had wild game dinners and plenty of cold Mexican beer to wash them down with. Enough, all told, to lift a tired man's eyes above the world of strict rules and hard work and up toward some of the finer things in life. But not Claudie; he hadn't even wanted to cross the Mexican border in the first place. He'd just wanted to buy some gasoline for our car and drive on down the Rio Grande to Brownsville, Texas, where the cotton-picking season was going full blast.

"It ain't over two hundred miles, Clint," he said. "I expect I must have been born to pick cotton."

"Listen, Claudie," I said, "here's one of your relatives that's really paid off. When have we made forty dollars before in one day?"

"I dunno."

"This is only the beginning of the harvest Jules Rabinowitz told us about in Beaumont. In Brownsville we'd be a thousand miles from Amarillo again. In a run of luck like the one we're in you don't go pick cotton; you parlay. And now how would you like to have twenty-five thousand pesos?"

"How much is that in money?" he wanted to know.

"Several thousand dollars anyhow. For fifteen dollars," I explained, "I can buy a lottery ticket that we could win twenty-five thousand pesos with, and we'll be off for Amarillo in style."

"If you don't lose," Claudie butted in, always seeing the bleak side of things.

"And if I win," I went on, "I'll figure exactly how much it's worth in cash. If I don't win, it don't matter."

Instead of waiting for this to soak in on Claudie, I went on over to the bartender, paid my money, and got myself a lottery ticket for the next drawing. Then I found that the shriveled little Mexican at the table next to ours spoke pretty fair English, so I contacted him. He turned out to be Juan Garza, the customs man at Nuevo Laredo, and I bought him some beer, figuring a little pull with the Mexican government wouldn't do any harm to a careful American investor down there. When I make a move like that, you can see I don't leave anything undone.

Early in the morning a couple of days later I and Claudie were standing by the butcher-shop billboard there in Nuevo Laredo when they posted up the winning lottery numbers, and Claudie seemed almost glad, I thought, when my number missed winning by several thousand.

"You really lost big," was what he said as he sniggered and shooed a green horsefly away from one ear.

"Claudie," I told him, "we've had two hopeful days. That beats picking cotton."

"Uh-huh," was all Claudie could think to say.

"You can have the losing lottery ticket to remember Mexico by," I told him.

He stuck it down in his jeans and said, "But now

let's us go to Brownsville. I've still got enough money left for gas and oil."

"Later on, maybe," I answered. "But, first, I'm going by the customhouse and tell my friend Juan Garza good-by."

That turned out to be the best idea I'd had in days, since we found Juan had himself a problem on his hands he couldn't begin to handle without help.

I sized things up, the way I always do before I make a move. There on the street in front of the customhouse was a long yellow sedan with a New York license, and in the back seat two big, ugly bulldogs were barking and showing their teeth at Juan. In the front seat were two women that had some kind of a grudge against Mexico, and they were taking it out on poor Juan Garza in stout, blunt English — but one of them had a broken accent, at that. She was a young blonde with a high forehead, and her hair, the color of goldenrods, grew into a pretty pointed V in front. She was wearing a little bitty red hat held on by a felt ribbon that went down under her chin, and she was so dadgummed mad that a lot of fiery pink color bloomed up in her cheeks and set off her bright blue eyes. Her temper up that way made her take deep breaths too, and every time she did I could see that the buttons down the front of her white silk jacket were hanging on for dear life. The other woman, a busty, square-faced brunette was older; and from the talk I could tell she was the blonde-that-was-so-mad's mother. Madder than a wet hen, too, she was. "But, Señora Glasscock —" Juan would say; then the women and the dogs would let him have it again.

"Imagine!" Mrs. Glasscock was saying out loud as I eased up to the driver's seat where she sat. "Just imagine!" Poor Juan just stood there, swallowing.

"Somebody will hear about this in Washington," she went on, her black eyes blazing. "I know a gentleman who is very high up in the Bureau of Reclamation, and —"

"Hold it, lady," I cut in on her as I took off my hat. "Hold it, please. What's the trouble?"

"I'll tell you what!" the old brunette answered. She spoke smooth and hard like a fellow I'd known once from somewhere in New Jersey. "Gersten is due to open tomorrow night at the Reforma in Mexico City."

"Open what?" I asked.

"Gersten sings. She's the Norwegian Thrush; you must have heard of her. But we'll never make it this way."

"Why not, ma'am?" I asked.

"It's nearly nine o'clock already," Mrs. Glasscock went on, "and we can't make it unless we leave right away. It's a long two days' drive. We've got our passports, our automobile certificate, and everything else in order. They told us in New York — they told us positively — there'd be bonded Mexican guides to drive us from here to Mexico City. But now this nincompoop says there are no guides today." She snorted and glared at Juan Garza, who seemed to shrivel.

"Ladies," I said, "kindly do not speak unkindly to my old friend Juan Garza any more. I and my associate here will have you in Mexico City in plenty of time to sing." I pointed to Claudie, who looked like he might break and run.

"You don't sound like any Mexican to me," Mrs. Glasscock stated, and she was blunt.

"Are you holding it against me that I speak such good English?" I asked. "Do you want us or not, ma'am?"

"I guess we've got to," she answered; so I turned and said, "Come along, Claudio. We have some business with Juan Garza."

Inside the customhouse I spoke to Juan. "I guess you noticed, Juan, how I took up for you. Personally."

"*Si, señor,*" Juan's grin showed wrinkles and relief all over his leathery face. "*Muchas gracias.*"

"Now, Juan," I said, "we might need a little help from you. In the first place, we need a good Mexican guidebook."

"Next door." Juan pointed, and I sent Claudie to buy it. "Get a good one, Claudie; we're going to be bonded guides and we've got an awful lot to learn."

"Now, Juan—" I turned to him and said; then I noticed that Claudie had not left to buy the guidebook.

"Go ahead, Claudie," I told him. "Don't just stand there like a fence post. We've got no time for you to piddle around."

"We can't speak no Mexican. How do we get to be bonded guides?" said old ironhead.

"That's why I sent you to get us a guidebook, damn it. All we'll need to know will be right there in the book."

"Then how do we get bonded?" Claudie asked without moving a peg, and I couldn't tell when I'd been more disgusted with the big burly jackass in my whole life. About this time the car horn started honking, and this set the dogs to barking out in front. Juan Garza turned the color of an old Chinaman that is about to be sick.

"Just a minute, Mrs. Glasscock," I hollered from the customhouse door. "There is some official business we haven't quite tended to yet." Then I turned back to Juan and asked him how long it took to get bonded.

"*Dos semanas, o tres,*" he said. "Two weeks — sometimes longer. Costs one thousand pesos, but first guides have to fill out forms and send to government. Like these." While Juan was showing me the long folded sheets with a lot of Spanish in fine print, I saw that the blanks were already filled in. Also I saw clipped to them little square papers all covered with signatures, seals and ribbons.

"What are these, Juan?" I asked him as I unclipped one of the squares.

"Bonds for guides; my friends Erasmo Rodriguez, Guillermo Guiterrez and Ricardo Lopez."

"What are you doing with them here?"

"I keep bonds until guides come back from cotton-picking season in Brownsville," Juan explained.

"We don't want to borrow but two of these nice bonds, Juan," I told him. "We'll hand them to you just as soon as we get back."

"But, *señor*—" Juan sounded pretty stubborn, but I noticed that Claudie was leaving to go for the guide-book.

"Juan," I said, as the bulldogs kept barking outside, "are you ready to tell those ladies they can't have bonded guides?"

Juan wasn't, but he wasn't quite ready to lend me the bonds either. Safe inside the customhouse he wasn't ready to do anything until I left him all the money I had on me—three dollars and a quarter—as security for two of the bonds I borrowed.

When Claudie came back, I handed him one of the bonds while I took a fast look at the guidebook he'd bought. I saw it was a very cheap, paper-backed job, but there was no time to send him back for a better one. On the folding map in the back I found the high-way we'd follow straight to Ciudad Victoria, then to Mexico City.

At first Claudie was a little balky about getting into the back seat with Mrs. Glasscock and the bulldogs, but I took over and explained to the ladies that I was the one that did the driving while Claudio was a sort of mechanic that fixed flat tires and fought off bandits.

Then I climbed into the driver's seat and kept talking. "I think you'd better let Gersten sit up in the front with me, Mrs. Glasscock. I will tell her how the Mexicans like their singing done. Claudio don't speak as good English as I do." It worked and as I drove off, Gersten looked at her watch, she said it was after nine-thirty already, and asked how far it was to the next town.

"Two hundred and forty miles to Monterrey. Right down the Pan-American Highway," I yelled loud enough for Mrs. Glasscock to hear. It was fresh in my mind from the road map.

"Very good, driver," Mrs. Glasscock said.

"A bonded guide is never called 'driver,' " I stated. "You ladies might not be able to pronounce my whole name, but you can call me Clint for short."

"What's that? Clint? That's not a Mexican name!" the old brunette's voice sprung at me from the back seat; then she said, "Driver, let me see your bond," and she said it the way they say, "Halt, who goes there?"

"Under the rules, lady, guides are not supposed to let the bonds out of their possession. But I'll let Gersten see mine." I pulled it out of my pocket and held it up before the beautiful Norwegian Thrush. She looked it over and spoke in such a sweet, silky, Norwegian accent that it was like violin music played at sundown. What she said was: "The name is a long, complicated Spanish name, Mother. I like Clint better."

At this she turned a nice Norwegian smile on me, and I said in a very sincere way, "Thank you, Gersten." She looked so pretty that I almost didn't see some Mexican soldiers that were waving us down. *Inspección Aduanal* the sign there said, and I was not ready for it, whatever it was. But it turned out they only wanted to see the Mexican certificate on the car, and they asked for it in plain English. Mrs. Glasscock had it, so we showed it and drove off. But I told the ladies I'd better keep it from there on.

Gersten soon brought up the subject that got me in the front seat in the first place; she wanted to know more about the way Mexicans liked their singing, so I told her. "Well, it's like this, Gersten: they don't like it too low, and they don't like it too loud. They like it sung pretty fast, too, but not too fast. I don't mean, though, that they like it sung real slow. Want to try one?"

Gersten blushed, and said she'd feel silly singing in a car, but I told her to go right ahead, she was among real friends. So she sang a song called "La Paloma," one she'd learned especially for the Mexican trade. The song was so dadburned pretty that as I listened it was like cranking my liver and lights through a clothes wringer. When she finished, I said, "Gersten, you haven't got a thing to worry about in Mexico. They'll

take on over you at the Reforma." Gersten patted my
knee, put a wide, fond smile on me and said, "You're
sweet to say so." About this time I looked in the rear-
view mirror and saw that Mrs. Glasscock was asleep
and Claudie was holding the dogs' collars, one in each
hand. He looked pretty miserable, I thought, but the
dogs looked fine.

We got to Monterrey in a little less than three
hours and pulled up in front of the Gran Hotel An-
cira at twelve-thirty noon. Mrs. Glasscock, wide awake
by this time, asked me in a very accusing way, "How
far did you say Monterrey was, driver?"

"Ma'am?" I said, reaching for the road map. I knew
we'd never hit eighty; still we'd done the two hundred
and forty miles in under three hours, and I was about
ready to burn up that cheap guidebook Claudie had
bought.

"The distance!" she said. "I thought you told
us it was two hundred and forty miles to Monterrey."

"We have made good time," I admitted. Claudie
tried to help, and said, "Time shore does pass slow in
Mexico." Then I found what I was looking for in the
guidebook. "Distances," it said, "are shown in kilometers, except where otherwise indicated."

"One of you men can come in the hotel and order
the food for us," Mrs. Glasscock stated. "We can't
speak a word of Spanish."

Just in time I saw a sign that said: "English spoken

in hotel café." So I told Mrs. Glasscock to go right on in. "English," I said, "is spoken in hotel café."

After I and Claudie had eaten close by and fed the dogs, I tore the guidebook in two and told him to go to work on his part while I studied the rest. "Dig out some dope on this country fast, Claudie," I told him. "A bonded guide has to know all about Mexico." I kept the part with the road map folded in it and found the highway to Ciudad Victoria right off.

We pulled out of Monterrey at two o'clock. We traveled in coarse, rocky country with nothing growing but weeds, cactus and other thorny things. We'd been going for nearly an hour when Claudie started talking. I'd never heard him put so many words together before. I rolled up the car window so I could hear better, and what I heard was: "Ah, magic Mexico! Land of variety! Land of breath-taking beauty! From the moment the traveler crosses the sleepy waters of the Rio Grande his pulse will quicken to the spell — the spell —" And there Claudie bogged down.

I knew it had been too good. It was more than Claudie could possibly have memorized. Then, in the rear-view mirror I saw that he was looking at the first page of the guidebook, trying to find his place. Finally he went on: "quicken to the spell of this quaint and ancient land. From palm-dotted shores to lofty snow-covered peaks, the variety of scene never ends. Weird shapes of shrub and cactus grace the landscape." Except Claudie called it "landscrape."

I noticed Mrs. Glasscock was looking out of the window at some buzzards circling in the sky, but Claudie went right on, looking, as he read, like someone breaking in a pair of new shoes. By this time he was following the lines with his finger. "On the central table-land the climate is mild. It varies but little the year round, as shown by the tables in Figure 1." In the mirror I saw Claudie close the guidebook like a preacher that's read today's text, so I opened the window again.

By this time I'd worked up a considerable personal interest in Gersten, anyway. I'd found that she was a girl with a very sweet nature to go along with her lovely voice and face and everything. She told me all about her early life in Chicago, Illinois, before she'd joined an orchestra and gone to Norway on a ship that took people for Scandinavian cruises. She sang blues songs with the orchestra, she explained, until the orchestra leader's wife took a shot at her in Oslo. That annoyed Gersten very much, she said; so she quit.

I told her I didn't blame her at all, and she went on to say that she liked Oslo so much that she didn't come back to the United States until she'd picked up a good stiff Norwegian accent. Gersten, the Norwegian Thrush, was only her stage name, she said.

"What's your real name, Gersten?" I asked.

"Bridget," she said, "Bridget Amelia Glassock. That was my maiden name, and I always get it restored."

"Well, Gersten, if it's all the same with you, I'd

like to keep on calling you Gersten. I've got so used to
it already," I told her, looking right into her pretty
blue eyes. She looked right back at me too, as she did
many a time that afternoon on the road south from
Monterrey.

It was nearly dark when we got to Ciudad Victoria.
We found the Sierra Gorda Hotel, the one that had
the biggest ad in the guidebook, and we left the ladies
there. I and Claudie slept in the car with the dogs.

The next morning it was pouring down rain from
low, slaty clouds — the kind where a man that's studied
weather the way I have could tell the rain had set in
for a spell. I and Claudie were due to call for the ladies in front of the Sierra Gorda Hotel at eight sharp,
but a few minutes before eight Claudie found something at the filling station that near about set him hog-
wild and made us a little late. It was the winning lottery numbers for the day, posted on a sheet there next
to the gasoline pump, and Claudie found the number
of our ticket on it. Twenty-five thousand pesos our
ticket had won.

"Take it easy, Claudie," I said, trying to calm him
down. "Try and get aholt of yourself. You are running
around this filling station like a chicken with its head
chopped off. We simply looked on the wrong day in
Nuevo Laredo; that's all. No wonder our number
missed yesterday by several thousand."

"*Our* number?" Claudie asked. Oh, he really was in
a stew and a fret. He left the cap off the gasoline tank

and started the car motor with the hood still up. He
wanted to hurry and cash in the ticket, but we soon
learned we'd have to wait until nine o'clock when the
banco next door opened.

"A banco," I explained to Claudie, "is about the
same as a bank anywhere else."

We stood in front of the banco until nine, and it
took us most of that time to figure out whose lottery
ticket the one he had was. Claudie wanted to claim
I'd given it to him, but I pointed out that this was
pretty unreasonable.

"Who bought it?" I asked. "Who picked out this
winning ticket, Claudie?"

"You did," he admitted, "but —"

"And here we are, about to cash in on it in Victoria,
Mexico. Right?"

"That's right," Claudie admitted, but —"

"All right. Where'd we be right now if you'd had
your way, Claudie? I'll tell you where: in Brownsville,
Texas, picking cotton."

This got him, and so we settled on half his and half
mine just before the big whey-bellied umbry came and
opened the banco doors. He admitted we had the winning number, but he wouldn't pay off right away. He
said it would take an hour or so to prove it wasn't
counterfeit. I told him we didn't have any hour or
so; we had to be off to Mexico City. In that case, he
said, we should go ahead; the tickets were printed in
Mexico City, and we could get our pesos quick there.

By this time the word had got around some way, and umbrys hurried up all around us — and little Mexican kids, too, jabbering like a bunch of hawk-scared hens. They wanted tips; and I told Claudie to hurry and turn all the money he had into pesos before the crowd got any bigger. So we bought our way out of the banco crowd, got into the yellow car and headed for the Sierra Gorda Hotel.

"Claudie," I said as we drove off, "we've got the same as twenty-five thousand pesos in that lottery ticket and in an hour everybody in Victoria will know it's on its way to Mexico City in this car. We can't afford to get robbed."

"Nobody could miss this here yellow car if he wanted to rob us," was the way Claudie cheered me up; then he added, "I believe a robber could see a car this color in the dark."

In front of the hotel we found Mrs. Glasscock and Gersten sitting on their baggage. Gersten was crying, so I jumped right out of the car and went over to her, since I cannot stand it to see any blonde cry — much less one as pretty as Gersten. Claudie listened up everything Mrs. Glasscock had to say, while I spoke to Gersten.

"We're a little late, Gersten," I told her, patting her hands between mine and watching her tears dry up. "I and Claudio had to go by the banco, but you'll still sing tonight at the Reforma. You can count on that."

It was plain that Gersten was glad to see me; and Mrs. Glasscock, from what she said, was getting satisfied to see the bulldogs and the car not run off somewhere with. I was about to get back into the driver's seat when Mrs. Glasscock spoke out. "I didn't like the way you drove yesterday. You didn't keep your eyes on the road. I believe I'd like for Claudio to drive."

"But, Mrs. Glasscock —" I said.

"Claudio will drive," she stated.

"But Claudio hardly knows the roads like I do," I told her.

"I'm not sure either one of you can find the right way out of Victoria," Mrs. Glasscock stated in a way that stung my pride some. But I was on solid ground here, as I knew the road map by heart, so I said, "Listen, madam, two highways come into Victoria from the north — the one we traveled and the one from Brownsville — but only one goes out, and that's the one to Mexico City."

"Very well," she said. "Driving is your department, but where we sit is not. Claudio and Gersten will sit in the rear seat, and I will sit in front with you."

Now here is where something happened that I will not blame you if you do not believe, for I hardly believed it myself until we were on the road several miles out of Victoria. Gersten said, "No, Mother. You know you are always more comfortable in the rear seat. Besides" — and at this Gersten gave me a sweet little sideways look out of her eyes — "besides, I want to ride in front with Clint." I watched the old lady bristle and then give in. She looked like an aunt of mine used to look right after she'd belched. But she saw that Gersten — the one, after all, that was going to sing that night — had meant every word of what she'd said.

We stopped twice that morning in the pouring rain to get gasoline. I tried to find the names of both towns on our map, but they weren't even shown — or if they were, they weren't spelled right. I was pretty busy, anyhow, since each time we stopped I really put out the talk I'd picked up in the guidebook. I knew it wouldn't do for the ladies to hear either one of us try to order gasoline.

I could tell I had Gersten in a very admiring frame of mind with the way I'd pronounce the mountain called Ixtacihuatl, the state of Tlaxcala and some other hard ones. Meanwhile, Claudie would take the gas cap off and tell the Mexican filling-station people by sign language and every other way he could that we wanted the car filled up. "Are we serviced, Claudio?" I'd ask him; he'd nod his head and answer, "Si"; then we'd be off. Did I mention that in Victoria I'd taught Claudie to say "si!" when he meant "yes"?

Along about noon we crossed a wide, muddy river on a ferryboat. The rain was still coming down so hard that we couldn't see the far bank when we started, and Gersten seemed a little scared as we pulled out of the slip into the current. Scared that way, she was even prettier than when she'd been mad. Her hand was there on the seat between us, so I reached over to pat it and make her feel better. This was when she took my hand and squeezed it and said, "I feel ever so safe with you, Clint." Just like that. Right then I could have swum the river with any sort of an excuse at all.

When we reached the far side of the river, I got out the guidebook map to see if there wasn't another river or so before we got to Mexico City. I could have used several like the one we'd just crossed, I figured. But the map didn't show rivers. I was about fed up with that cheap guidebook map, anyway, so I turned back to Claudie and said: "Claudio, when you bought this map I hope you got back all the change you had coming to you."

"I do too," Claudie answered. Then he went on, the way he sometimes will when he's brought in on things by being spoken to. He said he was pretty hungry.

"I'm sure we have no time to waste with eating," Mrs. Glasscock put in. "Isn't that right, driver?"

"In Mexico," I had to tell her again, "a bonded guide is not called 'driver.' But I'm afraid you're right. We'd better keep driving." I didn't know how many miles — or kilometers — the river was from Mexico City; the guidebook was no help on that. Also I did not wish to waste any time in getting Gersten to Mexico City to sing and that lottery ticket there to be cashed.

No food made the bulldogs pretty fractious, though,

and the old brunette got downright grouchy herself
on an empty stomach and the rain pouring down
and all. She kept harping on something that wasn't
bothering me a bit. She felt the mountains should
be higher and the roads steeper.

"Mrs. Glasscock," I finally said, "the Lord made
Mexico the way it is. A bonded guide cannot do much
about it."

I'd been expecting bigger mountains myself, from
the way Claudie's cheap road map looked, but either
it was wrong again or I was getting used to mountain
driving; I couldn't tell, and I didn't care much. I was
Mexico City bound, hungry but happy with Gersten
edging over toward me a little closer the farther along
we went in the pouring rain.

Once she gave me such a nice long look that I had
to look at her too; and when I glanced back at the road,
it was not the road I saw exactly. We had edged
down into the ditch on one side of the road, into the
red rocks and rank weeds, that is; and the noise of
the rocks against the bottom of the car was like hail
on a tin roof, only a lot louder. That started the dogs
to barking; and by the time I managed to get the car
stopped, Mrs. Glasscock herself was saying some
things I knew she'd be sorry for later. It turned out
that she had been dozing a little when we left the
road, and she couldn't get it out of her head at first
that we hadn't had an awful wreck of some kind.

"Nothing of the sort, Mrs. Glasscock," I said. "All

Claudio has to do is move a few of these rocks in front of the car and we'll be on the road and traveling again in a jiffy." But what I was really thinking about was that twenty-five-thousand-peso lottery ticket. I knew we'd be a pretty easy mark for robbers, stuck there in the ditch with a lot of big rocks out in front of the yellow car.

Before Claudie could get himself together and go to work on the rocks, the Mexicans came. I saw their car parked on the road above us, then I saw them coming down into the ditch where we were — three very hard, bristly looking Mexicans, and I knew there was no future for us with them. Even if they wanted to help, there wasn't one chance in forty they'd have said it in English; and I was not ready for Gersten and her mother to hear us try to talk Mexican to them. But as the Mexicans got closer to the car, they looked less and less like Mexicans that wanted to help.

"Robbers," I turned and said to the back seat. "Bandits. Hide your purses *and things — and things*." I looked hard at Claudie, sitting there stiff as a poker with a lottery ticket in his pocket that was good for twenty-five thousand pesos. Then I turned back to the Mexicans. They weren't five feet from the car, and the closer they came the rougher they looked. Something had to give somewhere.

All of a sudden, several things happened. Gersten put her arms — soft arms and strong — around my neck and said, "Oh, Clint," in a sweet, scared voice.

I turned the switch, gunned the motor and let the clutch out. The yellow car shot forward like a mule colt that's been hit with a bull whip, and we bounced ahead in the rain and over the rocks toward the road. It was rougher than a bucking horse. The bulldogs barked, and the ladies screamed, but Gersten never took her arms away. Finally I fought it back up the bank and onto the smooth road, and we went roaring down the road in the rain.

Gersten didn't say much, but it was enough. "You're wonderful, Clint," she said, and held onto the part of my arm above the elbow where the most muscles are. I couldn't tell when I'd felt so all-fired prosperous or brave in my whole life. I mean I was ready to take over, so I yelled so loud it surprised me, "Everything that's hid, let's leave hid. There might be some other bandits."

It was late in the afternoon when we came onto a stretch where the road was smooth and straight for a long ways, and I knew we were bound to be on the central tableland that Mexico City was in the middle of. The guidebook had said so. "The homestretch, Clint," I said to myself, as I figured we couldn't be more than an hour or two's drive from Mexico City — allowing even for that screwy map of Claudie's to be wrong again about the distance.

"Claudio," I yelled back at him, "kindly tell Mrs. Glasscock about the central tableland. We're on it, if you've been noticing." But Claudie didn't say a word, and I was about to speak to him again when he leaned forward and whispered, "Them bulldogs has done et up my part of the guidebook, Clint."

The sky ahead brightened and the rain let up a little as I drove on. And then I saw the outline of a tall steeple ahead of us. Mount Ararat couldn't have looked any prettier to Noah after the flood than that Mexican steeple looked to me after all the rain we'd been through that day.

"Look," I yelled, as electric tingles traveled up and down my spine, "I can see one of the Mexican cathedrals already. Mexico City next stop!"

"It's about time," was all Mrs. Glasscock allowed.

Gersten said again, "Clint, you're wonderful." Then she hummed a little tune, and in the late afternoon light she looked as fresh and soft as a new powder puff.

As we got closer, other buildings and spires showed up through the clearing dusk; and I found the excitement I'd felt was catching, even in the back seat. The bulldogs growled and barked some, and Mrs. Glasscock spoke of how she'd enjoy a warm bath and a bite of Mexican food as soon as they got settled at the Hotel Reforma. For the first time I noticed the old brunette had sort of a nice personality after all, and I said, "I and Claudio do not go to the Reforma often; it's very expensive, but we've made some good lottery deals lately, ladies. Tonight we will go to hear Gersten

open at the Reforma." Then I spoke to Gersten too
low for it to be heard from the back seat, "And after
the show, Gersten, let's us go take in a nice Mexican
night club."

"Oh, Clint," she said, edging over my way in the
seat, "I'd love it."

Now, according to Claudie's crummy guidebook
there was a lot of altitude around Mexico City that
bucks you up and lifts your spirits, and I allowed some
for all that in studying the way I felt; but, anyway,
sitting there beside the beautiful Norwegian Thrush,
I knew I'd never been so high or happy in my whole
life, or felt so sorry, either, for poor old Claudie —
rich too, as he was that day — riding back there with
Mrs. Glasscock and the bulldogs.

Pretty soon, as dusk gathered, we could see a wide
spread of lights ahead, and in the middle a heap of
bright ones flickered and glowed on the tall buildings.
One big neon sign said *Carta Blanca, Cerveza Exqui-
sita;* one said *El Jardín;* and others said other things
in Spanish, but I didn't see any sign right away that
said Reforma. I told Gersten that *Carta Blanca* was
Mexican for beer — something I'd learned from Juan
Garza in Nuevo Laredo.

In no time at all we were on the edge of town on
a main street with shops and crowds of people all
along. I followed this street a mile or more looking
for a Reforma sign of some kind until we rolled up

in front of a big building with a sign out front that said *Alto* and several Mexican soldiers alongside the sign. They seemed to want us to stop, so I did.

"This may take a little time, Gersten," I said, not knowing what the soldiers wanted but feeling up to it anyhow. Then I got out of the car and spoke to Claudie: "Come, Claudio, let's I and you go inside and deal with these soldiers."

"Very well. This is your department," Mrs. Glasscock stated. "Gersten and I will find our way to the Reforma from here. You can come on later and get your pay." She was out of the car by the time she'd said it. She climbed into the driver's seat quicker'n a flicker; she rattled the gears and drove off while all the Mexican soldiers yelled *"Alto."* Then the Mexicans turned to me and Claudie, and he was so rattled he gave them the only Spanish he'd learned by heart. Claudie said, *"Si."*

"The automobile certificate," the biggest soldier said. "I must see the automobile certificate."

"Here you are, my good man," I said, handing it to him. "The ladies were in a hurry. Now kindly give me it back, since we're in a hurry ourselves."

"Oh, no; you must turn in the certificate before you leave Matamoras," he argued.

"But —" I said, and I was ready to outtalk him so we could go on to the Reforma where the singing was to be done.

Then, as my eyes got used to the night I saw the

bridge ahead, the river below, and another big sign beyond; also, from the dopey look on the face of my burly cotton-picking friend Claudie, I could tell he'd seen the sign too. It read: *"Brownsville, Texas."*

"You must've took the wrong road outa Victoria," Claudie's great brain served up for him to say, and he said it.

"You don't say!" Oh, I can be sarcastic when I want to. "And what other great announcement do you wish to make, Dr. Einstein?"

"Well, it's about them robbers, Clint. When they come, Mrs. Glasscock put her purse down in front between her —"

"Between what, Claudie. Speak up."

"Between her dress and herself, sort of. You know — her bust; and I figured there'd be room for the lottery ticket too. So I asked her to hide it for me."

"Good, Claudie. Very good."

"But," he went on, "I never got it back. I didn't want to tell her what it was, and I hadn't figured out no other way to bring it up. Let's go find Mrs. Glasscock and get it back."

"I wouldn't have the heart, I'm afraid, with Gersten right there and all," I said. "Gersten that will not sing at the Reforma tonight."

"But, Clint —" Claudie started.

"We've had another hopeful day," I went on. "You've got to admit that, Claudie. If we found those women, they'd only spoil it."

"But how about that twenty-five thousand pesos, Clint?"

"No, Claudie," I told him. "It's only money, and it wouldn't be worth it. You've come to your cotton-picking place."

V

The Promised Land

"CLAUDIE," I told him, "the cotton-picking season down here around Brownsville started early, and it's bound to end early. Fact is, it's nearly over now. Unless we move north to the Brazos Valley where it's just good and started, you're near about through picking cotton for this year. Also, the Brazos Bottoms are between here and Amarillo and I know you'll never be plumb satisfied until you find that your kinfolks there won't care much about you either if they're rich."

What I said didn't seem to bother Claudie as much as I'd expected it to, and I saw his mind was in another numb spell. He was squatting down there on the levee by the empty irrigation ditch, pulling sand burs out of his overalls and looking down the long row of cotton he'd just picked. I sat on his half-full cotton sack in the shade of a mesquite tree and tried to give him some idea of a cotton-picking future in the Brazos Bottoms. I told him everybody in Texas knew about the mile-long rows up there, growing bale-to-the-acre cotton, the pecan-tree shade to weigh it in at the end of the rows, the watermelons galore and cantaloupes, and box suppers with pretty girls on Saturday nights.

"You talk like the Brazos Valley was the Promised Land, Clint," he finally said.

"It is, for a man that was a born cotton-picker, and anybody that had to learn on that bumblebee cotton in the Alabama wire-grass country deserves a crack sometime in his life at high cotton — the kind that grows along the Brazos River."

"But —" he started, and I stopped him.

"Listen, Claudie. You're not about to admit you don't want to go to the Brazos Bottoms, are you?"

"Oh no, not that," he said. "But how can we?"

"That," I stated, "is just what I was coming to. With about ten dollars of the money you've made picking for Mr. Martinez here, I can get to Laredo. It's only a couple of hundred miles. One week from today I promise I'll be right back here at noon with our car and trailer. Also, I've got to take these guide bonds back to my old friend Juan Garza. Now, if you will be so kind, please hand me the money."

Claudie wouldn't admit he had but five, so I took it, climbed through the fence there by the levee, and started walking up the hot dusty road toward the Laredo Highway. Over my shoulder I watched him buckle his leather knee pads back on and pull the cotton sack strap across his shoulder. Then, as he began picking down the long row, I yelled back a word of good cheer, a thing I'm always good at. "Pick hard,

Claudie, and collect your money. Be ready a week from today, and I'll be right here."

I'd have made it, too, if that little Mexican in a garbage truck hadn't run into me just as I got back to the edge of Brownsville. All his fault, too. The whole front end of my car was badly blunted, and the garbage truck was bashed way in on one side. Our trailer house wasn't ruined, but the wreck didn't do it any good, and it cost eleven dollars to get it fixed so it would roll again. And eleven dollars was every cent the best junk dealer in Brownsville would pay for the car, the shape the front end was in after the wreck.

So it wasn't noon when I found Claudie on the day I'd said; it was near about dark, but he was there on the levee where I'd left him the week before. He seemed to sag a little in all his joints when I told him about the car, and his eyes looked like mud, there in the dry dusk left by the sun that had done set and gone.

"But the trailer house is all fixed up," I explained.

"Uh-huh."

"We can sleep in it tonight. Come on; it's only a couple of hours' walk. Also, I have a surprise for you, Claudie. I've hitchhiked a tow for the trailer house. Early tomorrow morning we leave for the Brazos Valley."

"Who's gonna pull us?" Claudie wanted to know.

"I forget his name, Claudie. Little fellow I met today in a domino parlor. He's got a pickup, and he's going all the way to Tyler tomorrow. The road runs right alongside the Brazos River in Washington County, and he's going to drop us off there."

By this time we were walking in the dark down the Brownsville road.

Next morning the fellow with the ride woke us up before good daylight.

"See what I mean, Claudie?" I said after we'd put on our shoes and stepped out of the trailer. "Here he is. Here's Mr. —" I pointed to the bilious-looking little guy I'd made the deal with the day before.

"Just call me Jackass," the fellow said, "if I agreed to tow this old crate here halfway across Texas for ten dollars."

"Pay him quick," I whispered to Claudie, "before he changes his mind."

Claudie paid him, but he was so slow it was broad open daylight before he'd finished, and the last two dollars were in nickels, dimes and pennies he dug up from several different pockets.

Dark caught us in Columbus where Jackass had a flat tire and a bite of supper while he got it fixed. It turned out that Claudie didn't have but the price of one can of sardines left — all in pennies, too, and that's what we had to eat, without crackers, in Columbus.

"Here's the place," Jackass yelled back about nine or ten o'clock that night when he stopped. "You can't be more than spittin' distance from the Brazos River here."

We climbed out of the trailer, stretched ourselves and saw that we were close to a building of some kind there by the side of the road. And as our eyes got used to the dark night, we could tell it was a church with a steeple and big trees growing all around.

I'm no hand to mooch on church property myself, and I was about to speak to Jackass about this when I saw he'd already unhooked us. He drove off without a word, and about all I and Claudie had left to do was turn in for the night.

Quail all around woke us with their sharp friendly "bob whites" along about sunup, and a fresh clear day it was, too, starting off there in the churchyard. The big elm and oak trees put long shadows west in their own even shapes, but leaner and slenderer there in the early morning. And where the shadows weren't, the sun made bright sparklers of the dewdrops on the green grass blades. I thought a lot and spoke some to Claudie about what a fine morning it was, as he dug around inside the trailer house looking for some coffee that he couldn't find. Then I had to agree with him the day would have looked even better on top of a big breakfast.

The church was painted a neat white, and it had stained glass windows with angels and saints and Pharisees and all in them. Also, there was one of Belshazzar's feast in Babylon, but Claudie wouldn't even look at it, he was so hungry.

"Where's the cotton?" Claudie asked, and we looked all around for it. But all we saw was woods to the north and pasture land every other way.

"Where's the Brazos River?" he wanted to know next.

"Take it easy, Claudie; it's bound to be close by," I told him. Then I walked north a little ways through a clump of hackberry and bois d'arc trees with Claudie tagging along behind just for the pleasure, I supposed, that big contrary cluck would get out of it if I didn't find the cotton and the river. And pretty soon I had to stop, but just in time, since the clump of trees was on the edge of a high bluff.

Claudie came up without a word, and from the rocky ledge there we saw much more all at once than a man's eyes can take in so well that early in the morning. Beginning a hundred feet or so right below the bluff and stretching for miles and miles was this flat valley, all cut up into even green patches and dotted here and there with red cotton gins. On the nearby land we saw the cotton rows — the longest and straightest I'd ever seen, and loaded with open white cotton bolls.

"Look close," I told him, "and you will see what I meant about the Brazos Bottoms. The Promised Land couldn't have had much edge on what your eyes are laying on. And look right straight down below you;

look at that wide rusty-colored stream moseying slow along the bottom of this bluff. That, Claudie, is the Brazos River, just like Jackass told us."

Claudie studied the river a while and said, "But it runs between us and the bottoms where the cotton is."

2

We went back to the churchyard, where I'll admit, to be fair, it was Claudie that found the little scrub oak tree with a wild grapevine growing all over it, and it was covered with big clusters of blue-black grapes, all dewy and shining in the bright morning sun.

"I'll pick our hats full of these grapes, here, Claudie," I told him. "But you know I like them better with cream. Get that little stewer out of the trailer and see if you can't find a fresh cow around here somewheres. Then we'll have us a real breakfast."

Claudie left, and, sure enough, he was back in no time with the stewer full of milk. Mostly, though, it was foam. That came, I knew, from Claudie being such a fast milker, and this time he said he really had to hurry because he saw somebody coming before he got through.

And before we'd finished breakfast somebody did come — right on up to our trailer house there in the churchyard, too. I and Claudie noticed it first when we heard a gun go off not very far away. We stepped right out, and there she was — a tall high-hipped lady that looked to be about twenty-five or a little less. She was never going to be Miss America — I could tell that — and she was all broke out in the face with ginger-colored freckles.

"Good morning, ma'am," I said as she walked up and put her long black six-shooter back into the carved leather holster on her right hip. Claudie spoke, too, scared as he was: "Pleased to meetcha," the only thing he ever says at first to people.

She stood there about ten feet away and studied us with her arms folded. She was wearing a blue and white checkered sunbonnet pushed back from her brown and uncovering the freckles on her forehead all the way up to her fiery red hair. I mean she was full of freckles that showed on her arms below the short-sleeved gingham dress and on her knees, also, when she put one foot on a burned stump there and kept on looking at us.

But she didn't say a word, and that gave me a chance to do a little thinking. She'd shot too soon, that was one thing; she hadn't handled the gun like a woman long used to one; she'd seemed a little un-steady before she put her foot on the stump; and, while she stood there with a stiff upper lip, I noticed her lower one trembled a mite. Then I knew why she didn't talk; she wasn't sure what to say.

"This sure is a pretty church here, ma'am," I began, figuring I'd sort of limber up the air around us, but she only nodded her head a little bit. "Are you a member of the congregation here?" I went on, and I was about out of soap too, if you want to know the truth.

"No," she admitted, "but this church is in my precinct."

"Your what, ma'am?" I asked her.

"The precinct I'm constable of," and about this time I saw her badge in the shape of a star — for Texas, that is. Well, the Good Lord hadn't made her very pretty in the first place, and I am ready to state that whatever she might have had to start with along the line of beauty, the gun and the badge didn't bring it out any.

"Thank you, ma'am," I told her in the best manners I could turn up. "I admit we don't belong in this churchyard. That's just what I told the man with the car that left us here last night. Didn't I, Claudie?"

"Uh huh."

"And the one that has done the most wrong is the man that wouldn't take us any farther," I explained. "We told him we didn't want to mooch on any church property; still he went off and left us anyhow."

"But you're the ones I've caught," she said, as good an answer, I figured, as any man constable could have thought up.

It seemed the time had come for us all to meet personally and maybe put the lady constable more at ease, so I held out my hand and said, "Hightower is my name; Clint Hightower. And this is my partner, Claudie Hughes."

"Pleased to meetcha," Claudie said again.

"Which one of you fellows milked my little Jersey heifer?" the lady constable seemed to want to know before she shook, and there I stood with my hand out in the air, plumb empty.

"I didn't," I said, letting my hand ease back slow to my side. "I didn't even see the heifer that was milked, ma'am, but I sure can tell you this much right now about Claudie Hughes here. He loves all dumb animals, and he is very kind to cows. You know how a young heifer that's fresh will suffer with a full bag?"

The lady nodded like she did.

"Well, Claudie can't stand to see that. He'll give the cow relief every time. Was your heifer's calf with her last night?"

"No," she said, showing a little flicker of a smile, it seemed, with her mind on the calf. "I just started penning him up last week."

"A little bull calf, I'll bet."

"Yes, a little bull."

"Well, I'll declare," I stated. "How old?"

"Five weeks."

"Well, ma'am, many's the time my partner here has milked a fresh cow where he saw her bag was strutted in pain. He must have been the one that milked your heifer this morning."

"She does have a mighty full bag of mornings — ever since I penned up the calf," she admitted, and I could see the lady constable's nervousness was about gone.

Also, I thought her glance was almost thankful toward Claudie, who was looking down and rolling a little old rock around and around there on the ground with one foot.

She was ready to shake hands by now and tell us her name too. Disheroon it was, Mrs. Beulah Disheroon, but she wasn't wearing any wedding ring, and when she saw I was noticing that, she put her left hand behind her.

"My partner Claudie, here, is also a champion cotton-picker," I told Beulah. "We were headed for the Brazos Bottoms when we got stranded here. Could you tell us how to get there?"

"There ain't any bridge close by," she said. "If you go by Old Washington it's fifteen or eighteen miles to the bottom lands, but by Independence it's nearly thirty."

"That's too bad, Beulah," I said. "Claudie really loves to pick cotton. You don't happen to have a car, do you?"

"Sure," she said.

"Well, maybe —"

"What kind of work do you do?" Beulah asked me before I was ready.

"Well," I said, "I expect you can see I'm not exactly the cotton-picking type. Also, the burs stick my fingers. But when it comes to the finer things in life: music, poetry, romance —"

About this time an old dirty-gray Brahma bull came

down the road, grazing along the fence row, and Beulah saw him just when I did.

"There's Percy; he's out again, the old rogue," she said. "I'll have to go now and drive him back in the pasture."

"No thank you, ma'am," I told her. "Claudie can handle that for you. He's a fine hand with stock."

"Can he? Would he?" Beulah asked, smiling at us both and looking fairly chummy for a lady constable with her pistol barrel still warm in her holster.

"Where'll I drive him?" Claudie wanted to know. He was ready to move.

"You know where Mrs. Disheroon's pasture is, Claudie," I told him; "it's where you milked that poor little Jersey heifer a while ago."

"The heifer's pasture is the last place I want that Brahma bull," Beulah said. "He goes in the pen beyond the pasture. Just open the gap and drive him in."

As Claudie went off down the road, shooing the old bull ahead of him with a horseweed he'd pulled up, Beulah looked at me and I looked at her. She was a lady constable with a car that could pull our trailer house to the Brazos Bottoms. She had far-apart eyes that were blue like real deep water; she had red lips without any makeup, and used as I'd become to the gun she was wearing, I began to see a fine womanly softness about her that the holster didn't altogether hide.

Beulah sat down on the stump she'd propped her

foot against earlier, and I took the closest other one to
it thereabouts. That way she didn't seem to be so
much taller than I was. She smiled at me, and I
thought about her car and said, "Maybe I'm peculiar
that way, Beulah, but I really like freckles."

"I've sure got plenty of them," she said, blushing
and putting her hand up to her cheek.

"But they're real becoming to you."

"You're only saying that."

"A freckle," I explained while she tucked little
strands of red hair under her bonnet and looked a
long way off, "can be a thing of beauty. It all depends
on who wears the freckle."

I could see by now that Beulah liked to be told nice
things about the way she looked, so I spoke to her
some more along the same line. When I would, Beulah had a way I liked of looking down with her eyes
and smiling, but the smile was not down; it was right
straight at me. Beat anything I ever saw.

It turned out as we talked there in the churchyard
that Beulah would be pleased to give us a lift to the
Brazos Bottoms — but not that same day, she explained — the next day. I was so thankful I shook
hands with her there again and said, "But, Beulah, we
can't leave the trailer house here."

"Don't worry about that," she said; then, before I'd
turned her hand loose, we both saw that Claudie was
back, so Beulah told us both about the shady place by
a rock spring close to her home where we could park

the trailer house for the night. "I'll go get the car now and give you fellows a tow," she said.

"Oh, my, no, Beulah," I said. "I'll have Claudie do that, too. We can wait right here for him. Where's your car?"

"It's in a little lean-to on the east side of the barn," Beulah said. "An old-model Dodge sedan, and the key's in it."

"What'll we hook it on with?" Claudie asked, a lot sharper than he is most of the time.

Beulah seemed stumped for a minute, then she flashed a very wide smile and said, "There's plenty of baling wire in the barn. Claudie can help himself to it."

"Good," I told her; "Claudie understands baling wire fine."

"Trouble is," Beulah went on, "this baling wire is on the hay that's stored in the loft — only two strands around every bale."

"Undo about forty bales, Claudie," I said; "we don't want the trailer house to break loose from Beulah's car."

Then when Claudie started off toward the road, Beulah called out to him: "Don't break the wire off the bales, Claudie; just undo it, even if it takes a little more time."

"You're a mighty pretty girl, Beulah," I said, and we walked over to the little clump of hackberry and bois d'arc trees on the bluff where I and Claudie had first stood and looked down on the Brazos Bottoms. Beulah sat down on a big cedar log there, and on this same log where she sat, I sat too.

If you have not been kissed at ten o'clock in the morning by a lady constable wearing a badge and a gun, you may not believe what happened on the log on the bluff the very minute we sat down. But with bumblebees humming as they sucked pink and purple summer flowers all around us; with all the birds singing gay in the trees overhead, and the warm sun bringing out the beetles and crickets that chirped back and forth at each other in the tall grass on the bluff — with all these hearty signs that Mother Nature was on the job all about and Claudie gone again, what the hell else could or should have happened?

And long before Claudie got back with the car and wire, I'd found her arms were softer than they were strong, — or was it the other way around? Also I'd found that for a man who wasn't born to pick cotton, this bluff could be a great deal more like the Promised Land than anything you could see from it.

"I just love to hug and kiss," Beulah said finally. "Don't you? It's more danged fun than a barrel of monkeys." She was right, too, I knew; except I'd never thought of it before in quite that way.

3

The place where Beulah lived turned out to be an awful old settled one, built of cedar, Beulah told us, by slave labor away back when Texas was a part of Mexico. It had tall square columns in front, an outside stairway and two old stone chimneys at each end. And from the house place you could see forty miles or more of Brazos Bottom cotton growing across the river. You could see all this, too, from the close-by pecan grove where we parked the trailer house that day.

I tried to point out this pretty sight to Claudie while he unwired Beulah's car and she drew us a cool drink from the rock spring in the middle of the grove. But Claudie kept looking up at the sun that by this time was about in the middle of the sky. Then I figured everything out. This was his way of letting Beulah know that it was about noon and time for vittles. But before Beulah caught on, the telephone rang up at the house. Beulah said, "That's my ring," and ran to answer it. All the way Beulah's holster, with the gun in it and all, mind you, would give her a sort of a little spank on that side every time she'd hit the ground, and I thought what a fine picture of a lady constable she made that day.

"There's been a cuttin' scrape over in the Bottom,"

Beulah told us when she came back. "Near Snook. It's out of my precinct, but the constable over there wants his handcuffs I borrowed last week. I've got to go take them back."

"O. K., Beulah," I said. "We'll look after the place while you're gone."

"And cut some corn tops for the stock, too, won't you?" she called out after she'd started her car. "The knives are there by the water tank below the barn. Turn on the windmill, too, please. The stock need water." Then pretty soon there was only dust where Beulah's car had been.

Claudie is awful stupid, I'll admit, specially on an empty stomach; but still I wondered and thought a lot that afternoon, while he fed and watered the stock, about how neither Claudie nor Beulah nor anybody said a word before she left about us catching a ride to the Brazos Bottoms with Beulah when she went to take back the handcuffs.

It must have been about an hour by sun when Beulah came back. She allowed she'd missed eating anything at noon and she'd be glad to go cook us all some supper if we'd like for her to. There was hardly anything she could do, I told her, that would make us any happier than that. She'd ring the bell, she said, when it was ready.

The sun was low and hot-poker red in the west when we found out Beulah didn't exactly live on the place all by herself. Claudie was greasing a squeak out of the trailer house axle, and I was shaving when a tall skinny old man came trudging up the trail from the river with a long string of catfish.

"You see," he told us when I stopped him and asked him what he was doing there, "this here place is mine. This is the Nate Pinkney place, and that's my name. It ought to be by now; I heired it from my pappy and this is the seventy-ninth summer I've lived here."

"I see," I said. "Nice string of fish you've got there, Mr. Pinkney."

"Mind tellin' me what you doin' here yerself?"

"We're friends of Beulah, the constable," I stated, and Claudie nodded to back me up. "We've been helping her some with the stock, and she's in the house right now fixing us some supper."

"Beulah's friends are always welcome here," Mr. Pinkney said as he sat on the curb of the spring, doused the string of fish in it, and fired up his clay pipe. "Beulah's a fine girl. She's my granddaughter-in-law."

"Your what?" I asked.

"Yup, that's it; my granddaughter-in-law. Married my grandson." At this a lot of color flared up in the old boy's ashy-gray face, and he went on: "But the worst dadgummed thing that ever happened to her was hitching up with that mis'able, pesky rapscallion, Whit Disheroon, my daughter Sarah's boy."

"You don't say!"

"Yes, I do say. The intol'able young scamp."

"What all'd he do?" I asked, seeing the old man had a whole lot more of this to get off his chest.

"What'd he do? Whit? Why that sorry, scrawny, lousy, flea-bitten little peckerwood! He didn't make Beulah happy. That's what! You know, men, for fifty years they've called me the cussingest man in Washington County. I've been, too. But until Whit come along and give me something to cuss about, I reckon I really never come into my own."

"Tell us some more," I said.

"You bet I will." The old boy was really boiling. "You see, I raised him after my daughter Sarah followed her husband to the grave. That was Walt Disheroon, good fellow, but not much to him. I wanted Whit to be a vet. Fine trade with as much livestock as there is around here, so I sent him four years to the A. & M. school over at Bryan. When he got through he settled here and married Beulah, an orphan girl from Burleson County, and she made him as fine a loving wife as any man could ask."

"Good," Claudie said.

"Wait; not yet," the old man went on. "There was one flea in the ointment. Just one. They'd taught Whit at school to doctor dogs as well as livestock, and what do you suppose he went and done?"

"What's that?" we both asked.

"He went and bought into a practice in Houston where he don't doctor nothing but poodles and pooches and lap dogs and other kinds of useless varments for all them rich people down there. Whit's done took on so much culture and put on so many airs there ain't nothing to him any more. Why, he'd be lost around a sick horse or a clover-bloated heifer!"

"But Beulah. What'd he do to—" I started.

"Don't butt in on me now, young man. Can't you see I'm not finished yet? And Beulah—well, God damn it, she quit him, that's what. She quit him and come home. And I didn't blame her. This is the only home she's got—poor orphan—but she's welcome here as the flowers in May. So are her friends. But if Whit Disheroon ever shows his face here, I'll horse-whip him within an inch of his life."

"I don't blame you," I said and got mad right along with the old man. Also, I looked at Claudie to see how he was feeling about Whit. He looked awful wrought up, and when the old man saw that, it seemed to do him a lot of good. Only thing, Claudie hadn't had a bite to eat since those grapes, and what Beulah's grandpaw-in-law didn't know was that when Claudie gets awful hungry he looks a whole lot like the way he does when he's awful mad.

"Well, these catfish have got to be cleaned," Old Man Pinkney said. "I'll go up to the house and get it over with. Glad now I didn't catch any more."

"Stay right where you are, sir," I told him. "Claudie here was cleaning catfish before he could talk. Let him handle that while you sit down and rest a while."

They both took to my idea, and Claudie loped all the way up to the house with the string of fish.

Well, the old man talked on about how sorry Whit was until I saw Claudie leaving the house for the cow lot with a big wooden pail in one hand and a milk stool in the other. He'd had about enough time to clean the fish.

"Tell me more about Beulah," I said, and before the old man finished talking nice about Beulah, Claudie had finished milking and gone back to the house. I took all the talk in, too, and liked it, even the part about how everybody took her side when she left Whit. They all wanted to do something for her, so the first paying public job that opened up they elected her to it — constable of the precinct.

It was nearly pitch dark when a little breeze sprung up from the south, and the perfume of fried catfish that floated on it started my mouth to watering something fierce. I hated to cut in on old man Pinkney's talk, but I had to; and we went up to the house together. The old fellow drew a bucket of water from the cistern so as to wash the fish goo off his hands, and I went on into the kitchen.

Supper was ready; the fried catfish were piled high on a plate and the corn pone was done in the open oven. But nobody was there. It was so quiet everywhere that I went on through the house toward the front. I was about to go out onto the porch when I heard Beulah giggling a very happy giggle — a lot like the one I'd heard before.

"Let's us hug and kiss one more time before they come, Claudie," she said. "I think it's more danged fun than a barrel of monkeys, don't you?"

I waited for Claudie to answer her question, but he never said a word. Everything was quiet again until old man Pinkney rang the dinner bell.

4

No fancy fish sold under French names and soaked in spicy sauces at big hotels could ever taste better than the fried catfish we had that night for supper. We ate every single catfish right down to where the bones wouldn't even draw flies. And all during the meal Claudie wouldn't look me in the eye one time. He had a very fond look on his face, but it was all used up on Beulah and the catfish.

After supper Beulah started to wash the dishes, and old man Pinkney asked me and Claudie to go out on the veranda with him. But Claudie said he believed he'd help dry the dishes.

"Oh no," I said, "Claudie cleaned the fish. I'll help with the kitchen things." But he was his regular contrary self, so we both stayed on to help Beulah until everything in the kitchen was spic and span. Still, Claudie never did even look me in the eye.

"Come on out on the porch, fellers," the old man called to us when we'd finished inside. "It's nice and cool out here." But I still didn't go out until Claudie did. Beulah went, too, and took a wicker rocking chair right between the ones I and Claudie sat down in.

I let my arm hang down next to Beulah's chair and found her hand was right there. We held hands as we rocked; also, every time I'd say anything, she'd squeeze my hand, and I expect I said about everything I could think up about the half moon, the cloud bank over in the east, the sheet lightning that flashed dim behind it, the stars, the gargling song of the tree frogs, the lightning bugs and the dogs barking a long way off in the night.

When the moon moved across the porch far enough to light up Claudie on Beulah's other side, I looked to see whether she was holding his hand too. She was.

The moon was low in the west when old man Pinkney got up, stretched and spoke some of his rheumatism. He said he believed he'd go wash his feet and turn in. He was a little tired anyway, he allowed, after fishing all day and making the climb from the river with such a big string.

"Claudie needs some rest, too," I stated as the old man went on inside. "His liver always bothers him when he misses his sleep. Also, tomorrow is a cotton-picking day for Claudie."

"Howzat?" Claudie asked.

"Remember, Claudie," I told him, "the Brazos Bottoms that we're already in sight of. It's tomorrow we're going."

"Tomorrow ain't botherin' me," he said, almost smart-alecky, I thought.

"Come on, now, Claudie," I said, serious as I knew how, "I mean, sure enough, ain't it about your bedtime?" and Beulah gave my hand a hard squeeze.

"I ain't a bit sleepy," the big contrary lug said — "why don't you go on to bed yourself?"

There was a new something like sandpaper in his voice that I didn't like at all, and I said, "I'm not about to. I never felt wider awake in my life."

"I never neither," Claudie answered, and Beulah said it was past her bedtime; she really ought to turn in.

"Oh, no, not you," I and Claudie both said, and we all three rocked on.

If Claudie thought he could outwait me, he was dead wrong; he ought to've known that, but as things were going, more and more of nothing at all was happening to both of us. I mean it was awful. By then I'd found it wasn't doing me as much good as it had earlier just to hold Beulah's hand. It began to feel like shucks if you want to know the truth.

I started to have a whole set of very poisonous thoughts about Claudie as he rocked away there in his chair that squeaked with every rock. At times I figured that if he rocked and squeaked his rocker one more time, I'd blow up or something. But all I could do was sit there, getting madder and madder at him until all the stars up in the sky looked red and yellow and blue to me. I found I'd built up inside me a terrible mountain of hate toward Claudie — a mountain that felt like it had a volcano, maybe, inside of it; and I finally said, "O. K., Claudie; enough is enough. You've got to go on to bed. I wish to speak to Beulah privately." And what do you suppose the big lug said to me? Not a damn word. He just kept on rocking, and I could tell he was pretty mad at me too.

Of course, Claudie is a very large guy and built in the shoulders like the men in clothes catalogues, but in mind I trimmed him down to my own size. I could see myself picking him up by the scruff of the neck and the seat of the pants, then dragging him as he kicked and squealed all the way to the trailer house. Afterwards, I'd brush the dust off my hands and go back up to the house where Beulah would be waiting for me.

But when the moon went down Claudie was still there, rocking and squeaking his chair; and when everything would get quiet, I could hear a new noise in the dark. It was Claudie grinding his teeth. The rain set in along about midnight, and by that time I was madder than ever. There was a feeling all around in the air that something had to give somewhere in a big way. Something had to bust loose.

And it did. I mean lightning struck. It was a blue-white bolt, big as a stovepipe, stabbing the ground right out in front of the porch with a blinding blaze of fire. And right along with it the thunder cracked rough and hard in our faces, and a sickly, scorched smell came into the air.

Limp as it left me and all shook up inside, I felt better. It was like the good Lord had spoken some of the things I'd been feeling, and I found I was ready to tell Beulah good night. Claudie was too, so we both went back to the trailer house and turned in without another word.

5

Next morning the sky was clear, and the whole Pinkney place had a neat, well-scrubbed look from the rain. The mocking birds were singing in the pecan grove there by our trailer house, and underneath the trees two peart little scissortails fussed over a worm.

"Come on, Claudie," I said, cheerful like, "wake up. Today's the day we go to the Brazos Bottoms. Beulah —"

Then I remembered I was mad at him and why. He got up and buttoned his shirt, but he didn't say a word. Claudie was still not speaking. Now, many's the time he's been silent before breakfast that way, but only because he couldn't think up anything to say. Many a time. But I could tell this was different. I could just tell, that's all. Well, I was mad enough not to speak any more also, and I didn't. Then I noticed Claudie still would not look at me, so I quit looking at him too. But I did see out of the corner of my eye that he was putting on his suit of clothes. Being blue serge and double-breasted, the suit would swelter him in the heat, I figured, and make him too sweaty for Beulah to care for.

I got out my yellow sport shirt with the open collar and combed my hair back pompadour, the way women often say they like it best, all without even one more glimpse at Claudie. I did notice, though, through the Cardui calendar mirror on the trailer door, that he'd put on the ready-made green polka dot bow tie that's always been too little for him. You know the kind — on an elastic band. I didn't see him get the talcum powder out, but I smelled it and knew he had. Then Claudie shaved — even while the bell was ringing up at the house.

"After all," I finally had to say, "aren't you carrying this pretty far? There ain't but one woman up there."

But do you think Claudie would so much as answer me? Not Claudie. And I'll admit it was beginning to bother me some.

Claudie was parting his hair away over on one side — where it never stays parted, and I was glancing at him in the mirror while he did it; so naturally I didn't see old man Pinkney when he came up outside the trailer house.

"Come on," he was saying, "what's got into you danged fellers? The eggs is cold, and I don't aim to fix another breakfast this morning."

"You don't?" I asked as I stepped outside. "I thought Beulah was the cook."

"Not this time," he said as Claudie, the dude, stepped out, his hair loaded with bear grease and parted nearly straight over his right ear.

"Why?" I asked the old man.

"Beulah's gone, that's why. The damndest thing. Right in the middle of the storm last night she got in the car and left."

"Where'd she go?" I asked.

"Houston, in the pouring rain. She's gone back to that mis'able little whelp, Whit Disheroon. How about let's eat them fried eggs before they get plumb clammy, men?"

"I'm ready," I told him. "Come on, Claudie."

But old numb-brain didn't seem to hear me. He was standing up straight — all six and a half feet of him — in his double-breasted blue serge suit and his too-tight green bow tie with the polka dots. He was looking a long ways across the Brazos towards all the cotton in the bottoms beyond while everything we'd said soaked in on him. Then he sort of went limp all over. He grinned at me real friendly and said, "O. K., Clint. I'm hungry again."

Claudie was back to normal.

V I

Forty Years of Firewood

SOME OF THE TALES old man Nate Pinkney told me
and Claudie went all the way back to the days of the
Indian fights. His pappy had been an Indian fighter
from one end of the Brazos Valley to the other, and
when he told us about his pappy's forays against the
Choctaws, I figured some of them would have made
Joshua in Canaan look like Nedrick in the First
Reader. Old man Nate would talk about Indian fights
at the drop of a hat; he was always ready. I and Claudie were just as ready to listen, too, since free meals
went with the listening. So, with Beulah gone in the
car and nobody else around to give the trailer house a
tow, we sort of settled down there. We found the fare
of grits, sowbelly, fried catfish, black-eyed peas and Indian fights was agreeing with us. Also, it did not call
for any manual labor on my part, and Claudie soon
got so he could look at the Brazos Bottoms without
getting real restless. Matter of fact, Claudie seemed
about cured of his cotton-picking fever by this time.

I borrowed a book on Indian wars from the old
man, and every day while Claudie helped him with
milking the cows and feeding the stock, I read up on

Indian trouble all the way from Florida to Canada. I figured I might as well learn about what caused these fights, and from what the book said, I could tell that the Indians had always been in the wrong. There wasn't a history in the whole house written by Indians.

I guess we'd been there a week or more when we learned that there was at least one Indian still around. It was a warm, cloudy evening, and we'd had supper with old man Nate on his back porch before moving out into the chairs under a big umbrella china tree in his back yard. He was telling us for the second time in two days about his pappy's Choctaw fight at Pilot's Knob, when we looked up and saw a tall man and a short woman walking along the bois d'arc hedge toward the house. They were followed by two lean, hungry-looking brindle hounds.

"Who's that?" I asked, breaking in on the story.

"That's Sheb Sprunt and his Indian wife, Josie," he said. "Sheb rents the south eighty acres of my place." Then he went on with his yarn, but he lost Claudie, since Claudie never knew before what Indians looked like, except from copper cents and cigar stores.

Sheb and Josie stopped about ten steps away from us and stood there close together by the cistern. Sheb was a scrawny, skinny, young fellow wearing dirty brown britches and a washed-out duckin shirt. He had an odd squint in one eye. Josie's skin was about the color of bock beer by lamplight, and her eyes were inky black. She was what I'd call squatty and square in the way she was set up. You could almost see corners through her faded calico dress.

"Mr. Pinkney," Sheb called out, "me and Josie want to go to the reservation tomorrow. 'Zit all right with you if we do? We'll be back Saat'dy night or Sunday."

"It's a pity," the old man said, "that you can't wait until you get all the corn gathered and in the crib."

"Josie's brother's gonna be made chief of the Waxahachie tribe, and he writ her to come." Sheb had made his speech. He turned and nodded to Josie, who grinned and showed her teeth. They were square and very white.

"How are you figurin' to go?" Old man Nate asked.

"We sold enough corn to get my brother's car fixed up."

"That's what I was afeared of," the old man answered, "and it'll never get you there. That Indian reservation is way down below Gruntsville — must be over a hundred miles — but I reckon I've got to let you go." Then, as they nodded and walked off, old Nate turned back to us and polished off a few more Choctaws before it got good and dark.

When he had finished, I said: "Mr. Pinkney, I think I and Claudie had better go on back to the trailer house and get us a good night's sleep. That sounds like a long trip to the Indian reservation."

"You ain't going, too, are you?" the old man wanted to know.

"Yes," I told him. "We'd better be moving on. We

don't want to wear our welcome out here, and I know Claudie wants to see them Indians."

Next morning, bright and early, Claudie found the baling wire and hooked the trailer house on behind this battered-up old Chevy. I told Sheb to drive slow, since there was a mean wobble that cropped up in the trailer at about twenty-five. Then, before Josie got in the car with him, I told her not to let Sheb drive too fast. She said, "Sheb bad driver; can't drive fast," and with that to think about we climbed into the trailer and Sheb pulled out.

On the way Claudie fussed some about leaving. He said, "I'd like to see them Indians, all right, Clint, but that's the nicest place we ever left without being run off."

"Claudie," I told him, "I sometimes think you haven't got any more ambition than a dadburned mule. Can't you see it's time to get a move on? We've been listening to old man Nate and eating his food for a week. If Sheb and Josie don't make it back, we'll fall heir to that corn gathering; and you know how I feel about manual labor."

"But we ain't gettin' any closer to Amarillo or El Paso thataway, Clint."

"From what I've seen of your rich relatives," I said, "they're more help to you at a distance than they are close up. Let's see them Indians first."

"My old man allus said a rollin' stone don't gather no moss," Claudie grumbled.

"There you go, Claudie," I told him. "Stubborn, too, like a mule. Man cannot live by moss alone."

It was after noon when we reached Gruntsville, and from there Sheb drove east a few miles through the deep piney woods to where a big sign said: "Waxahachie Indian Reservation 1/2 Mi. North." We followed a dusty, woods road north, with the branches and brambles scuffing and rattling against our trailer house, until we came to a little clearing.

All around was thicket. The undergrowth of palmetto, Cherokee rose and briars was so heavy you couldn't see ten feet outside the clearing. The trees were tall and thick; pine, magnolia, hickory, and beech, and here and there a sprinkling of dogwood.

The clearing was no bigger than an acre or an acre and a half; a number of cars were parked in it, and a lot of people and a few grunting razorback hogs milled about. Mostly the people weren't Indians, though; they were Texans. Also, the Texans seemed to have things in charge. Several grown Indians and a lot of little Indians were huddled here and there, hovering around the fringe of something that you could tell was about to take place.

Over on one side of the clearing, there was a new platform all covered with red, white, and blue bunting, and alongside it a big earthen crock. "Free Lemonade," it said on a sign, and the Texans were drinking the lemonade.

On the platform stood seven very uncomfortable-looking Indians, all dressed up in hot, heavy-looking robes and feathers. Josie said the one in the middle was her brother Joe Eaglebeak, and I noticed Joe had that same square look about his face and person that Josie did. Then I saw all the other Indians did too. The headpieces with all the feathers in them were much too big for these Indians, and you could see only the lower part of their faces — all except Joe Eaglebeak. He had shoved his feathers back to where they sat at an angle on his head like some of the hats the English women wear in the horse race pictures. The platform Indians all looked sweaty and tired in their hot, heavy Indian suits.

I sidled up to one of the Texans, a big, bald one dressed in a seersucker suit; he seemed to be having something to do with what was going on. I said, "The feathers don't fit them Indians very well, do they?"

"You are looking at all of the Indian costumes we could find in Houston," he told me, without even looking my way. "Matter of fact," he explained as he walked off, "we needed three more because we've got ten Indians on the Council."

Then he climbed up on the platform and said in a big voice that it was two o'clock and the program was going to start. Everything got quiet, and some people took a lot of pictures of the seven Indians in the feathers and the big Texan in the seersucker suit. They said it was for the newspapers.

As everybody gathered in close around the plat-

form, the big seersucker Texan said they were going to
have a double-header. They were going to inaugurate
a new chief, Joe Eaglebeak, and they were going to
break ground for the new gymnasium that the government was building for the Waxahachie tribe. The Texans cheered and even gave out a few Indian war
whoops; then the Indians out on the edge of the
crowd cheered too. Josie cheered, seeing as how Joe
Eaglebeak was her brother, but the seven Indians up
on the platform were too bogged down in feathers and
robes to do anything but stand there and sweat. Joe
Eaglebeak grinned and nodded his head every time
his name was mentioned, and I noticed that his teeth
were big and white, like Josie's.

While they were making a chief out of Joe Eaglebeak, I asked another one of the Texans who was standing around just who the big shot in the seersucker
suit was.

"That's B. Roger Blight," he told me. "He's a big
political boss from Tyler."

"What's he doing way off down here?" I asked him.

"He's the contractor that's going to build the gymnasium," the Texan explained.

When they got around to the gymnasium part of the
program, Mr. Blight said there would have to be a
very ceremonious ground-breaking. He called on Joe
Eaglebeak to go over in the far side of the clearing and
start digging at a place marked with a little stake. They
gave Joe a spade, and he began to dig while the state

senator, an old man with a long haircut, made another speech. They took some more pictures of the senator speaking and Joe digging, then everybody but the Indians started leaving. The Texans took the feathers and robes along with them, and the next thing I knew I and Claudie and Sheb Sprunt were the only people left except the Indians. There weren't over seventy-five members of the tribe around, counting the children and the real old ones. They were chattering and making a big to-do over Josie. According to Sheb, she was about everybody's cousin in the whole tribe.

The Texans had left the jar of lemonade, and the Indians all moved over to get what was left. Then somebody asked where Joe Eaglebeak was. In the crowd around the platform nobody had noticed that he wasn't drinking lemonade. We looked over at the far side of the clearing, and there was Joe, still digging. Nobody had told him to stop.

Late that afternoon we went with Sheb and Josie down a little trail in the woods to Joe Eaglebeak's place. It was not over fifty yards from the clearing. Joe and his wife, Joey — who looked a whole lot like him — lived in an old, run-down, two-room house that swayed low on the east side where some of the supports were gone. I noticed that there were porches on all four sides of Joe's house, so I said, "Lots of porches you've got here, Chief."

"Need much porches," Joe said. "Porches good for

sit. In winter Joe Eaglebeak follow sun around house. In summer follow shade."

Right beside Joe's place was about two thirds of a nice big, new-looking frame house. It must have been twice as big as Joe's house — leastaways, it would be when finished.

"Nice new place you're building there, Chief," I remarked.

"Not building," Joe said. "Tearing down. Don't like inside smell of new house. Old house best."

"Why did you build the new house, then, Chief?" I asked him.

"Don't build new house," he told me. "Government build new house. Good for firewood. Last maybe one year for firewood. Joe Eaglebeak chop no trees long as government house last. Time to eat."

We all sat down to supper on one of the porches with Joe and his wife, Joey; and they fed us cold possum and corn pone. When the food was put out on the table, little Indians showed up from everywhere. They swooped on and off the porch like a flock of teal, and every time they'd pass the table, they'd grab handfuls of food.

After supper Joe Eaglebeak said, "Time for radio," and went in the house. Then the radio came on full blast. It boomed; it rattled the windows; it made the house shake on the east side where it was swaying; and it drowned out everything else. We could see Joe inside as he worked turning knobs. He got all sorts of music and talk about soap, skin lotions, politics, and cigarettes, but he never turned it down. It even seemed to get louder, and finally Joe came back to where we were sitting on the porch with Joey. He grinned and said something, but it was lost in the roar of the radio.

Along about sundown I yelled at Claudie and told him I thought we'd better get back to the clearing. Joe walked with us up the trail; and as soon as we got out from under the blanket of radio racket, I turned to Joe Eaglebeak and said, "How's the game around here?"

"Plenty game," Joe said.

"Lived here all your life, Chief?" I asked him.

"Except in German war," and as he said it, Joe's skin seemed to tighten up across his face. He almost looked like a different Indian. "In German war," he went on, "Government draft Joe Eaglebeak to Oklahoma. Private Eaglebeak in Fort Sill, Oklahoma, twenty months. No game in Oklahoma."

I explained to Claudie about the Field Artillery School in Fort Sill; then I asked Joe, "Did you learn to shoot cannons there, Chief?"

"Nope," Joe said. "Joe no shoot cannons. Keep horse lot clean in Oklahoma. War not good for Joe Eaglebeak." Then he turned back toward home, and I and Claudie went to the trailer house and turned in for the night.

The next morning, about daylight, we heard Sheb
and Josie trying to get their old Chevy started, and
Claudie allowed he was pert near ready to go back
to the Pinkney place.

"You really want to get in on that Brazos Bottom
cotton-picking, Claudie?" I asked.

"Well, uh —"

"No, Claudie," I explained. "I'm afraid that old
car'll never make it back with the trailer house, and
I'd rather be here or there than stranded somewhere
in between. Also, we'll be in on the ground floor
when Mr. Blight starts to build the gymnasium. I'll
get you on here, doing heavy anyway, and we might
even both get jobs timekeeping, or straw bossing, or
something that docs not take any manual labor."

We told Sheb and Josie good-by, but only after
they'd pulled our trailer house over to the edge of the
clearing. We knew we'd need the shade.

As the dusty old Chevy disappeared up the woods
road, I almost felt stranded again and blue. In the
early morning light the clearing looked pretty bleak
and dreary. The bunting on the platform was all limp
in the dew, and some rusty-colored hogs were rooting
around the hole Joe Eaglebeak had dug. It didn't look
like a very good place to build an Indian gymnasium
— or any other kind.

The sun wasn't very high when it started getting so
hot and muggy that the air quivered and shimmied
across the clearing. There were lots of flies and gnats

about. When I began to feel a little itchy about the armpits, I checked up on myself and found that I was alive with wood ticks. So was Claudie. I don't know many things that will get a man's dander down further or faster than a passel of wood ticks in the early part of the day.

Along about nine or ten o'clock we saw a big black sedan come into the clearing from the north, and when it pulled up even with our trailer house, out hopped a fat citizen with a thick, chubby face and little eyes set very close together. He wasn't any Indian either; he didn't even look like a Texan. He said he was looking for the Waxahachie chief, and I pointed to the trail leading toward Joe Eaglebeak's house.

After he had gone, Claudie said that he did not like this fat guy's looks one bit.

"I don't either, Claudie," I told him. "I'm afraid he ain't our kind of folks." Then, while Claudie fixed us some breakfast, I sat in the shade of the trailer house and thought a while about a number of things; but mainly I thought about how badly stranded we were, particularly in case we needed to make a quick move for one reason or the other. We needed a car in the worst way.

In an hour or so I and Claudie noticed that the lemonade stand was going again full blast, and the Indians were all gathering again around the platform on the other side of the clearing. They were being spoken to once more, and we could see from where we were that the speaker was the fat fellow with the close-together eyes who had come in the black sedan. We couldn't hear what he was saying, but he seemed to have his heart more in it than the speakers had the day before. He was waving his arms in the air like a man fighting bees, while the Indians all stood around listening and scratching themselves.

"Wonder if these Indians have a speakin' every day?" Claudie asked me.

"I don't know," I said, "and I don't much care, but I hope they don't cut out that daily lemonade. Let's go have some."

Just as we got over to the platform, the Indians all took a vote on something or other. "All in favor hold up their hands," the fat speaker said, and the Indians all held up their hands. We drank our fill of lemonade as the meeting broke up.

Pretty soon we saw what the meeting had been about. Indians started boiling out of the woods on all sides. They went over to the black sedan where the fat man handed them signs on long sticks, and they started marching single file around the clearing. The signs said:

B. ROGER BLIGHT IS UNFAIR TO AMALGAMATED ASSOCIA-
TION OF HELPERS, HOD CARRIERS AND BUILDING TRADE
APPRENTICES, LOCAL 1131.

The Indian pickets, as they walked by the trailer house, all looked very mad and warlike.

Pretty soon a big truck filled with sand came down

the road from the north. It stopped at the edge of the clearing where the Indians were marching. The driver got out and said it was the damndest picket line he'd ever seen, but he wasn't going to cross it. Then another truck came and stopped the same way; then another and another, until by sundown the trucks were backed up all the way to the Gruntsville road turnoff.

It was nearly dark when Mr. Blight, wearing a fresh seersucker suit, turned up. He walked by the stopped trucks and came to the trailer house where I sat watching the pickets. He was in an awful fret. His face and the back of his neck were as red as a Denton County beet, and his eyes were all bloodshot.

"So you've organized the Indians," he said as he walked up to me with his hands on his hips.

I called Claudie to come and said: "Take it easy, Mr. Blight. A haughty spirit goeth before destruction. Why weren't you fair to the Amalgamated?"

"I'm not unfair to the Amalgamated," Mr. Blight said. "I never heard of any union in here until an hour ago when they told me my trucks were tied up."

By this time Claudie was standing there, about a foot taller than Mr. Blight, so I said: "Now, Mr. Blight, if you will be so kindly, I'll thank you to have a civil tongue in your head. Let's get this clear. We didn't organize these Indians."

"Oh, yeah?" he said, but I could see that Claudie's size and my firm, polite way were telling on him.

"Certainly not," I said. "Maybe we can unorganize them, though. I know a lot about Indians, and my associate, Claudie here, does too. We're sort of Indian experts."

"What's your name?" he asked. He was getting a lot more friendly.

"Clint Hightower, and I think that I can help you with these Indians if you will let yourself cool off a little," I said.

"Well," Mr. Blight explained, as he eased up in the tone of his voice, "this is sure one hell of a mess. You see, I agreed when I got this contract that I'd use Indians for common labor. Now the union has tied up all my labor and my building material, too."

"Let's get down to business," I said. "Do you want these Indians unorganized or not?"

"What's your price?"

"Well," I said, "I and my associate have us a nice trailer house, as you can see, but we do not have any car to pull it. We're getting awful tired of hitchhiking rides for it."

"Do you mean — ?" he started and choked, turning red in the face again.

"I mean," I said, "we want a car that will pull this here trailer house."

"Why, I'd see you in hell first. The law —" he choked again.

"You keep forgetting, Mr. Blight, that we didn't or-

ganize the Indians. We only want to unorganize them,"
I explained.

"But —" he said, and I broke in:

"If there is a strike on this time tomorrow, we don't
get anything. If there ain't, we want a car."

"You've got more gall than a government mule, but
you've made yourself a deal," he told us and left. He
was still mad.

It was pitch dark by the time Mr. Blight left. Claudie fired up a lantern, and we went down the trail to
Joe Eaglebeak's house. We found him sitting on a
stump in the yard smoking a corncob pipe and listening to the radio. It was on full blast.

"Chief," I yelled as loud as I could to make him hear
me above the radio, "tune that thing down; I want to
talk to you." Joe went inside and turned it down a little.

"Joe," I asked him when he came back, "who was
that fat fellow in the black sedan?"

"Union organizer," Joe said.

"I thought so," I told him. "Who's head man in the
new union?"

"Joe Eaglebeak, President," he answered.

"Good for you, Joe. I'm proud of you. Tell me about
the union. What all do you know about it?"

"Not much." Joe lit his pipe again and sat down as
he said it. "You know much about unions?"

"Oh sure; they're a lot like the Army, Joe," I told
him.

"Union like Army? Army not good for Joe Eagle-beak."

"A great deal like the Army," I went on; "and another thing: that big, fat fellow in the black sedan sounded just like a top sergeant to me."

"Sergeant?" Joe dropped his pipe in the grass as he got up. "Sergeant?" he said it again to himself, and fighting lines showed up around his mouth. "Sergeant no good."

"Joe," I said, "it looks to me like you are going off somewhere again to clean horse lots. You may like it, but how about the other Indians?"

"Sergeant no good," Joe kept saying to himself as he looked for his pipe in the grass; then, when he found it, he struck out for the tall timber. I and Claudie walked back up the trail to the clearing.

The next morning when the fat organizer came to the clearing in his black sedan, the Indians were waiting for him. There were forty or fifty of them milling around him about a minute after he got there. They all had their picket signs, but they weren't marching any more. This time the Indians were doing the talking, and above it all I could hear them yell, "Sergeant no good." The fat man didn't have a chance. One of the Indians hit him over the head with a picket sign; then there was an awful mixup, with Indians pushing and shoving and chattering like a bunch of women at a rummage sale.

I got Claudie to go with me, and we ran over to the

crowd. We dug the organizer out the way football umpires dig out the man with the ball. He was pretty badly ruffled up when we got him in the clear, and Joe Eaglebeak had hold of him by the coat collar. I asked Joe to turn loose and get things quieted down so I could talk. "This ain't a fair fight, Joe," I said. "You Indians have this good man outnumbered." Then I turned to the organizer and said: "I don't believe these Indians like you very much, but the way they are abusing you is against my sense of fair play. I and my assistant here want to help you, mister, but not in any Indian fight."

He was too out of breath to talk, but with all the Indians standing around and muttering at him he seemed to be almost persuaded that it was about time to leave. Then I said, "I'm afraid I can't promise to hold them off much longer."

That was enough for him. He bolted for the car, but when he did the Indians swarmed after him again. It was all I and Claudie could do to hold those Indians off, but with some help from Joe Eaglebeak we did, and the man in the black sedan sloped for the Gruntsville road. The Indians all went off down the trail that led to Joe's house.

After the dust and the Indians had cleared away, the trucks all came into the clearing; and the drivers started unloading sand and gravel and lumber. Mr. Blight came along after a little while, and he was the most relieved customer I'd seen since the time we

pulled Claudie's Uncle Zeke out of the bear trap back
in Alabama.

"You fellers didn't take long," he said.

"I think I'd like a red automobile," I told him. I figured I'd better strike while the iron was hot.

"Let's get a green car," Claudie put in.

"We'll take red, Mr. Blight," I said. "Maybe we
can get a red one with a little green trimming somewhere on it."

About this time we looked over toward the trail
leading to Joe Eaglebeak's house, and there came the
Indians again. Joe was in the lead. They went over to
the platform, got the "Unfair" signs, and started to
march around the clearing. All the truck drivers quit,
folded their arms, and stood there watching the pickets. Mr. Blight looked at me like you'd look at some
carcass the dogs had drug up from the creek.

"There they go again," Claudie said — as stupid a
remark as I'd heard him make all day.

I went over to Joe Eaglebeak, who was leading the
picket line. I took him by the arm and said, "Chief,
what the hell's up? I thought we'd fired that fat organizer."

"Fired organizer," Joe said and kept on marching.
I marched along with him until we were even with the
trailer house, then I asked Joe to come in for a minute
so we could talk things over. The other pickets
marched on while Joe went in with me.

Inside, Joe sniffed and looked around; then a nice

friendly look came across his face — almost like that of Indians on calendars. He said, "Joe Eaglebeak like inside smell of trailer house."

"O.K., Joe, and thanks," I said, "but what's going on out there?"

"Joe Eaglebeak big union chief now," Joe stated. "Indians strike."

"Listen, Joe," I said, "you're fixing to louse this gymnasium job up if you don't watch out. What the devil is it you are striking for this time? What do you want?"

"Big house in Florida for Joe Eaglebeak."

"Florida?" I said. "What do you know about Florida?"

"Know from radio," Joe said. "Union chiefs get Florida houses."

"Wait a minute, Joe," I argued.

"Blonde bathers, too, for union chiefs in Florida. Bathe squaw in ocean," Joe went on.

"Do you know anything about the game in Florida, Joe?" I asked him.

"Never thought of game." Joe looked a little stunned at this.

"Well," I said, "there's no more game there than there is in Oklahoma."

Joe looked pretty hard hit, and I went on while I had him bothered. "Joe," I said, "I once knew a wooden Indian who used his head more than you are using yours right now."

This seemed almost to hurt Joe Eaglebeak's feelings, and he got up and started to leave. He was talking to himself, but all I could hear was, "Bathe naked squaw in ocean."

"Hold it, Joe," I yelled, remembering a chapter from old man Nate's book on Indian fights. "There's one more thing about that house you want in Florida. There's a war on over there, you know."

Joe sat back down, and I saw the skin tighten up on his face again. He said: "War in Florida? No more war for Joe Eaglebeak. Had war in Oklahoma."

"Of course you did," I said. "Now you listen to me, Joe. Did you ever hear of the Seminole Indians?"

"Seminoles? Sure," Joe grinned and nodded.

"All right," I went on, "the Seminole Indians have got them a war on over in Florida. It's been going on a hundred years or so. Big Chief Osceola started war. No peace treaty yet." I found I was beginning to talk a little like Joe. "No war in Texas; plenty game here, too. Big Texas house is what you want, Joe. Government calls it gymnasium. Let them build it. If you don't want to live in it, you've got forty years of firewood."

"Forty years of firewood?" Joe asked.

"Of course, Joe," I told him. "Forty years anyhow."

"Forty years enough," Joe said.

"Now you are talking, Joe," I said. "Let's burn up them picket signs."

"Indians burn platform, too," Joe said. "But, first,

Indians need smart fellers' help to build gymnasium.
Indians make no mistake if Clint and Claudie work
too.''

"You don't need us, Joe," I argued. "I'm no good
at manual labor."

"You no work, Indians no work; Indians strike," Joe
took hold of the picket sign and started to raise it up.

"Hold it, Joe," I said. "Claudie will work on the
gymnasium. I might be a straw boss or something."

"You no work, Indians strike," and he said it like
an Indian that comes from a long line of fighting Indians.

"O.K., Joe, you win," I told him. Joe nodded and
grinned until all his square teeth showed. We shook
hands on it.

We had a big bonfire that night in the clearing. We
burned the platform and all the picket signs. We all
drank our fills of lemonade that B. Roger Blight fetched
from Gruntsville. He brought it in a red Ford coupe
with green wheels. It was second-hand, but it would
run. He handed me the registration on the car, made
out in my name, but I saw that the blank headed "Oc-
cupation or Business of Owner" was not filled in.

"What goes here?" Mr. Blight asked me.

"Just put it down 'manual labor,' " I told him.

V I I

Sam The Management

AFTER THREE MONTHS' WORK on the Indian gymnasium, I and Claudie were ready to see how far away from there we could get — without actually leaving Texas, that is. Also, it was winter time by then, and I'd got me a bellyful of the cold drizzle that the raw east wind blew in for a week straight along about Thanksgiving.

Claudie'd worked every day, doing heavy labor on the gymnasium job; and while I'd been too nervous and bothered for anything like that, I'd brought in a line of jewelry, almanacs and liniment that the Indians went for in a big way. I cut Joe Eaglebeak in on a certain percentage of the profit, but he never asked me how much, and it didn't amount to a lot.

What really decided us to move quick was that Claudie heard from some of his folks back in Alabama that his Cousin Windy had moved to El Paso and was in on something pretty good there.

With some money saved up from our Indian work, Claudie'd wanted to try to make Amarillo, but I knew better. "No, Claudie," I said; "not this time of the year. There ain't anything but a few strands of barbed wire — a very poor windbreak — between Amarillo and the North Pole. El Paso is different. There's a hell of a lot of weather in this state in the winter, but there's less of it to get betwixt you and the sun in El Paso. Remember also the light in Jules's crystal was brightest over El Paso until Amarillo flared up so."

A week later I and Claudie were sitting on a bench about noon soaking up the warm sun in the park with the alligators in the middle of it — the one there next to the Cortez Hotel in El Paso.

"Hasn't the time about come for you to think again, Claudie?" I said. "I mean about Windy."

For the last three days I'd had Claudie study hard for a whole hour trying to think up Windy's last name. All Claudie could call to mind was that Windy was his Aunt Earline's boy by her second marriage. He knew right off who her first husband was and her third, but that was no help in finding Windy that had lighted up Jules's crystal ball so bright.

I sat there in the park a solid hour, looking at the alligators while they looked back at me and blinked their droopy, mean eyes; then I said, "All right, Claudie, your time's up," and he walked around and around the bench, scratching himself.

"Windy Willie is all I kin 'member," he said.

Then I got this terrific idea. Claudie should write his folks back in Alabama for Windy's address. This got it, but we hung around the general delivery window at the post office for over two weeks before the letter came. It turned out Windy's last name was Smith — William Smith. Then we found that not a single one of the William Smiths in the El Paso telephone book would admit to coming from Alabama or being kin to Claudie either.

Claudie wanted to give up on Windy, and, if you want to know the truth, I was about ready myself to forget him — but not before I'd sat down and written Jules Rabinowitz what a faker he was.

Then, the very next day, we found Windy through a pool-hall contact of mine, and found out right off why he wasn't in the telephone book. It was so a man in his position would not be bothered by salesmen, tradesmen and moochers, Windy explained later. Windy was living in a big brick house out in the high part of El Paso toward Mount Franklin — the address the fellow gave me at the pool hall.

Windy remembered Claudie well, he said that morning as we studied the fine plushy room he asked us right into. There were plenty of sofas, settees and pictures of scenery on the walls and rugs on all the floors. When I told Windy how glad I was to meet him, I promoted Claudie right in the same breath. I stated Claudie was my partner.

Windy wore tweedy-looking clothes and dark horn-rimmed glasses, and on his tie, I remember, he had a handpainted horse. He was heavyset all over — even in the face — and looked like a man that had put on a lot of well-heeled mileage in his thirty-five or forty years. His cheeks were pinkish tan with lots of little red veins showing through. His hair was wavy brown all over and cut to look like it hadn't been.

Windy asked Claudie how he'd been doing all these years, but before Claudie could speak up Windy went on to apologize for the house he'd asked us into. "Just camping here," he said. "Some very dear friends of mine, the Dillinghams — they own a big slice of the copper smelter in El Paso — are away on a trip around the world. I advise them on investments and look after some local interests for them. I agreed to stay here while they are away. I've been puttering some in the garden this morning with a hobby of mine — bulbs. There's nothing like a hobby to get a man's mind off of his worries."

"Zat your car out in front?" Claudie asked. We'd parked our Ford behind a cream-colored Cadillac roadster, and I could tell Claudie was sniffing for a real asset this relative of his owned.

"No, my car's in the shop," Windy said. "It's a foreign make, and they've had to order the parts from somewheres in Europe. But the Dillinghams want me to use that little old Cad out there, and it'll just have to do until mine's fixed up."

Claudie said, "Uh-huh," and Windy talked on. From some things he said I could tell he'd been to college, where he'd been a great athlete. He spoke of being a four-letter man in college, and claimed that, fat as he was getting, he still had many of these same talents that made him one.

Windy never said it right out, but it was plain to me from the names he spoke of that he'd cut a real swath in high West Texas society. He had plenty of well-heeled friends that he mentioned accidentally — people that owned ranches, oil wells and automobile agencies all over West Texas. He spoke of some friends that owned a race-horse farm, too, located in that part of Kentucky where the grass that grows is all blue. He was on the best terms with several Hollywood stars, and all these celebrities he called by nothing but their first names. Big stars, too, with swimming pools Windy had swum in personally. Windy didn't brag about these things, understand; they just sort of came out from what he said. And of the Washington people that Windy spoke of by name — all very high up, like senators or ambassadors or judges — he didn't so much as mention just a congressman, not even once.

Windy had been married to a beautiful opera singer when he was very much younger than he was that day in El Paso, but her career had interfered with his, and they'd had to call it off. He was deeply in love at the present time, he went on to say, with a moving picture star who wished very much to marry him, but he wasn't taking any chances on any clash between his career and that of another star of any kind. He was too cultured, he explained, to mention her name to us, and I said, "Of course, Windy. I can understand that."

"What's your line, Clint?" Windy asked me after the longest.

"Mainly," I told him, "I am a planner — large projects, gymnasiums and —"

"Speaking," Windy cut in, "of large projects, the Elephant Butte Dam up on the Rio Grande is one of the biggest I've ever been on. It's enormous. At first the government wasn't even going to build it at all. The Secretary of the Interior wasn't for it, and even our senators said it couldn't be done. That's the way it was when I came out west a few years ago. Now we've got the dam — millions of gallons of water backed up there. Well, it all goes to show what co-operation will do. Everybody working together. After it was finished, the chief engineer on the job called me aside and said, 'Bill,' he said, 'you ought to be proud of this dam. You —'"

"The telephone's ringing off the wall," Claudie said, and Windy went into the next room to answer it. He said, "Yes sir," about four times and "All right, sir," — good, sound southern manners all right; then he came back, smiling. "That's my old friend Dillingham," he explained, "calling from New York. Just wanted to be sure I was all right."

Somewhere a clock was striking twelve, and I said, "Why don't we go somewhere and eat something?"

"I'm for it," Windy said, "but you fellows have to let me treat you. Where do you want to eat?"

"At the Paso del Norte," I told him. "But it's on us. I and Claudie'll meet you there in an hour. I may have to make a few arrangements first."

Well, it was all I could do, in the hour I gave myself, to talk the man in that little bank down by the Southern Pacific station into a fifty-dollar loan on our red Ford, but I knew we couldn't keep up long with anyone in Windy's league on no more than the fifty cents in cash that I was down to and the dollar seventy-five that Claudie had. He didn't want to mortgage the car, but I explained that it wasn't often we had the chance to travel in such company as Windy's, and Claudie's own kin too. "This may be our big day," I told him.

At the Paso del Norte Windy ordered a porterhouse steak with about everything fancy they had to go along on side orders, and so did I. Claudie said he'd like a settin' of eggs fried, but I only told the clean, starched little waitress to bring him the same as mine and Windy's.

As we ate, Windy talked to us just like we'd been old friends of his that had been riding around in Cadillacs all our born days. It was not until we'd finished eating that Claudie spoke up — the first thing he'd said all during the meal. He asked the waitress for toothpicks. Imagine it! I caught his shins under the table with my heel and said, "Not here, Claudie"; then I told the waitress to bring us the check, without any tooth-picks.

"Oh no, fellows," Windy said. "This is on me. You must allow me to have the check."

I noticed that Claudie was grinning all over and nodding his head, but I put up a good argument with Windy before I lost it, since I really could tell his feelings would have been hurt if I hadn't. But at the cashier's stand, when Windy started to pay the check and for the fifty-cent cigars he bought around, he looked inside his wallet and found that the smallest amount of money he had on him was a one-hundred-dollar bill. I never saw anybody so embarrassed. I mean, I really never did. So I took the check and paid it there while Claudie went into an awful coughing spell over his cigar. Claudie could never get used to fifty-cent cigars, but for a man that shouldn't have ever left the pot-licker part of Alabama anyhow, he was trying.

Out in front of the Paso del Norte Hotel there was a doorman dressed up like an admiral in the Navy, and Windy spoke to him, very democratic, and said, "How's tricks, Eddie?" Then he turned to me and Claudie and said, right where the doorman could hear, "I'll tell you right now, I've sat in some of the highest society in New York and Newport and Rhode Island, but I don't know when I've been with finer folks or enjoyed their company more."

"Thank you, Windy," I said; "thank you very much."

"Well, fellows," Windy said, "I expect I'd better get back to my place. I've got to make some long-distance telephone calls, and I haven't studied the *Wall Street Journal* yet today."

"Let's all go over to Juarez," I said. "They have some nice shows and nightclubs over there. Why don't we just make a day of it?"

"I've never been there," Windy said. "There's nothing to it unless you go to the Tivoli Casino — that's the big gambling place, and I hardly ever gamble. Fact is, I've almost sworn off, except small games of chance with associates."

"Oh, come on, Windy."

"But —" Claudie started.

"Not now, Claudie; can't you see your cousin's talking to me?" I said.

"Come to think of it," Windy weakened, "we might try it once. It might be good for me to relax at the Casino."

"I and Claudie are ready to go now," I stated; and Windy smiled the friendliest smile you could imagine and said, "O.K., fellows. Hop in."

Then I and Claudie personally climbed into that big cream-colored Cadillac, and Windy drove us over the Rio Grande bridge to Mexico. I mean finally we were in high cotton, and with Claudie's own kin.

2

When we got to the Tivoli Casino in Juarez, a whole passel of little Mexican kids swarmed around the car, yelling like a bunch of crows in a cornfield. They started shining the bumpers and the bumper guards and everything all over the car. I gave a dollar to the biggest one and told him to split it up with all the rest of them, and this started a fight amongst them that still wasn't over when we went on in.

It was the first time that I and Claudie had been inside the Tivoli; but, since Windy hadn't been there, I led the way and called the head waiter "Juan." Headwaiters in Juarez will always answer to "Juan" anyway. I could see that Windy was proud to be with people that knew their way around in Mexico.

In the middle of the afternoon, that way and all, the place was pretty empty; but when they saw what a fine customer they had in Windy, all dressed up like a Hollywood hero on vacation, people came alive everywhere around. The Management, a fellow named Sam, came out and greeted us personally. He was soft, pudgy and bald as a nest egg, but he had bright black eyes. He used a sort of Mexican accent on every word he spoke; but I remember saying to myself that if this guy was any Mexican, he had come a long way — maybe from somewhere beyond China — to be one.

Sam The Management shook our hands and said he would consider it a personal favor if we would send for him when the headwaiter produced anything that we even suspected was less than the very best. We told him we would, and then he ordered a round of drinks on the house — tequila for Windy and me, but Claudie only drank mescal, a much cheaper type of drink.

It should give you some idea of how they liked us at the Tivoli Casino when I point out that The Management put on a floor show for us that afternoon about five o'clock — one with four or five Mexican girls in it — that wasn't due to go on until ten or eleven that night. They beat on tambourines and sang some songs in Mexican, and then they came right around our table and did us a dance, wearing pink dancing costumes that were all the same size. But the girls were not. I am sure that those same girls lit up by soft lights on a stage late at night would have looked much healthier and better. That way you don't see warts, moles, wrinkles around elbows or skinned knees. Also, we probably wouldn't even have noticed that the one we later learned was named Lolita had such a terrible cold.

After the floor show we walked down a long corridor hung with green curtains and went through a heavy door that had four Chinese dragons painted all over it. It was the door to the gambling room, and as we walked in, a plump Mexican woman in rose-colored clothes started playing a piano.

Windy told Sam The Management right off that he wished to present a check on his New York bank for Mexican money worth about five hundred dollars. The Management smiled at us all and said United States cash would do.

"Very well," Windy agreed, "I'll make out a check for five hundred dollars, American."

"Checks we do not cash," Sam explained. "It's house rules."

"I sincerely trust you are not telling me that you decline to accept a check on my New York bank." Windy's eyebrows were away up close to where his hair was parted.

"The rules of the house apply to New York banks, too," Sam The Management said, still very polite. "You see, I have studied law, and I interpret the rules."

"Try some of them hundred dollar bills on him," Claudie urged, and Sam's little eyes shined like cut glass.

"No, it's a matter of personal pride with me," Windy argued. "I can see how The Management might not like to cash a check on a Mexican bank or even a Texas bank; but if this is a joint where a man cannot even cash a New York check, then I shall have to withhold my patronage."

Windy seemed half hurt and half mad — standing there holding his check book, bound in leather with gold lettering on it; and I do believe that he would have left and not gambled at all if The Management had not finally given in and said, "All right, my friend; I like your looks. I will cash one check on your New York bank for five hundred dollars."

With this Windy whipped out a gold fountain pen and wrote the check. Then he got a handful of different-colored chips, and the gambling started.

First, Windy played chuck-a-luck — the one where the houseman flops over a little silver cage that is full of dice. He said anybody who could win at chuck-a-luck was in a real streak of luck, and he simply wanted to run a test on himself. He was right, too. And when he had won a hundred and fifty or two hundred dollars — he didn't even bother to count it — he said he was ready to shoot craps.

Sam The Management said, "Fine." He called another houseman, who took a brown canvas cover off of the big table in the middle of the room, and there was as pretty a layout for a crap game as a man could ever dream up. I told Claudie that if the Lord ever allowed them to shoot craps in Heaven, it was hard to see how a finer dice table than this could be provided. It was green velvet in the middle with all the figures that showed the odds printed there in gold. Around the edges the table had little mother-of-pearl flowers and medallions and things set down in the wood and smoothed and polished and shined.

"Aren't you going to gamble?" Windy asked, and there I stood with less than fifty dollars in my pocket.

Claudie shook his head, and I said, "No, not right now."

It turned out that Windy spoke a lot when he gambled, and everybody that was in the room, including The Management, the Mexican woman in the rose-colored dress that had been playing the piano, and the dancing girl named Lolita — all of them — came over to watch Windy shoot craps.

First, he rubbed the dice between the palms of his hands and seemed to be talking to himself when he said: "This is not the most dignified way in the world for a gentleman to flirt with the fates and court the charms of Lady Luck; I usually prefer the stockmarket or drilling for oil. However, one must find one's amusement where he is, and it is well to find it in some counterpart to the risks and vicissitudes that go to make up life — come seven!"

Well, Windy was hot as a pistol that night. Pretty soon he had a pile of chips that looked almost knee-high, and every one of them worth a hundred dollars. He just couldn't seem to miss; he would put chips down on the gold letters that said "eight for one" if you rolled eleven; then he would roll an eleven. He would put chips on the gold letters that said "twelve for one" if you rolled an eight the hard way — with two four's; then he would roll two four's. All this time Sam The Management stood there pale around the gills, fidgeting, putting his hands in his pockets and then taking them out again and looking for all the world like a man that is about to fly apart.

Finally Sam spoke up and said he believed he wished to bring Windy some new dice, since a change now and then made for a fair gambling game — also, it was a rule of the house that the dice could be changed whenever The Management said so.

Windy said, "Fine"; then he started betting hundred-dollar chips against himself; I mean, there on the gold letters he put bets that he would not make a seven or an eleven and also bets that he would not make his point after he had come out on it; and, sure enough, he picked exactly the time when his luck changed, because the money he won from then on — several stacks by now of hundred-dollar chips — was all won by betting against his own rolls.

By this time Sam The Management was really fit to be tied. Then I noticed there around the table several Mexican soldiers that had just popped up from somewhere. Sam said he believed it was time to change back to the dice Windy had been shooting with first, and Windy bowed to all the people and soldiers before he said, "O.K., that's fine with me, but just now I believe I will give myself a little rest and recreation at the bar. I've had a pretty busy time of it, ladies and gentlemen, and I thank you for your kind attention."

Windy handed The Management five one-hundred-dollar chips and said, "Now, will you be so kind as to bring me that check on my New York bank? I will take it back, and here are your chips."

Windy's pile of hundred-dollar chips was so big that I hardly noticed the difference in the size after he had taken out five. The Management brought him the check, and Windy held it up in the air and tore it into small pieces; then he dropped them into a great big brass spittoon that was right there beside the gambling table.

I and Claudie went right along with Windy to a little table in the next room where the bar was, and we all had a lot more drinks, but this time Windy would not let them be on the house. He paid for our drinks with a hundred-dollar chip and told the waiter to keep the change.

Then the floor show came again and put on their act, and I thought the girls were a whole lot prettier than they had been that afternoon. They seemed to like us more, too. Windy gave each one of them a hundred-dollar chip and said it was partly for the show and partly if they would be quiet and not do a thing for the next thirty minutes. He spoke of the need to meditate. And he did, and so did I and Claudie as we drank some more tequila — except, of course, Claudie was still drinking only mescal.

Along about midnight Windy said a strong hunch had come over him that we should go and gamble some more. Claudie allowed that it was later than he liked to stay up, especially if he was in Mexico, but Windy said the night had only started. He was really in fine spirits.

Windy laughed and laughed and said, "Listen, fellows; I've got another sweet little run of luck tucked away in my system, and you must come and help me get it out. Come watch me while I break this joint." You can see the liquor was beginning to change Windy's personality some by this time; but Claudie — can you believe it? — actually tried to argue there with his cousin. Windy only laughed and laughed and called for the dice.

"But, first," Claudie said, stubborn as a mule, "let me hold some of them hundred-dollar chips for you."

Windy was plainly not worried at all about the future, but only to please Claudie he gave him two hundred-dollar chips, and Claudie went straight to The Management and cashed them in for United States money.

"That's a little present for you, Claudie," Windy said; then he went back to the dice table, where by this time there were some other people shooting — mostly American men and women; and one Mexican — the biggest one, I believe, I ever saw. Also, there was Lolita, the dancing girl with a cold, shooting dice all by herself; and when Windy started shooting again, Lolita came over and stood right beside him. I noticed that from time to time he'd give her a hundred-dollar chip to go over and play chuck-a-luck with — just so she wouldn't be there in the place where he needed elbow room, Windy said.

From this time on Windy seemed still to be winning a lot, but he was also losing some. He had all of his pockets so full of chips that whenever he lost, he'd simply dig into one of them and pull out a bigger handful and bet it. Once I heard him say, "Many's the time in Monte Carlo I've seen ten thousand go faster than that measly five hundred."

Then, after a little while, I noticed Windy was over between the piano and the chuck-a-luck table having a very serious talk with Sam The Management; and when he came back, he had another handful of chips. They didn't last long, and pretty soon Windy was writing checks left and right from his leather-covered checkbook. But it didn't seem to bother him one whit. The waiters kept bringing tequila for Windy, and I and Claudie drank some more too.

Along about two or three o'clock in the morning the people started to thin out, but it must have been close on to four when Windy said he believed he'd had enough. All the other customers, the floor show girls and all the Mexican soldiers had long since gone.

3

Outside the casino we got into Windy's Cadillac and started toward the bridge across the Rio Grande to El

Paso. Just one block before we got there, Windy's head seemed to nod, and the big Cadillac veered a little bit from the middle of the road. Then, before I knew it, there was a little Mexican pushcart right in front of us, and we hit it. The racket was something awful, and all kinds of fruits and berries and Mexican melons flew up and spattered the windshield. In no time at all Mexican policemen started coming on motorcycles from every direction, and they took us to a little office a couple of blocks away where some more Mexican policemen were sitting around inside under dim lights.

One of the Mexican policemen spoke pretty good English, and after he'd taken our names and all, he said there was nothing he could do but put us up for the night in the close-by *juzgado* — Mexican for jail. Also, he pointed out, the bridge to El Paso had been closed since midnight.

At this, Windy was more than a little put out. He started talking in a loud voice and turned red as an apple around the neck and in all the parts of his face except his nose and cheeks. They were as red as a fire engine.

Windy told them how he was an American citizen and spoke also of the Constitution of the United States. Then he went ahead to brag on us a lot. He said that I was so high up in the United States Government that I was practically a Secretary of War and Claudie was the heavyweight champion of the State of Texas.

He spoke well, too, of his friends, the Dillinghams, and he threatened to get every policeman in Juarez fired if they detained him so long as one more minute. But when he started to walk out and asked us to go with him, several Mexican policemen got in the door and threw their guns on us.

One little Mexican came up from behind Windy, holding a rifle with a bayonet on it in his left hand and the barrel of a hog-leg pistol in his right. Just before he hit Windy over the head with the pistol butt, I reached for him; but it was Claudie that actually grabbed him. The little Mexican reeled and fell against the rifle, and as he went down on one knee, the bayonet on the rifle nicked the bottom part of his ear. The blood spurted. I have seen many a stuck pig stuck, but I'll swear that for the next few minutes this little Mexican's ear would have held its own with any stuck pig — up to a six months' shoat, that is.

With the sight of all that Mexican blood and hearing a lot of fast Mexican words the bleeding one said to the others and they said to him and to us, I knew we were in for a very squally time in Juarez that night. Some more Mexican policemen came in, and before you could say scat the place was full of them; also, they all had their guns leveled right in our faces — Windy's too — and they had the triggers on these guns cocked; every one of them. They had no trouble at all in moving us next door to the *juzgado*, where they put us all three in one cell.

The clang of the iron door to our cell rang out loud and rough on the night air, and by the little sliver of moonlight that came in the barred window, I saw the rats taking off. Biggest rats I ever saw. Inside the cell there was no place to sit down, and by this time of night it had turned pretty cold too. We found some blankets on the floor, but they must have been there for a long time. They wouldn't even bend.

In a few minutes Windy was asleep, snoring away there on the cell floor. So was Claudie.

I climbed up on a little shelf that folded down from the wall and looked out of the cell window with the heavy steel bars across it. I looked at the adobe houses and church spires still and quiet and brown in the clean moonlight. I looked beyond at hard Mexican mountains that looked soft in the light of the moon, and I watched the white puffy clouds as they drifted across the valley of the Rio Grande and put their fuzzy shadows on the ground. Fact is, I do not know when I have seen a prettier night in all my life than the one I saw outside the *juzgado* there in Juarez. Then I went to sleep on the floor of the cell in the only place left for me — there between Claudie and Windy.

It was broad-open daylight and they were clanging an old chain against the iron bars when I woke up. I found I was stiff in all my joints and shivering from one end to the other. Claudie's face was blue. We got up, stretched and spoke, but it seemed that for some reason nobody could think up much of anything to say.

Not even Windy that had had so much to say the night before. Then the guard was giving us some breakfast; three bowls of chili and three flat leathery tortillas.

The hot chili brought tears to Windy's eyes that stayed there after he finished eating. Windy spoke very confidentially to us and said that he didn't have but one real weakness; it was the one we'd seen in him the night before. It must have been the drinks, he told us, and he was repenting plenty, over what he'd done.

"Why, Windy?" I asked. "The wreck didn't seem to me to be all your fault."

"That's not it," he said. "I must have cashed between ten and fifteen thousand dollars' worth of checks."

"But, Windy, for a man of your position, what's a little sum of money like that?"

"The difficulty," he explained, "lies in the fact that I do not have any money in the New York bank."

Here Claudie had to get in on things. "If them checks wasn't no good," he asked, "why'd you give up them chips for the five-hundred-dollar check?"

"That," Windy stated, looking through the bars and away off toward the little patch of blue Mexican sky, "is a matter of honor with us Smiths."

After what seemed a long time, a whole gang of Mexicans came marching in a kind of military formation right up to the door of our cell. They opened it up with a big key and marched us out to look head-on at fifteen or twenty guns, all leveled right at us, and these same guns all cocked like they'd been the night before.

We marched where these Mexicans told us to: four blocks to the gray stone building we found was the Juarez courthouse.

We stood up in front of the bench where the wrinkled little old brown judge sat and listened while the policemen from the night before told their story. It was all in fast Mexican that we couldn't begin to understand, but the judge spoke to us in English. He said Windy's case would be dealt with first because it was easier. Windy owed the number of pesos that amounted to $9.50 in American dollars for driving his Cadillac while drunk. Also, he would have to pay $21.90 for the damage he had done to the pushcart and all of the ripe fruit and melons in it.

Windy took us off to one side and said wouldn't I and Claudie put up this piddling amount of money to pay him out. "I lost all the dough I had on me last night," he said. "If we can get ourselves out of Mexico and into the United States, it's the best thing, even though we have to do it one at a time."

Claudie had the money he had cashed the chips in for — two hundred dollars. I knew he had put it away somewhere in his shoes, but I could tell from the look on his face he wasn't about to dig it out.

"Can't you see, Claudie," I said, "as soon as Windy gets out he'll start to work on our case, and with all the pull he's got —"

"Uh-huh," Claudie said.

"Won't you, Windy?"

"Of course, fellows," Windy said. "Claudie's my own blood kin, and you're his friend. I can do a better job springing you from the outside, I'm sure."

When Claudie wouldn't budge, I dug down in my own jeans and found it took just about all the money we had left from mortgaging our car. So I paid the $31.40 to the rusty little clerk there in the court, and Windy left.

I waited until I heard the Cadillac motor start outside; then I turned and asked the little brown judge how much I and Claudie owed.

His honor looked very serious and bothered. He said nobody in the State of Chihuahua could figure out the punishment.

"Oh, come on, Judge," I said; "couldn't you give us a sort of an estimate —"

"You must not understand," he went on slowly. "Thees is not local matter; thees case cannot be dealt with in Ciudad Juarez or the State of Chihuahua. You have violate the laws of the Republic of Mexico; you have challenge the peace and dignity of our country; you have shed the blood of a Mexican soldier. It is a national crime."

Here we were at war with Mexico, and there stood the little Mexican policeman whose ear we'd nicked the night before, grinning at us. I looked at Claudie, and in my mind I could see him in striped clothes making little Mexican rocks out of big ones, but at first I couldn't tell who that smaller guy was right there beside him. Then I knew. I was wondering why I'd ever left Alabama in the first place.

It got so quiet in the courtroom I could hear some chickens clucking outside and a mission bell that rang a long ways off. The time was passing slower and slower until I heard the court room doors swing open and in came Sam The Management from the Tivoli Casino. He marched right up to the bench, and I mean he really hustled.

Then Sam The Management spoke to the judge, and he went straight into a lot of Mexican talk — fast like a machine gun. Oh, but he made a fine speech. There was passion, a lot of it, in his voice, and at times righteous wrath like you'd expect from one of the Old Testament prophets. I couldn't understand a word he said, but I could tell from the way he said it all he was for us. He pounded the table, and he shook his fist, and sweat poured off of his face — even in the winter time there, and all.

When Sam The Management got through, the judge said something in Mexican to the soldiers, and they all put their guns on their shoulders and marched out. Then he thanked Sam, and he told us in English he was convinced that the whole thing was simply the kind of mistake that any government could make about even the best citizens of some other government. He pointed out that if he had any other way of telling us how sorry he was that we had been detained in Mexico, he was ready to say it then and there.

"No hard feelings, Judge," I said, "and my partner here, Claudie, has no hard feelings also."

Outside the courtroom I spoke to Sam The Management in my politest way. "I and Claudie will never forget your fine speech," I told him. "Mr. William Smith must have told you about the awful kind of trouble we were in."

"I'll say he did," Sam answered, still hot. "He also told me if I didn't get you two out of jail today he would stop payment on all those checks he wrote last night."

About this time a street car came along headed for the river bridge and El Paso. We told Sam The Management good-by and caught it. As we crossed the Rio Grande I thought a lot about the fine judge of character I was and how right I'd been about Windy — to pay him out of trouble when Claudie wouldn't; but, of course, I didn't have the heart to rub such a thought in on Claudie. Also, I did not wish to hurt the feelings of a partner that had two hundred United States dollars there in the soles of his shoes.

VIII

A Quilt for Claudie

CLAUDIE spent the first fifty dollars of our Juarez money to pay the bank off and get our car unhocked. Then, with some of the rest of it I made several fine contacts there in El Paso and got in good with some people that had real pull; I mean such as a Texas Ranger, two notary publics, the secretary of the Barbers' union, and the Champion Wild Cow Milker of the Fort Worth Stock Show — Ladies Division.

The Champion, Willie Sue Grundy by name, was a big, bouncy brunette, and she was terribly nice to me and nice to Claudie also. She was the one, come to think of it now, that got us to leave El Paso around the middle of December. She wanted a lift to Fort Worth so she could try to win the Wild Cow Milking title again; and she told us when we got there she had a very jealous husband in Fort Worth, so that was the last we saw of the Champion.

In a few days I managed to get Claudie a nice position at the Fort Worth stockyard packing houses. He was in charge of a goat — the black one that led the sheep down a chute to be slaughtered. Then Claudie would lead the goat back for more sheep, over and over again, all day; and that was just about Claudie's speed.

The winter was mild enough when we first got to Fort Worth, and the old-timers around the domino parlors spoke real often about it. "Clint," they'd say to me, "man and boy, these Texas winters ain't what they used to be." That was the talk until Christmas Eve, when a blue norther — one that our almanac hadn't said a word about, either — swept down from the Rockies to the Gulf of Mexico and put a skim of ice on every creek, pond and wet place in the whole State of Texas. It was early in the morning, an hour or two before daybreak, when the north wind struck. It rocked the trailer house and woke me up; it moaned and sighed around the eaves and whistled in through several cracks that Claudie had meant to fix but hadn't.

I braced my cot against the wall, pulled both my quilts tighter around me, and went on back to sleep. Then, along about daybreak, my teeth chattering woke me up again, and I found I was so cold I was blue-numb and shivering all over. I looked at Claudie, snoring away on his pallet, and since he looked as warm as a depot stove, I borrowed one of his quilts to see if I couldn't warm up and get in a little more sleep before time to get up. But right away Claudie's sneezing woke me back up. He sounded like the air brakes on trains do right after they stop.

Claudie got up, though; he dressed in about all the clothes he owned, and he said he was the coldest he'd been since the day in Alabama when they broke the ice in Chaney Creek to baptize him. I noticed his nose was running, so I dug out some mutton suet and coal oil for him to put in it.

As Claudie went sniffling off to work without a word about the quilt, I almost felt out of sorts with myself for what I'd done. I needn't have, though, since by that time it had got so cold that one quilt more or less couldn't have made a great deal of difference. Then I got to thinking about Christmas coming only once a year and how that fierce blow out of the north had brought the kind of weather that went with Christmas in storybooks and songs; enough, all told, to put a whole batch of ideas in a man's head about stepping out and buying a nice present for somebody, so as to help celebrate such a special season of the year. What a dandy thing it would be, I thought to myself, if I went downtown and bought Claudie a nice warm quilt as a surprise for Christmas.

Now, I did not have the kind of money to buy Claudie a good quilt — or any kind of a quilt, for that matter — but I knew my heart was in the right place, and I had the whole day before me, so I set out for town on the next streetcar that came along. It was some warmer inside the streetcar — out of the wind, too — and with my mind thawed out a little this way, I worked out a fine program before I got halfway to town. If I could open up a charge account, I could buy Claudie a nice quilt on credit and pay for it later.

I got off the car right across from Cashman's — by far the biggest and the best department store in Fort Worth. I figured that if I was going to get credit, the best would be none too good, and it would be an honor to have a charge account at such a store as Cashman's. If, on the other hand, I wasn't going to get credit, I didn't want to be turned down by any second-rate store.

I crossed the street and looked into Cashman's show window, where tinsel, holly and little red bells were scattered all around with other kinds of gew-gaws on the sparkling artificial snow. I looked over the dummy figures standing around in loose, carefree poses and dressed up in fine clothes that fit; I saw the gay, happy looks on the faces of the dummies — faces that showed no worry, no grief, and plenty of credit. I wondered how I'd take to the life of somebody like those guys there in the window, wearing new bedroom slippers and a silk smoking jacket and filling up a pipe from a big jar of tobacco by a brick fireplace. Then my teeth were chattering again, so I went into Cashman's.

It was on the ground floor that I first saw the floor-walker, and he must have seen me at about the same time because he started moving my way. I went ahead, pretending that I wasn't even noticing him; but wherever I went, he kept on edging closer to me until

I found I was not liking this floorwalker at all. He
was so clean — freshly shaved and dressed up — that it
was enough to give a workingman the pip. His light
yellow hair was very curly and parted right down the
middle, and his cheeks were as pink and shiny as over-
ripe apricots. He had on a batwing collar, striped
pants and patent leather shoes, and in his coat lapel
he wore a big white flower.

I watched him as he glided along from counter to
counter. I saw how the people that were clerking in
the store would spruce things up when he came by;
they'd straighten out things that were already in
even rows and flick dust off of counters that looked
clean enough to me in the first place. When the floorwalker spoke to the clerks, he had a way of lifting up
his eyebrows and batting his lids like a man with a
wild gnat in his eye.

I was watching the pert, bright-eyed girl at work
behind the candy counter when the floorwalker came
up from behind and spoke to me. "To which department of the store do you wish to be referred to?" was
what he wanted to know, in very elegant grammar.

"I'm just looking around," I told him. "Later on I
will make up my mind what it is I wish to purchase."
And I raised my eyebrows right back at him when I
said it.

He turned toward the candy girl and asked, "Have
the specials come down yet from the stockroom, Miss
Fothergill?"

"No," she answered. "Not yet, Mr. Twilley."

Then I made my move. "Mr. Twilley," I said, "I wish to open a charge account. The name is Hightower — Clint Hightower. I live at the Dolly Dimple Trailer Courts, and —"

Before I could finish, though, he said, in a very prissy way, "That has to be taken up with the Credit Department. It's right there." Mr. Twilley pointed to a close-by sign that said "Credit Department," about like you'd point out a big red barn to somebody that had nearly walked right into the side of it. Then he offered to step over to the Credit Department with me. No, I told him, he needn't bother; but he said, with both eyebrows up, "Oh, it would be a genuine pleasure," and I knew, somehow, right then, that I wasn't going to do my best on any charge account with this sprucy character hanging around.

Well, I was right. Somehow, I never could get going with the heavy-set fellow that was Assistant Credit Manager. He had a mighty lot of curiosity, but of all the points he took up with me, the one that seemed to bother him most was that I did not exactly have a job at the present time.

After he'd thought it all over, the Assistant Credit Manager put his shoe-button-sized eyes on me and turned me down while Mr. Twilley, that fancy floor-walker, stood right there hearing the whole thing. As I turned to walk away, Mr. Twilley bowed and said, "Sorry, old fellow."

I wish people in this great big world would not say, "Sorry, old fellow," and I've noticed it's even less help when it comes from hotel clerks, floorwalkers, or people that represent the United States government.

I was on my way out of the store when I passed by Cashman's Santa Claus, and I could hardly believe it when I saw the awful shape he was in. I'd thought Claudie had a bad cold that morning, but it was nothing like the cold that Cashman's Santa Claus had. His eyes were watering, and his nose, together with a circle all around and into the fringe of his whiskers, was plumb raw and about the hue of the little red wagons the women were buying for the kids close by. But Santa's cold was so plain to see that the mothers were steering the kids away from him like they would from an old well or a wasp nest.

I went up to him and said, "Listen, Santa, aren't you in pretty bad shape to be handling this particular job?"

"I ache all over," he groaned. "Thank God, it's Christmas Eve — the last day." Then he caught his breath a couple of times and sneezed his whiskers loose on one side.

I saw that under his whiskers he needed a shave, personally, and I felt so sorry for him that I said, "I believe you'd better go on home, Santa, before you catch your death of cold. You look awful."

Santa was hooking his whiskers back over his ear while all the kids around giggled and pointed to him, when I saw another fellow dressed just like Mr. Twilley, the floorwalker, coming our way. But he had a better look than Mr. Twilley's on his face, so I spoke to him as he came up, and said, "I don't think Santa feels very well. Somebody ought to take his place."

The other floorwalker led Santa over toward the freight elevator, and I went right along with them. Santa was explaining that he had to go on because he needed the ten bucks they were going to pay him, when I spoke up again.

"Tell you what," I said to the other floorwalker, "Santa's got an awful cold, and he needs to go home. I'll finish the day for him. He can take five dollars, I'll take five, and it won't cost Cashman's a cent more — but I want a fresh set of whiskers."

In ten minutes, or fifteen, I was the new Santa Claus. Mr. Twilley had been so busy haunting the clerks over at the other side of the store that he never did know about the change. He didn't recognize me, either, when he came by about noon, because he said, "How's the cold, old fellow?"

I said, looking him right in the eye, "Mr. Twilley, I never felt better in my life."

About two o'clock that afternoon, they gave me an hour's relief for lunch, but I didn't even bother about any food. I got out of my whiskers, red clothes and boots, and went down to the bargain basement where they sold quilts. Right off I found some blue, silky-looking ones that I knew Claudie would take on over, but the price was way too high. I looked through them all until I found one that was a little damaged; it looked rusty on one side, and it had been torn in two places. When the little quilt saleslady agreed to mark it down to $4.98, I said, "Kindly put that one aside for me. I'll take it on the lay-away plan."

It was after eight that night — and the store was going to close at nine — when I saw Claudie come in. He walked right by the place where I had a whole passel of kids telling me what they wanted me to bring them, and, of course, he didn't begin to know who I was.

I supposed that Claudie must have been there to buy me a present, so I watched him as he worked his way through the crowd of last-minute shoppers. He looked over the fountain pens, the silk pajamas, the bathrobes and the leather handbags. Then he sauntered around the perfume counter for a while, and I figured I must have been wrong, after all, about who was going to get this present. He stood there a long time, looking at some big cans of men's talcum powder — something I could use, all right, with no way to take a bath in the trailer house — but I couldn't help thinking that forty-nine cents a can wasn't much for Claudie to put into a Christmas present for me.

He wandered around some more and finally came to light at the men's jewelry counter. He got him a clerk after the longest, and I saw him pay his money. Then he left the store with a little bitty package.

I couldn't see how anything that size could do me much good, but I went right over and found out from the clerk that Claudie had gone and bought me a gold-filled, mother-of-pearl tie clasp and paid $4.98 for it. It was the shape of a beetle, and it worked the way a clothespin does. The more I thought about Claudie buying me that gold-filled tie clasp, the better I felt inside and the more stuff I wanted to promise those kids they'd find in their stockings.

At nine o'clock, the doors were closing, and I was about to go turn in my suit and collect my money when a nice little old man came up to me. He had on a black overcoat with a velvet collar, and he was holding a derby hat in his hand. His hair was thin and white, and he was a little stooped in his walk — all signs of a very old man; but his friendly gray eyes were clear and bright like you see in younger people that have always behaved themselves very well.

"Santa Claus," the old man said in a kind voice, "you must have had a busy day."

"Pretty busy," I told him, "but I'm not much tired. I'm almost sorry it's over." His nice manner seemed to make me want to talk to him, so I added, "Matter of fact, it ain't really over, because it will be some time before I forget all those kids."

I could see what a hit that made with him. He nodded and said, "Tomorrow, I wish you would come to my apartment. You see, every year I have a Santa Claus at my Christmas dinner."

"What's the pay?" I asked. I was for taking him up, being already in the groove on this kind of work.

"It's not for pay," the old man said. "I mean I want you to be my guest."

But I thought of Claudie having to eat Christmas dinner all by himself, so I said, "Much obliged, Mister. I wish I could, but you see I've got a partner, and I'd better eat with him tomorrow."

"Bring him along," the old gentleman said. "Come to Suite 88B at the Texas Hotel around one o'clock. I'll be expecting both of you." I told him he could count on us, and he left as fast as he had come.

Then it dawned on me what a mess I was about to make of things. Why I hadn't seen it in time I could not tell. I and Claudie couldn't go to Christmas dinner and not take along a present; that was a cinch. But how? My five from the store was going for Claudie's quilt. Claudie was gone, and all the stores would be closed on Christmas Day. Then I knew that Claudie's quilt would have to wait. I rushed down to the basement and unbought the quilt; then I went shopping again for the old man's gift.

The basement clerks were putting things away as fast as they could, so I had to hurry; but I soon found exactly what I was looking for — a beautiful picture in a gold frame with a wire on the back so it could be hung up. From the time I first laid eyes on it I could tell it was just the present I wanted to give that fine old gentleman.

The picture was one of a lady playing a piano and wearing a low-cut dress, but from the way she sat in the picture, you could only see her back, all pink and soft-looking. The piano was one of those flat ones, and on it was a big vase full of flowers in all colors. The price turned out to be only $4.98, and I told them to wrap it up in the red wrapping paper with green holly. I bought it with my pay from Cashman's.

As I went out of the store, carrying the present, I passed Mr. Twilley, that dude that had been walking the floor and raising up his eyebrows all day. He said, "Merry Christmas," like he was saying to everybody that was leaving, so I said, "And Merry Christmas to you, old fellow."

When I got to the trailer house, Claudie was sitting inside with his feet in a pan of steaming hot water. He said he believed he'd got his heels frostbit a little at the stockyards. He seemed downhearted somehow, but when I walked in with that Christmas-wrapped package under my arm, you should have seen the look that came across Claudie's face. Just like a little boy, I thought, as I put the package under my cot.

It was so cold by this time that the only way to get warm was to go to bed. I gave Claudie back all his covers and borrowed an extra blanket for myself from the people in the trailer next to ours. We made it fine during the night, but next morning, after we'd had breakfast, Claudie gave me my present; and there I was, fresh out of any present for Claudie. "Christmas gift!" he said as he handed me the little package.

I opened it and looked as surprised as I could. Then I thanked him and said, "Claudie, this is about the prettiest tie clasp I ever saw. I am touched by this more than you think." Claudie just stood there over by the stove, waiting, and I could tell he had already thought up what he was going to say when I gave him his present.

"Claudie," I went on — but I could not look him in the eye — "here's the way it is . . ." and then Claudie wasn't waiting any more for his present. For a man that is baffled by many a strange gate and some ordinary barbed-wire gaps, Claudie is smarter than you'd think about some things. He could tell that all he was going to get was an explanation — something you can't unwrap on Christmas morning.

He pointed under my cot. "What's in that there package?" he wanted to know.

"I was going to tell you about that," I said. "It's a present that I and you will give to the nice old man that has asked us both to Christmas dinner today." Then I told Claudie about the picture of the lady playing the piano, but I did not show it to him, since that would have spoiled the beautiful way it was wrapped.

Outside the door to Suite 88B, we got all ready to speak a Christmas greeting to the old man, and then I punched the button. The door swung open on a very classy room with several mirrors in it, and just as it opened we heard a clock inside strike one. By the door stood a colored man all dressed up in a stiff white shirt, a dark suit and a black bow tie. I said, "Merry Christmas," and the colored man said the same to us as he took our hats. I decided to leave the Christmas package with him, too, until the time came to give it. The colored man bowed and said, "Come in, gentlemen. Mr. Cashman is waiting for you in the library."

"Mister who?" I asked.

"Mr. Cashman," he said again.

"The one that owns the store?"

"That's right," he answered, with a grin.

When we walked into the library, the gray little old man was standing there alone. He had on the kind of smoking jacket I'd seen those dummy figures wearing the day before in Cashman's show window. There was a fireplace in the library too, like the one in the show window, except that this one had a real fire blazing away in it.

After we'd wished him a Merry Christmas, Mr. Cashman wanted to know our full names, where we were born, and a lot of things I wouldn't have thought mattered one whit to him. He was sorry about Claudie's bad cold and glad it wasn't any worse; in fact, he was so dadgummed polite and easy in his way that he made me feel almost used to this much class. When he sat down and said, "Gentlemen, it gives me great pleasure to have you dine with me today," everything was about like that part of the Twenty-third Psalm where it says, "My cup runneth over," and so on.

"It pleasures us also," I told Mr. Cashman, speaking for Claudie too, since by that time Claudie was so flabbergasted that he was just sitting there in a big easy chair, sniffling and swallowing. The colored man brought us gold cups full of eggnog, and Mr. Cashman told us about his annual custom of having the Cashman's Santa Claus in to Christmas dinner. "This is the twenty-first consecutive year I've had this pleasure," he told us.

Claudie was lapping up his eggnog too fast, and I was even hurrying a little with mine to keep him from looking plumb coarse in company that was strictly so top quality, when the doorbell rang.

"That's Featherstone Twilley from the store," Mr. Cashman said. "I asked him to join us when I learned he was all alone today."

I looked, and the colored man was bowing that spiffy floorwalker into the library. He was dressed within an inch of his life, and Mr. Cashman introduced him to us. Claudie said he was pleased, and I guess he was; I said I was pleased too, and Mr. Twilley said, "How do you do, I'm sure."

"We're fine," I said, while Mr. Twilley looked at us like a lady in high heels might look at a horse lot she had to walk out of. But he didn't let on that he'd ever seen me before, and, naturally, I didn't let on. He turned and handed Mr. Cashman a box of cigars —

Christmas-wrapped — and the old gentleman said they were his favorite brand. Mr. Twilley turned on a cocksure smile that seemed to say he'd rot before he'd produce even one cigar that he didn't already know was Mr. Cashman's favorite brand.

I figured it was time to send Claudie to get our present for Mr. Cashman, and I was about to do it when Mr. Twilley spoke up and said he simply couldn't wait to see Mr. Cashman's new Van Gogh. Claudie, who hardly knew what was going on, said, yes, he'd like to see it too. So Mr. Cashman led us into the living room, where some fresh eggnogs were served to us all.

Now that library had about everything I reckoned a room ought to have, with soft, plushy furniture all around to sit on, or in; with hundreds of books in shelves; and several pictures on the wall showing people in red coats on horseback; and over in one corner a marble statue of a woman without a stitch of clothes on. But the living room Mr. Cashman showed us was enough to make the library look downright dinky. All four walls were lined with pictures, since, as it turned out, Mr. Cashman was a sort of an art collector on the side.

He had some very plain-looking religious pictures, and they were so old that the paint was all cracked on them. I remember, too, he showed us one of a beautiful English woman in a big hat, painted, he told us, by a fellow named George Romney. Then there was a country scene that was lit up by a little light built into the frame at the bottom, and the animals and people in it looked so real you'd have expected them to move about any minute. When Mr. Cashman told me and Claudie he'd paid eighty-five thousand dollars for another picture he showed us, I told him I thought it was worth every cent of it.

All the time Mr. Cashman was showing us around, Mr. Twilley was standing in front of a picture that I figured was about the poorest of the lot — one of a dreary-looking woman who looked like she'd had smallpox most of her life and liver trouble the rest. It turned out to be the picture drawn by the artist named Van Gogh, and Mr. Twilley was liking it so all-fired much that he seemed a little stunned. I mean he was slobbering over the picture and bragging on Mr. Cashman's taste in art, and the old man was eating it up. Mr. Twilley turned to me and said, "And do you not think it is superior, Mr. Hightower?"

Now I did not want to run down Mr. Cashman's new picture, but I wasn't about to agree with that floorwalker, so I said, "I can't tell how good it is, Mr. Twilley, since I never saw the person it is a picture of." Claudie nodded his head so as to agree with me. Mr. Cashman added that he could understand my point of view.

As we wandered around the living room, listening to Mr. Twilley drool over the pictures, I got to wondering where Mr. Cashman was going to put the picture of the woman playing the piano when we gave it to him; also, I wondered when the right time would come to let him unwrap it. I found this had been bothering Claudie, too, because when we were about to go into the dining room to eat, he pulled me off to one side and asked, "Hadn't we ought to give Mr. Cashman his present before we've et?"

"Not right now, Claudie," I told him.

Well, we found that Mr. Cashman had some of the prettiest pictures of all in the dining room, and while we ate turkey, turkey dressing and cranberry sauce from enough plates to take care of a dozen people, Mr. Cashman told us about these other pictures. Some of them were painted in European countries several hundred years ago, he said, and Claudie allowed they were in pretty good shape to be so old.

Mr. Twilley was showing off how much he knew, when Claudie blurted out a question. "You haven't got any picture of a woman playing a piano, have you, Mr. Cashman?"

"I don't believe I have," he answered, and I stung Claudie with a stony look that kept him from going on.

As soon as the meal was over, we all went back into the library, where the colored man brought in a big tray, and on it was a silver pitcher with a long spout and several little saucers with cups no bigger than thimbles. One thing about rich people, I always say, they sure do live dainty.

Mr. Cashman, himself, poured us out little dabs of black coffee, and Claudie, whose hands are bigger than

my feet, looked pretty funny holding his saucer up and
pouring coffee in it. But he was never one to drink
coffee that hadn't been saucered and blown first, and
this time Claudie made it without spilling a single
drop.

Mr. Cashman opened up the cigar box Mr. Twilley
had brought him and passed it around. He asked Claudie to take two if he liked the brand, and Claudie took
two while Mr. Twilley sat there looking like a poi-
soned puppy. Myself, I wanted to take two, but my
manners got the best of me.

After we'd smoked a while and listened to Mr. Twilley brag on Cashman's Store, Mr. Cashman himself,
and the Cashman art collection, I noticed the old gentleman yawn a couple of times — very polite yawns,
though, with his pale hands held up to his mouth.
There was a feel of about-time-to-go in the air, but
still we had not given Mr. Cashman his present, and
still it did not seem to be the right time to do it. I was
worrying about this when Claudie said, "Mr. Cashman, we brung you a present."

"That's very thoughtful, gentlemen," Mr. Cashman
said. "You needn't have, I assure you; but I am very
grateful."

Claudie went into the little anteroom and brought
back the present, still Christmas-wrapped and all. He
handed it to Mr. Cashman, who stood up to take it.
Claudie stood there beside him as he snipped the ribbons with silver scissors, and Mr. Twilley looked on

from the red plush chair where he was sitting by the fireplace. His eyebrows were high, wide and handsome.

Poor Claudie, I thought; wait until that $4.98 picture is sprung on Mr. Cashman — a man that is used to paying eighty-five thousand dollars for pictures.

But it didn't work out that way at all. When Mr. Cashman saw the picture, his eyes brightened up the way they must have a long, long time before over his first Teddy bear. He said, "Gentlemen, this is a beautiful picture. It is just as I told you a little while ago; I did not have a picture of a lady playing a piano. I thank you from the bottom of my heart."

I knew Mr. Cashman must have been putting on an act, but when I looked at Claudie I could tell it was an act that was good enough for him — and then some. Claudie was grinning from one end of his long face to the other, and the whole thing started getting next to me, myself, as we stood there in the nice warm library with the weather so cold and raw outside. I forgot all about Mr. Twilley as I remembered some scripture about it being more blessed to give than to receive, and I knew I'd a damn' sight rather feel the way I did than the way I'd have felt if I hadn't received anything out of it personally except the same picture of the lady playing the piano.

I noticed the colored man was bringing Mr. Twilley his hat and coat and gloves, so I told Mr. Cashman we'd better be going ourselves. He said, "Gentlemen, this has been a very happy Christmas."

"Thank you, Mr. Cashman," Mr. Twilley spoke up. "It has been my pleasure, I am sure."

Then Mr. Cashman spoke to me and Claudie and said, "Before you go, I should like to do something for you so that you will always know how much your visit has meant to me."

"Oh, no," Claudie said, "we won't never forget it nohow."

"But, nevertheless," Mr. Cashman went on, while the colored man brought us our hats, "after all, I am established, and so is Featherstone. Yet I can tell that you gentlemen have not until now had the full measure of your success. Is there not something that I can do for you?"

"Well —" I said, and I knew I did not want to argue much more with Mr. Cashman. I looked at Mr. Twilley, who was still hanging around to see how it was coming out, and Mr. Cashman went on, "Remember, it is my sincere desire to do something for you and Claudie."

Claudie said he believed he'd like another cigar; and while Mr. Cashman was trying to talk him into taking two, I was looking down at my mother-of-pearl tie clasp and thinking. Then Mr. Cashman turned to me and said, "And you, Mr. Hightower?"

"Mr. Cashman," I said, "I believe I'd like to open

up a charge account at your store. A five-dollar account will do, I expect."

"Certainly," he answered, and he turned to Mr. Twilley. "Featherstone," he said, "you will see to it that this account is opened first thing in the morning."

"Yes," I added, speaking to Mr. Twilley. "First thing in the morning, old fellow."

Then I and Claudie said good-by and left the warm place behind the door marked 88B.

I X
The Delegates

CLAUDIE is a sucker for a bargain; turn him loose in a good-sized town with some money in his pocket, and there ain't any telling what all he'll buy up. Anything; just so it's a bargain. That's how Claudie came by such things as his imitation ivory mandolin pick — but he don't own any mandolin; a silk watch fob; a dozen golf balls that he's got about as much use for as a hog has with a handsaw; *Bentley's Revised Manual for Bird Watchers* — all items no good at all to a man that can do only very manual labor and sing bass.

So I wasn't surprised that cold January night in Fort Worth when Claudie came back to our trailer house from losing his job at the packing house and brought nothing but two excursion tickets to Galveston and back. He'd spent all his pay except carfare on them.

"Only $3.98 apiece," he said. "Good for thirty days on all trains."

"Now, Claudie," I said, "if we're buying tickets on trains, just why Galveston instead of Amarillo where Jules saw the big light?"

"They ain't no excursions to Amarillo," was Claudie's idea of a complete answer.

"O.K. Just one more little bitty question, Claudie." I put it to him straight. "What would we use for money in Galveston?"

"Oh, I know we can't afford to rilly go," he said.

"Then why in the hell did you buy the tickets?"

"Kind of a bargain I'd never let get away," said Claudie, still proud of what he'd done.

Well, I am not a man to let anybody's railroad get away with anything like that, and Claudie ought to've known it. So I asked him, "Did you happen to be so smart as to pick up a railroad timetable too?"

He pulled one out of his pocket and said, "The lady that sold me the tickets give me one free."

I looked the timetable over and said, "Claudie, the next train for Galveston leaves Fort Worth at eleven tonight. Gets us there at seven in the morning. That's the train we'll take. Leave us not argue, Claudie. I've already decided for us to use up these here tickets. We might make out all right in Galveston after all. And these tickets are round trip. We won't get stranded." I was brushing the wrinkles out of my coat with the padded shoulders and out of the different-colored britches that I always wore with it. Claudie put on his double-breasted blue serge suit, and we packed my corn remedy along with our razor in Claudie's wicker suitcase. Then, with the little money we'd have spent for a bite of supper, we got our shoes shined at a close-by barbershop and paid our carfare downtown. We got off in front of the Santa Fe station stony broke.

What a mob there was at the train! And a band, too — playing loud patriotic music. They were sending off a lot of men and women that had big white "Delegate" badges on their coats, and as soon as I got up close enough to figure things out, I explained to Claudie what it was they were going to — the Annual Convention of the Texas Chamber of Commerce in Galveston, Texas — right where we were going, too.

When the porters all up and down the train started to holler "Board!" I and Claudie climbed right on. We looked up and down the car for some beds that hadn't been taken, but the delegates and their wives kept beating us to them; so we went through a green curtain marked "Men" at one end of the car and found ourselves in a little room with black leather seats and tin washbasins all around. It was a better deal than fighting them aisles with the delegates that seemed to know their way around on the train. Also, it gave us a chance to clean up a little, which I did, and shaved too, while Claudie tried to get a drink of water out of a little spigot on the basin.

It was about this time that two conductors came into the little room and asked us for our tickets. Claudie forked the excursion tickets over, and the conductor said, "Now let's have your Pullman tickets."

"Give the man everything you've got, Claudie," I said, "except the part of the tickets that will get us back from Galveston."

"But I did," Claudie told me. "He's even got that

part right now, but he'll never get out of the room with it." In Claudie's voice I could tell his dander was getting up.

"Here is the return portion of your tickets," the conductor was saying in a sassy way as he handed them to Claudie. "Now you will have to go ahead to the coach — fourth car forward."

I looked around and Claudie was standing in the corner bracing himself like a man that was not about to go to any coach. "We're not bothering nobody in here," he said.

"At Waxahachie," one conductor said to the other one, "we'll call the officers and put these bums off."

This riled me and I said, "Listen, Mister. Between here and Waxahachie you are fixing to have the roughest ride since you started conducting if you don't leave my partner there alone."

"One more time —" the talking conductor said, and he was red as a beet in the face, "do you go to the coach or not?"

"And why should these folks go to the coach?" somebody said in a raw red whiskey voice as he came through the curtains marked "Men." He was a big citizen — nearly as tall as Claudie himself — and he was wearing a long "delegate" ribbon on the lapel of his coat. He had a round real tanned face, nice friendly eyes, and more sandy hair in his eyebrows than he had on his head.

"What's the trouble, fellows?" he asked us, paying

the conductors no more mind than he did the wash-basins.

"The conductors don't like our tickets," I told him.

"Why, that's an outrage," he said to us and the con-ductors. Then to the conductors only he said, "In Texas, people do not push other people around on trains or anywhere else. You'd better leave these dele-gates alone or the Chamber will ride some other rail-road next time." And at this he pulled two big silk "Delegate" ribbons out of his pocket and pinned them right on Claudie and me — just like that.

As the conductors backed up toward the curtains, one of them said, "O.K., we'll see you in Waxahachie if you're not in the coach by then."

"You'll do nothing of the sort," our new friend told him as he reached in his overcoat pocket and pulled out a quart bottle that was still over half full. "Now go peddle your coaches somewhere else. We're just before having a little drink in here," he yelled at the conductors as they ducked back through the curtains.

Well, I've run across some danged nice people in my time — some bartenders, Texas Rangers, Salvation Army captains, and one mayor of Dallas — but the best of the lot would look downright crummy if you put him alongside Cecil, our friend on the train. Cecil Snavely his name was, and he was a prince from the word go.

"Don't stint yourselves, fellows," he said when he passed us the bottle; "there's more where that came from." Then, when we'd all had a drink around, he passed the bottle again and said, "Here's the other half of that first drink."

My, but he was cordial to be no drunker than he was. He had the outside pocket of his coat stuffed with big black cigars, and we smoked along as we drank. I could tell that Cecil was used to good strong cigars, and when he smoked he'd put as much of the cigar in his mouth — down one side — as the part he'd leave dry so it could burn. And these cigars were so strong that they near about choked me and Claudie down, but we'd have smoked them or bust, that night on the train.

Later Cecil said, "Time for another drink, fellows; a bird cannot fly on one wing." We all laughed and had another.

It will show you how much pull Cecil had with the railroad when I point out that later on the conductors called "Waxahachie next stop" out there in the hall, but neither one of them so much as stuck his head back through the curtains marked "Men."

Cecil went on then and told us a very sad story about himself; about how he'd come to be nearly fifty years of age already, and hadn't found himself a woman yet that was for marrying him — at least not one that he himself had wanted to marry. He admitted that there was one he'd been trying to keep company with for several years, but she was so dadburned cultured and civic that she wouldn't have him. She lived in Wichita Falls, only fifteen miles from Burkburnett where

Cecil himself lived; she was nearly as old as Cecil was, but she spent all her time organizing musicales, bazaars, and rummage sales, speaking to literary societies, and heading drives to raise money for beautifying Wichita Falls. Cecil went on to say he was only a used-car dealer in Burkburnett for years, and hardly in the lady's league; but even when he sold out and bought an agency that didn't sell any kind of cars except brand spanking new ones, she still wouldn't have much of anything to do with him. Eleanora Jenkins was her name, Cecil said, and her old man had been in the Texas legislature at one time, so I could see how Cecil was outclassed, no matter what kind of cars he sold.

By this time I was feeling so sorry for Cecil I was about stone-cold sober. I looked at Claudie, the big clumsy oaf, and, sure enough, there he sat, leaning back against the black leather with his watch fob showing over the pocket with no watch in it and never had been, with the silk "Delegate" badge pinned uneven on his coat lapel, and with great big tears running right down his wide cheeks. When Cecil saw this, he said didn't we want a nightcap, since by then it was around two-thirty or maybe three o'clock in the morning and time for people to turn in.

"You bet we do." I spoke for Claudie too, and we all had another neighborly drink together.

I think I'd have suspected Cecil of being pretty drunk there on the train if the things he kept on saying hadn't been so true to life. I mean like what he told us about true friends. "True friends are the finest thing in the world," Cecil said over and over; and I told him I and Claudie were really his friends all right. "Matter of fact," I said, "we've never run across a finer friend than you in the whole dadblamed State of Texas. We'd like to do something for you just to show you how much we think of you."

"You've done it already," he insisted. "I was awful blue and lonely when I got on the train tonight. You see, the other two delegates from Burkburnett called their trip off at the last minute. They're Eleanora's brothers — the ones that run the chicken ranch — and they were going to be my guests. Now you fellows will have to take their place all the way."

"It's a pleasure," I said, and Claudie nodded.

It turned out that Cecil had a whole room — Drawing Room "A" — in that same car, and it had plenty of space for us all three to sleep.

2

When I woke up in the top bed the next morning the train was stopped and Cecil was in the little room next door shaving. Claudie was sitting there scratching himself awake on the shelf that the porter had made into a bunk for him to sleep on. They were whispering something about how warm it was in Galveston for January. That's how dadgummed nice Cecil was; he'd only whispered to Claudie until he found I was awake.

"Cecil," I stated, "you are a real gentleman and a true friend."

"True friends," he said again, "are the finest thing in the world. Where you fellows stopping?"

"We haven't exactly made up our minds," I answered.

"That's good," he said. "I've got a whole suite at the Galvez, and you've got to stay with me."

"I will if Clint will," Claudie said.

"We sure do thank you," I told him. "Matter of fact, we might have stayed at the Galvez anyhow."

"I don't know how," Claudie muttered to himself, and I froze him with a stony look.

By this time Cecil had finished shaving. He splashed his face with some strong-smelling green water like they have in only the best barbershops; then he made us agree to ride back with him to Fort Worth on the same car that night. "It'll be right here at eleven," he told us. "We'll meet on the car after the banquet."

We agreed to do it, and as the porter gave Claudie's double-breasted blue serge suit a good hard brushing, we fired up three of Cecil's big black cigars.

But at the Galvez it was too much, when we got ourselves into the plushy rooms Cecil had there, to go eat breakfast on him too. We'd all drunk a lot of the ice water that Cecil ordered up to the suite when he said, "Let's us go down to the dining room and have some scrambled eggs and ham."

"No, much obliged," I told him, as all-fired hungry as I was. "You go ahead. I and Claudie've got some folks we'd better look up first thing."

"Sure you won't come on?"

"Believe not, thanks," I said.

After Cecil left, I and Claudie sat there for a while in big soft chairs watching the bright blue ocean waves boiling themselves soapy white on the sandy beach. Claudie spoke of being hungry as a she-wolf, and I told him to forget it and look at the ocean while I took a little time to think.

There was another big hotel close by — the Buccaneer — so I pointed out that we might try picking up a bite of breakfast there for washing the dishes or mopping some floors or the like — the sort of thing Claudie can do as well as the next one. Claudie said he was ready, so we drank the rest of the ice water and went over to the Buccaneer. We still wore our "Delegate" badges; and when we walked into the Buccaneer lobby, two fine ladies met us like long-lost friends.

"You're late," they said, sort of accusing, but — you know — not really put out. They were very clean and well-dressed women, both a little on the heavy-set side of middle age, and they had on badges that said "Chamber of Commerce — Ladies Auxiliary."

"We've already started the Auxiliary breakfast," the biggest one with a pompadour hairdo and steel-rimmed glasses said. "We were afraid you men would be shy about representing the Chamber where we girls have you so badly outnumbered."

She led us into a big dining room where we saw at least an acre of women eating breakfast and not another man in sight. They all cheered when we walked in, and the two ladies that got us first marched us right up to a platform at the far end of the room where a dozen or so women sat at a long table eating away at big breakfasts. They put us in two of the six vacant seats at the long table, and there was where I and Claudie ate all the ham and eggs and jam that some dressed-up darkies brought us. Lots of hot coffee, too.

It was a larrapin' breakfast, and we'd about eaten our fill when in came another guy that got cheered and led right up to our table too. He was a short roundish citizen of about twenty-five, with pink cheeks, bright eyes, slicked-back yellow hair, and a lot of big teeth showing as he smiled at everybody. Oh, but he was feisty, and just above his "delegate" badge he was wearing another little dinkus that said "Executive Director" in gold letters.

He took up one of the vacant chairs next to us; he grinned wide, shook hands with both of us, and said how glad he was to meet us; he asked how we were, and before we could tell him, he asked us how we'd been. I was ready to say "Fine," but he was still ahead of me. His name, he said, was Elbert P. Jarvis, but

everybody called him Booster; then he told us all over
again that he was glad to meet us, but by this time he
was seeing ladies out in the dining room that he must
have known before, since he was smiling big and bowing to them here and there. Booster had a look on his
face just like a little-bitty guy that has caught a great
big fish.

3

Soon everybody was through eating, and I was wondering why the thing didn't break up when a lady
about four seats from ours tinkled her glass with a
knife or fork and said she was calling us all to order.
Things quieted down at this, and I got the first full
look at the lady talking.

She was pretty special; that was plain from the first
glance. She had a lot of even curls the color of sulphur
arranged on her head, and in them she wore a brown
comb that sparkled on the side next to me. She had
big blue eyes and an open face that looked soft and
forty-odd, and from the side she was shaped like a pi-
geon in the spring of the year — topheavy.

"Greetings," she said in a hearty voice, "and welcome. As incoming president of the Ladies Auxiliary
of the Texas Chamber of Commerce it is my pleasure
and privilege to open the meeting and introduce our
guest speaker. But first we have a special treat." Then

she went on to say that the hint had been put out to
the Chamber that as many as six members could come
to the Auxiliary breakfast, sort of as observers and special guests. But shyness, she pointed out, must have
overtaken the others. At this she nodded our way and
said, "Please present yourselves, gentlemen. We are
proud and pleased to have you with us."

"Clint Hightower, a delegate from North Texas," I
told the acre of well-scrubbed ladies; "and on my right
here is my associate, Claudie Hughes. He does not
wish to get up and talk, but he will sing "The Eyes of
Texas' for you."

All the ladies smiled and cheered as Claudie got up.
He was baffled at first, like he often is when my mind
works away ahead of his, the way it did that morning;
but with a big breakfast under his belt that way, and
dressed up in his blue serge suit and all, I knew he'd
come through, and he did. It's a good thing for a real
bass singer to have a lot of women around when he's
called on for a song, and Claudie proved it right there
at the Buccaneer. His voice filled the room like water
fills a bucket, and when he was done I thought the ap-
plause would never die down.

Next, the lady president pointed out that the affairs
of the Ladies Auxiliary were in such good shape that
the breakfast was the only meeting they needed to
have all day, but, of course, all the ladies were invited
to the final banquet of the real Chamber that night.
Then she named the new members of the Auxiliary

Committees and asked them all to stand up to be cheered.

After that was over, she introduced the feisty little Executive Director and said he really needed no introduction because he was so prominent; he was a well-known live wire, Booster Jarvis, the Executive Director of the Junior Chamber of Commerce, the person whom we would have the privilege of hearing next.

Booster Jarvis stood up, showed his teeth from ear to ear, and shook his own hands over his head like prize-fighters do when they haven't lost a single round. He told the Ladies Auxiliary about what the Junior Chamber of Commerce had done during the past year, and it was a hell of a lot — co-ordinating efforts; keeping in touch with developments; and always putting the old shoulder to the wheel. They'd been having committee meetings, he went on, and subcommittee reports. They'd been co-operating with some people and standing squarely behind others; viewing some things with alarm and giving unqualified support to some other things. They'd been pretty rough all year on people that had been against betterment. But all this good stuff was lost on the Ladies Auxiliary; they'd heard Claudie sing about Texas. Most of them weren't taking their eyes off Claudie, and even Booster Jarvis could see it as he went on and on. He got only a little spatter of cheers when he came to the best part of his speech — the part about how not a single member of the Junior Chamber of Commerce in the whole State of Texas would admit that there was another state in the Union that could so much as hold a candle to the State of Texas.

After a while it got so everything Booster said sounded just about like what he'd been saying before, and my mind strayed back to Cecil Snavely and all the things he'd told us the night before about Eleanora Jenkins that wouldn't have him; then I noticed Booster had quit talking so loud and turned to softer subjects. He was talking about the new president of the Ladies Auxiliary. Where I picked his talk back up was: "And, ladies of the Ladies Auxiliary, I am sure that no one is more responsible for the fine degree of co-operation between the Junior Chamber of Commerce and the Ladies Auxiliary of the Chamber, or for the accomplishments of both groups too numerous to mention here, than your incoming president. What a tower of strength she has been in the Ladies Auxiliary! What a grasp she has shown of the many problems the Auxiliary has solved! And now you have crowned her efforts with the highest office in your power to bestow. On behalf of the Jaycees all over this great state, I salute her — Eleanora Jenkins!"

As fast as my mind works, it must have been a second or so before it all hit me. I mean like a ton of bricks. Here was the big blonde that wouldn't have our friend Cecil Snavely because Cecil wasn't civic or social enough. Then, seeing all those women still stuck on Claudie for his singing, and the stuff about to go to waste, another of my ideas struck me like electricity. Why not run Cecil Snavely for president of the Chamber of Commerce? The women had been won over by Claudie; and any program we could sell them, they ought to be able to sell to the men. It was plain that here was the way to get Eleanora for Cecil.

So when the cheering after Booster Jarvis's speech died down, I got up and spoke to the Ladies Auxiliary. "You ladies might have wondered what I and Claudie are here for, and I'm about to tell you. We're campaign managers for Cecil Snavely of Burkburnett. He's running for president of the Texas Chamber of Commerce. Would you ladies like another song from Claudie Hughes, the Assistant Campaign Manager?"

The way they all cheered told me they would, so Claudie got up and sang them "Beautiful, Beautiful Texas." He wasn't scared this time; I could tell he knew he was singing Cecil into a happy home, and Claudie outdid himself. It wowed everybody, except possibly Booster Jarvis, who sat there at the table with nothing but the sickly dregs of a big smile left on his face.

4

Right after this the meeting broke up. I and Claudie worked our way through the women that were all bragging on Claudie's singing. They kept trapping

him with their gush until I got tired. With too many
women around, a man can be about as lonesome as he
is by himself, so I went on back to the Galvez Hotel.
There wasn't anybody there except several hundred
delegates telling each other how glad they were to see
each other and what fine fellows they all were, so I
went on back up to our suite. Cecil was sitting there
alone with pretty bloodshot eyes. He'd heard about
the campaign we'd started, and while he wasn't exactly against it, he said he didn't believe he would be a
very good president of the Texas Chamber of Commerce.

"Cecil," I told him. "You can't be too meek about
this thing. The meek can afford, like in the Bible, to
wait around until they inherit the earth, but at your
age it's no way for a man to win out with the likes of
Eleanora Jenkins. She'll be glad to have you when
you're president. You should have seen how glad she
was when she heard we were going to run you for
president of the Chamber."

"Eleanora?" he asked, and he looked scared, I
thought. "Where's she?"

"Eleanora's right here in Galveston, Cecil," I told
him. "I and Claudie just had breakfast with her — and
the others in the Ladies Auxiliary. She's the new president."

On this last item Cecil looked like a man that
needed some kind of a prop to hold him up; it was too
much and it plainly had him licked; Cecil, that had

been hell on wheels the night before with those conductors, was stalled with four flat tires. "I'm afraid,"
he said, "I haven't got much of a chance. Those executive directors pull all the wires in the Chamber, and
they've got Dennis Derryberry of Galveston picked
for president. You see, Clint, I know something about
Chamber politics."

"But not about women," I said. "You admit that
yourself. Leave it to the women and me. We don't
need to do another thing; it's in the bag."

Cecil then dug a couple of at least fifty-cent cigars
out of his pocket for us to smoke. He gave me a ticket
and one for Claudie too that would get us into the big
banquet that night at the Galvez ballroom. Seven
o'clock sharp, the tickets said on both sides. Then Cecil
left to go to a meeting of some kind of a subcommittee
of the Chamber that he admitted he wasn't even chairman of.

After Cecil had gone, I just happened to glance out
of the window of our suite. I looked down on the lawn
there in front of the Galvez where palms and olean-
ders were growing around the stone benches. And sitting there on one of the benches was old ham-handed
Claudie, looking better in his blue serge suit than
he'd ever looked before; also, sitting not very far away
on the same stone bench was Eleanora Jenkins.

I went right down, so as to waste no time at all
about telling Claudie a thing or two. But when I got
there I found I was on the wrong side of a little hedge

in the Galvez front yard; their bench was on the other side of it, and I could hear them talking — Eleanora, that is. Claudie was only saying, "Yes, ma'am," every so often as Eleanora told him what fine folks hers were; how all her ancestors had belonged to the aristocracy back in Virginia before they'd come to Texas.

If Eleanora had ever stopped talking long enough to listen to Claudie, she could have seen he was not somebody that she could make very much of an impression on — even a good one. But she never did let up. Why, even when she'd wind up with one subject she'd say "and" or "but" before she paused for another breath, so there was never any place for Claudie to come in. And this, of course, was just his dish. For being too stupid to think up anything at all to say, he was getting credit for being too polite to interrupt her, and very aristocratic, as well, I supposed. For that and for running under Cecil I could have slit his throat.

After a while they walked off toward the East Beach where all those tourist courts were, and I went over and sat for a long time on the stone bench where they'd been sitting. I looked at the path of the winter sun on the ocean, slick and shiny, a little way out from the beach, like a fresh-peeled onion, and I thought and thought. I mean about Cecil and what a hell of a life that would be for him if he got hitched up with all that talk. I figured maybe it would about serve

Claudie right if he did run under Cecil and take Eleanora away from him. Then I thought also: "Look,
Clint, who is this you are being, God or the Federal
Government or somebody deciding for Cecil what he
wants and what is good for him?"

5

It was a lot later, and the sun's path across the ocean
had turned the color of polished brass, when I noticed
Eleanora and Claudie strolling up from the East
Beach. As they got nearer I could see that she was
talking still. Her head was held high, and she had a
very joyful look on her face. Claudie seemed to be all
tuckered out. Even his "Delegate" badge looked limp.

They walked right into the Galvez together in broad
open daylight, and I thought, "Suppose they meet up
with our friend Cecil? That will really be the pay-off,
now won't it?"

Right then nothing I could think of to do seemed
quite good enough to do it, so I didn't move a peg
from where I sat until I saw by the clock outside the
Galvez that it was a quarter of seven and the banquet
only fifteen minutes off.

I went up to Cecil's suite and nobody was there —
not even Claudie. I shaved and bathed and sprinkled
some of Cecil's green toilet water on my face and hair;
then I got dressed for the banquet. It was after seven,

and I was about to leave when I discovered Claudie's wicker suitcase had a dozen or more of Cecil's fifty-cent cigars in it, and I said to myself, "Now, Clint, by God, you've seen everything! First, it's Cecil's girl Claudie swipes, and then it's his cigars."

When I went down to the banquet room, the only seat I could find was way off in one corner with some friendly people from Goose Creek. I tried to locate Eleanora or Cecil, or even Claudie, but my back was to most of the banquet, and by that time it didn't seem to make much difference anyway.

After all the delegates had eaten their fill, the president of the Chamber, a big bushy-headed guy with a booming voice, got up and started calling on people here and there to stand and be introduced. Everybody was cheering for everybody else. This went on for nearly two hours, and by the time they got through, I didn't notice anybody in the whole banquet hall that hadn't been cheered except possibly my own self — and, of course, Claudie. I still hadn't seen him anywhere.

Finally — and it was late — they got to the business of the meeting. Somebody up front rose and nominated Dennis Derryberry of Galveston, Texas, for president of the Texas Chamber. And before you could bat an eye somebody else up there moved that the nominations be closed. It was like sheet lightning in April, it was so fast. I stood up, but by the time I could they were all saying "Aye," and Dennis Derryberry was the new president. They'd given Cecil the old steam roller, and with not caring a tinker's dam about who was vice president — or secretary or treasurer either — I got disgusted with it all and left.

I asked one of the bellboys the way to the station, and since I didn't have any money on me personally, I walked.

When I got to Drawing Room "A" of our car, I went in to take some weight off of my feet — my corns were killing me by this time — and there was Claudie, already asleep on his bunk. He had on all his clothes but his shoes and his watch fob that were on his wicker suitcase by the bunk.

"Wake up, Claudie," I yelled and shook him hard. "I've got to talk to you before Cecil gets back to the car."

"He ain't gonna —" Claudie started to say, and I cut him off with "Just what kind of a deal is this any-how — you running under our friend Cecil? Also you can tell me now about them cigars of Cecil's in your suitcase."

"Cigars?" Claudie asked, rolling his eyes. That was the whole trouble. He still wasn't awake enough to make a bit of sense.

"Cecil didn't get elected, after all," I told him.

"That don't matter, Clint," he said. "Eleanora didn't keer whether Cecil was president or not. All she wanted was Cecil the way he was. But she couldn't stand them strong cigars he smoked — or the way he smoked 'em."

"Claudie," I accused him, "you're lying to me."

"Well, she's Mrs. Cecil Snavely now," he grinned. "I was the witness at the wedding, and when Cecil swore off of cigars for life, he give 'em all to me."

The train was moving by this time, and Claudie was plainly pooped out but happy as a goose in a rice marsh. Before he went back to sleep, he kept saying to himself, "Fifty-cent cigars, too. What a bargain!"

X

Five Pillars

THEY WOULDN'T TAKE Claudie back on at the Fort Worth stockyards, even after I went out myself the next day and spoke with his foreman. Best I could figure it out, there was a sort of personality clash between the black goat and Claudie. So I told the foreman what he could do with his job, just so I wouldn't feel the trip out there had been useless.

All we had to do, I figured, was hit a big lick of some kind so we could move on Amarillo in style; also we had plenty of time for that, since if you are anywhere else in the winter you do not go to Amarillo.

We moved over to Dallas, where I found Claudie a part-time job in a saddle factory and made some fine contacts myself. One of them was Crawfish Wartoff, that had his trailer house parked next to ours at the trailer camp out on the Preston Road. And it was through my contact with Crawfish that we went that spring to see Mr. Gissel. It must have been late May, or early June.

I and Claudie went early in the morning to the fourth floor of the red brick building there across from the Dallas courthouse. And on the glass part of a door that you could not see through, I found where it said in big black letters, "Rudolph Gissel, Dallas's Leading Private Detective."

"Come on, Claudie," I said; "this is Mr. Gissel's office right here."

But the door was locked, and Claudie said, "See, Clint? They ain't nobody there." He spoke like he might have known it all the time; then he added, "I've still got enough time to get out to the saddle factory. The foreman thought he could put me on the extra shift today."

"All that a locked office means to certain people is 'nobody there,'" I stated; "but to me it simply means that Mr. Gissel has not come in yet. After all, it's still pretty early in the morning, Claudie."

"But —" Claudie said; then he just stood there, big and dumb and stubborn like a one-eyed mule in the wrong lot.

I put both hands on my hips and looked up hard at him before I went on. "Claudie," I said, "when are you going to learn that it don't do you a bit of good to argue with me?"

"I guess I —" he started, but his mind seemed to peter out here, so I went ahead.

"Now and then, Claudie," I said, "I have to have a little help from you. Not often, I'll admit; but sometimes. Now, when Mr. Gissel comes, I'll do all the talking, but I happen to want you along when I speak to him, and I have my reasons. I want him to size you up and see that I've got something to offer besides just brains. That way we are more apt to get this job."

"What job's that?" Claudie asked, and I was so disgusted with him I didn't even bother to answer.

As a matter of fact it wasn't any particular job anyway. It was only an idea I had had the day before when I'd learned all about Mr. Gissel from Crawfish Wartoff, his brother-in-law. Crawfish had told me and Claudie about how Mr. Gissel was working himself to death in the private detective business. This didn't mean a thing to Claudie — nary a thing — but to me it meant that Mr. Gissel had more cases than he could detect singlehanded. Also, it came to me in a flash that I and Claudie were the ones to step right in and help him out. I'm no hand to boast or brag, myself, but I'll admit that sometimes I have ideas that are so terrific they fairly dazzle me.

"Another thing," I told Claudie while we waited; "you can't seem to get used to an active mind like the one I've got. It must be kept busy. For instance, you know that special job I got last week with the Texas Rural Almanac? Well, all I was hired to write up was one year's weather forecasts; but before I quit I wrote up three extra years for the price of only one more. Now — with it the spring of the year and all — my mind is ready to go again, and —"

"You're in the man's way," Claudie cut in; and, sure enough, there he was, the one that turned out to be Mr. Gissel. He was a short, bald little man in his shirt sleeves, and he had a cigar in his mouth that he was not smoking since it had gone out.

As I moved away from the door, Mr. Gissel reached into his hip pocket and pulled out a key ring that must have had forty keys on it. He was pretty needful of a shave at the time, and I kept wondering, I remember, how anybody could have as much dandruff on his shoulders from no more hair on his head than Mr. Gissel had.

"Hightower is the name," I began as Mr. Gissel finally found the right key and got it in the lock of the door with his name on it. "And this is my associate here, Claudie. We are friends of your brother-in-law, Crawfish Wartoff."

"Come in, fellows," Mr. Gissel said in a heavy, husky voice for a guy no bigger than he was, and in we went. "What can I do for you this morning?"

"Nice day," I said, taking my own time to look him over and the office too. It was not as big an office as detectives have in moving picture shows, and until Mr. Gissel raised the window, I noticed the air in there was pretty close. Mr. Gissel picked up an ash tray loaded with cigar butts and threw them into an already full waste basket. Then he sat down in a swivel chair behind a desk that was covered with papers, paper cups, paper clips, and over on one side the peelings from several oranges. There were no chairs for me and Claudie, so we stood there by the desk.

"O.K., fellows; what is it?" Mr. Gissel said, and by

this time he'd slid down into his chair and put his chin in his hand in a way that you'd expect in a detective that was used to figuring out hard cases every day of his life. Probably murder cases, too.

"Crawfish Wartoff thinks a lot of you, Mr. Gissel," I said; "and he's worried about you, too. Says you're working yourself half to death."

"Crawfish, he's been listening yet to that fool wife of mine. She's Crawfish's older sister. But you tell Crawfish I'm all right."

"Don't you have some cases you could use a little help on?" I asked. "Some help from me and my associate, Claudie, I mean. Also, we'd prefer murder cases."

"No," Mr. Gissel said and started shuffling papers from one side of the desk to the other.

We stood there watching him until he'd shuffled the papers back to about where they were when we'd first come in. Then he looked up and said, "You damn fellers haven't left?"

"I thought you were looking over your desk for a case we could handle — maybe a murder case," I said.

"No. Go away now; I'm a busy man," Mr. Gissel fussed as he swiveled his chair around and put both feet on the window sill.

As I and Claudie walked down the hall toward the elevator I knew it would not help matters for Claudie to say, "it's too late now for me to get on today at the

saddle factory." But that is exactly what Claudie did
say.

We'd rung the "down" button for the elevator and
waited a while when I noticed Mr. Gissel was out in
the hall calling us back. Then to the girl in the elevator that had come by this time I said, "Pardon us,
ma'am. We are not going down yet." And as we
walked down the hall I spoke to Claudie and explained, "Nice manners count for a great deal, especially in the South."

Back in the office Mr. Gissel was lighting up the
rest of his cigar and saying, "There is an old file here,
and the time is nearly run out on it, already. It's a contingent case."

"A what case?" Claudie asked.

"Don't mind him," I said, "go right ahead, Mr. Gissel."

"A contingent case is one when you don't get no pay
if you don't deliver the goods," Mr. Gissel explained.

"Of course," I said, "next to murder cases we like
contingent cases best of all."

"This one can be solved, all right," Mr. Gissel went
on, "if you've got enough brains and guts."

"Between the two of us, that's exactly what we've
got, Mr. Gissel," I said. "This is going to be your big
day, and —"

"All right, all right," he cut in. "Here's the dope.
Old lady ten or twelve miles out on the Irving road

claims she lost a valuable sunburst she'd had insured."

"A sunburst?" Claudie asked.

"Yes, a sunburst," Mr. Gissel said. "Brooch full of diamonds. Case looked suspicious from the first, but the adjuster for the insurance company didn't get to first base. He's pretty dumb though. Well, he's a lodge brother of mine, so he offered the case to me. I went out to see the old lady, but before I could get started I got bit by a bad dog at the front gate. I've been so busy since then I haven't been back. Now you guys might can do something with it. I'm sure it's a fake loss."

"How do you know?" I asked.

"The adjuster told me," Mr. Gissel answered, and by this time his eyes had narrowed some more in the way of a detective. In fact, one of them seemed to be closed altogether. "Do you want the job or not?"

"That's what we're doing here," I told him.

"All right. The insurance company paid off twenty thousand dollars on the loss. If you can find the sunburst or prove the loss was a fake, the company will get its money back. I'll get five hundred dollars for the job and you can have half of it."

"As nice a case as we've been on lately, Claudie," I said so Mr. Gissel could hear.

Mr. Gissel didn't want to stake us anything for expense money, but I and Claudie stayed there until he let us have ten dollars, then he told us the old lady's

name and how to get to where she lived. Right pretty
name she had, too: Miss Ernestine Myrtleblossom.

It took most of the ten dollars to pay what we owed
at the trailer camp. But Claudie scratched up enough
more to buy a couple of spark plugs and a gasket we
had to have before our car would run. Also, I bought
a dime tablet and some pencils so I could take plenty
of notes, the way the best detectives do.

2

It was two, maybe three, o'clock that same afternoon
when we turned off of the Irving road and followed a
long shady hackberry lane to the front of Miss Ernestine Myrtleblossom's house place. Claudie drove, of
course, so I could ride back in the trailer house and
think out the case.

I could tell the red brick house had been mighty
handsome and full of rich people at one time or another, because it was so big and had so much pretty
carving on the wood that was left around the eaves and
all. There were three tall columns in front that must
have been painted white once, but a long time ago,
and then there were places where two other columns
had been, giving the old house a sort of snaggled look.
One of these columns lay there in the front yard and
showed a little rotten on both ends, while the other
one was plumb gone. The yard was shaded by big pecan

trees and overgrown with tall scraggly weeds that almost choked out the blooming mimosa and pink and white lilacs.

The picket fence in front was about gone, with just enough of it left and patched up with chicken wire to hold a feisty little white Spitz dog that was prancing around inside. He was barking shrill, mad barks, and as I stepped out of the trailer the hair on the back of his neck stood up like the hair on the head of some fellow that's been off to college somewhere.

"Claudie," I said, "you stay in the car. Remember, you are only the chauffeur."

"I ain't gettin' out nohow until you do something with that nasty little dog," he said.

I stood at the gate and called "Hello" several times; then the screen door onto the front porch swung open, and a little old lady with white hair came out and stood at the place where one of the big columns had used to stand. First she spoke to the dog. "Come back, Ginger. Come on back, you naughty fellow." Then she called out to me, "It's all right; he won't bite." But I stayed on the outside of the gate until Ginger had gone back and the old lady had put him in the house and closed the screen door.

I took off my hat as soon as I went through the front gate, and I left it off all the way as I walked up to the porch. Then, just before I got there, I put it back on so I could be taking it off as I spoke. As you can see, I have a good set of manners with women folks, and here I was, already further along with the case than Mr. Gissel, that only got dog-bit. Also, I was dressed in the best clothes I owned in this world, and with a tablet and a sharp pencil in my hand I knew I could cut the mustard if anybody could.

"Good morning, ma'am," I said; "it's a nice warm day, isn't it?"

"Oh, yes," she answered in a little bitty voice that sounded a whole lot younger than this old lady could have been; "it's almost summer now."

While we went on and passed the time of day, I kept thinking to myself that she was almost like a little old bird of some kind — when he is not flying, that is. She wasn't over five feet tall; she was thin as a rail, and I figured she wouldn't weigh seventy-five pounds wringing wet. Her white hair was thin and wispy. She had pale blue eyes and skin so thin I could see the blue veins in her temples and on the backs of her hands.

"Hightower is the name," I said. "I had my chauffeur stop when I saw what a elegant place you have here."

"This was a pretty place when I lived here as a child," she said, looking at the old column lying there in the yard, "but it's badly run down now. Is there something I can do for you?"

"Nothing atall, ma'am, nothing atall." I looked down at my tablet and pencil before I went on. "I am a student of old places, and I thought I might like to write up a essay some day about this one of yours."

She smiled and a thousand wrinkles seemed to show

up in her face, but they were happy wrinkles and her eyes were brighter when she said, "What a nice thing that would be. Won't you come in?"

"Yes, ma'am," I told her. "I'd love to come inside"; then, when I looked out toward the front where Claudie was still sitting in the car, the old lady said, "Oh, your chauffeur; wouldn't you like to ask him in, too? Maybe I could give you men some lemonade and cookies."

"I'd be glad to," I told her. "I'm very democratic about things like that."

Claudie came, grinning, when I called him, and Miss Myrtleblossom took us into the parlor. It had nothing in it but old dark stiff furniture and a lot of pictures on the walls — oil pictures of Miss Myrtleblossom's folks, she told us, that had long since gone on to claim their reward. And while she was getting us the lemonade and cookies, I studied these pictures on the walls — about as fierce looking a bunch of ancestors, I figured, as such a sweet old lady could possibly have. The men all had dark beards, big noses and eyes like hawks' eyes, but the women in the pictures were little and slender and pale in black dresses, just like Miss Ernestine Myrtleblossom herself.

Then we looked at all the carved wood in the room — on the doors, the windows, and more so around the big old mantel over the fireplace. The wood was all done in the same pattern as outside along the eaves, except finer, of course, being on the inside.

"Mind your manners, Claudie," I told him before Miss Ernestine came back, "and remember to let me do the talking. Also, only one extra helping of whatever it is she brings out."

After Claudie had eaten up the last cookie on the plate Miss Ernestine brought, and the lemonade was all gone, she took us both around to look at the rest of the place. She told us how it had had a name once, but hardly anybody called it that any more. It had been called "Five Pillars."

It was plumb sad to see how nice the house must have been when it was new, or even when it wasn't very old. I could tell the way her ancestors had lived was the way people should live in this world if they are really going to get down to brass tacks about enjoying life. Why, there was even a third floor that had been for dancing at one time, but the only part of the house that was still being used was the parlor and the bedroom on the first floor between it and the kitchen. The old lady did her cooking on a coal oil stove in the corner of her bedroom. All the other rooms were bare and barny-looking, but they had a sweet, musty smell like churches on week days.

Then Miss Ernestine took us out in the back and showed us what had been the old stable. It had cobble-stone floors, places for a dozen or so horses, and it was plain to me that the horses in the old days hadn't had a bad life themselves. Then there was the old carriage there by the stable, and weather-beaten as it was, you could see it had been a fine one in its time — rubber tires, some black fringe still around the top, two whipstocks and everything.

Back in the house, we sat in the parlor again, and I made some notes in my tablet. Then the old lady said something that really almost got me — but it didn't quite. What she said was, "If you men would like to stay here for a few days until you can complete your notes on the place, you'd be most welcome to do it. There is a room where the grooms used to live above the stable, and I've kept it in fair order. You could stay there."

"Not unless you'll let me furnish you some help around this place here, ma'am," I told her, figuring I didn't want the case to be too easy, like shooting fish in a barrel. "There is plenty of work for a man to do. I can see it everywhere."

"My goodness, gracious, yes; there certainly is," she said, "but I wouldn't think of letting you take any time away from your essay."

"That wasn't exactly what I had in mind, ma'am," I told her. "My chauffeur here, when he is not chauffeuring, is not busy at all; and I'm sure he would be happier at work than he would be at ease. Wouldn't you, Claudie?"

I kept my eye right on Claudie until he grinned and said to Miss Myrtleblossom, "Yes'm. I shore would."

"In no time at all," I told her, "you will hardly know that front yard. My man Claudie, here, is a fine

man with a hoe." It was pitiful the way Claudie's face
fell as he looked at all the horseweeds out front, but it
was beautiful to see how happy I'd made Miss Myrtleblossom.

I had Claudie drive the car through a side gate and
pull the trailer house up beside the stable; then, after
I had looked over the room there, I decided that I
would live above the stable myself and let Claudie
stay in the trailer house. I explained this arrange-
ment to Claudie. "You see," I told him, "I am more
the Five Pillars type than you are."

3

That afternoon Claudie cut weeds, and the old lady
told me the story of the place. It was built a long time
ago, she pointed out, in the days when times were
pretty good — before the Civil War that is, and when
cotton and slaves made all these plantation owners so
rich they could hardly think of enough ways to spend
their money. Later on, though, when Miss Ernestine
was a little girl, there'd been hard times, hard money,
mortgages and trouble. She told me about how her
mother died nearly twenty years before and left her
all alone in this world, but she willed Five Pillars to
Miss Ernestine.

"Was that all she left you?" I asked, keen as a blade.

"No," she admitted. She sat and looked out the window for a while before she went on. Then she told me her mother left one other thing, a very valuable piece of jewelry that her grandmother had hidden out from the carpetbaggers when a gang of them came through, taking everything that hadn't been buried or nailed down.

"This, Clint," I said to myself, "is it. This has to be the sunburst." I felt like an old pointer looks when he's smack on a covey. Not a twitch, even in the flanks.

Well, of course, I was right. It was the sunburst — one that had been given to Miss Ernestine's grandmother when Miss Ernestine's mother was born — the year before the Civil War broke out. The one promise Miss Ernestine had made her own mother was that she would never part with the sunburst. So, she went on to tell me, for years and years — twenty or more — while the house near about fell down and the yard grew up in weeds; for years and years while she lived off a little patch of garden and butter and eggs, Miss Ernestine had hung on to the sunburst. Why, she'd even sold every stick of fine furniture in the house, she said, except something to sit on in the living room and something to sleep on in the bedroom — all so she could hang on to the sunburst like her mama said and keep the insurance premiums paid. But she'd finally run out of furniture, then out of chandeliers that hung from all the ceilings, and there hadn't been anything else to sell.

Then she described the sunburst to me. It was an antique piece of jewelry, she said; mounted on a gold base, and even the pin that you'd pin it on yourself with was made of purest gold. On the front of it there were forty-odd diamonds, with the biggest one in the middle — several carats — and others all around the center where they were littler, but still there weren't any puny diamonds right out on the very edges. Her lips trembled and tears came in her eyes when she talked about the sunburst, and if you want to know the truth, the whole thing started getting next to me — inside of myself — while I sat there and made notes and watched Claudie out the window digging away at the horseweeds in the front yard.

What a life, I thought. This poor little old lady all by herself here, living on the remnants of elegance, all tattered and torn, while the weeds and the grass move in on her year by year. Less and less to eat and harder and harder to scrape up the money to pay the insurance premiums. I almost forgot I was a detective, I was so taken with her story; but when I took ahold of myself, I asked her the kind of question that I knew would have made Mr. Gissel proud if he could have heard me. What I asked was, "And where did you keep this sunburst, Miss Myrtleblossom?"

At this I thought she drew a pretty fine bead on me with her faded blue eyes, and for a second they looked more like the men's eyes among the ancestors there on the wall than those of the frail, pale little women in the pictures. "Where *did* I keep it?"

she asked it right back at me. "Why do you say 'did'?"

For a man that seldom makes one, I found I was about to make a mistake. You see, I wasn't supposed to know she didn't have this sunburst any more. So I said, "Excuse me, ma'am. You looked bothered there a minute. I hope nothing's happened to the sunburst."

"Well, it certainly has," she said. "I lost it last spring."

"How?" I asked. You can see I was calculating fast. If a man is going to be a detective he might as well be a good one.

"It was like this," she went on. "I kept it in a little lavender jewel case that I always hid at a certain place right here in Five Pillars. I have never told, and I never would tell, where that place is. And no stranger could ever find my jewel case; it's so well hidden. But sometimes I'd take the sunburst out and wear it when I was alone here in the house. It was a precious link with the past, Mr. Hightower, can't you see, and it seemed to give me a sense of strength and security. Then one day — it was on a Sunday —"

About this time Claudie came in, and I could have wrung his neck. I mean particularly the way things turned out after that. He said the sun was about down and he was hungry.

"There's another half hour of daylight, Claudie," I stated. "Remember, you didn't get started until late. Couldn't you work a little longer?"

"He'll do nothing of the sort," Miss Ernestine spoke up. "You men sit right down here and relax while I go and fix you a bite of supper."

That was the night we learned what it was that had put such a strain on Jules Rabinowitz's crystal ball back in Beaumont. I found the whole thing written up in the *Dallas Times Herald* that Ginger, the little Spitz slept on, and the paper wasn't over a month old.

"Amarillo Magnate Endows Hospital," the headline said, so I moved Ginger over a little so I could read it all. The paper went on to tell how Weathers Hughes, the richest man in the Texas Panhandle, had put up over two million dollars to build a new hospital there. He was so rich, it said, the people of Amarillo were hoping for another million soon for a nurses' home.

"Is this one of your tribe, Claudie?" I asked him, before Miss Ernestine came back.

"Sure, he's the one we all called 'Stink Foot,'" Claudie said. "Usta have sores. Onct he come to our house and stayed all spring. Mama cured his sores with rattlesnake salve."

"Well, we've got to finish this job here in a hurry and get on out to Amarillo before he gives any more of his money away."

"Who's that?" Miss Ernestine had come back.

"Oh, just some rich relatives," I told her. "Some we've been missing."

"Your supper's ready," she said.

4

The next several days went awful slow. I mean for me, at least. Miss Ernestine wanted me to know all that I should know for the essay, and everything she'd tell me reminded her of several other matters; but since she could only talk of one thing at a time, she wound up each day with more dope left to talk about than she'd started with. I mean, sure enough, the more she talked, the farther behind she was with her story. She told me all about her family — both sides of the house; the Indian fights her ancestors fought; the wars her folks went off to; the dances, the feuds, the weddings, and the funerals, but she seemed about as apt to rise and fly as she was to talk any more about this sunburst. I finally used up my tablet and had to send Claudie to Irving to get a new one.

In a day or so Claudie had the front yard looking neat and spick with not a weed in sight. So I put him to hoeing Miss Ernestine's garden; then when he'd finished, I moved him around to the rear of Five Pillars where I could see he had the better part of a week's work cut out for him — if it took me that long to solve the case, that is.

The food Miss Ernestine served us was fair to middling, although not exactly the kind of vittles Claudie needed for the heavy work he was doing. It was more the kind of food that women serve women in tea shoppes — you know, skimpy and delicate-like — sand-

wiches, tid-bits, crumpets, spicy things, salads and such
— nothing that would really stick to a workingman's
ribs.

Finally, late one afternoon, and after we'd been
there nearly a week, I got Miss Ernestine around again
to the sunburst. The sun was low in the west, and I
knew Claudie might stumble in any minute and break
it up; but I couldn't miss the best chance she gave me
when she paused for breath in the middle of the story
about the uncle that went to war with Hood's Brigade
and lost a leg at Gettysburg.

"I've just decided, Miss Ernestine," I told her,
"there's too much good stuff you've told me to waste
it on any essay. I guess I'd better do a whole book on
this place."

"I'd hoped you would," she agreed with a little
show of pink in her cheeks. "I've always believed someone would write a book about Five Pillars."

"But I need to know the rest of the story about the
sunburst. That may be the best part of all."

"Oh, yes, the sunburst." She put one thin hand
against her cheek. "Now where was I on that?"

"You kept it in a jewel case that you hid somewhere
in the house here. But sometimes you took it out and
wore it."

"Of course," Miss Ernestine smiled. "How forgetful
of me. In the last few years, it seems, I've been getting
more forgetful than ever before. Well, I usually wore
the sunburst to church, too. And that's how I lost it.

It was on a Sunday morning in the spring. The day was rainy and blustry, I remember — about a year ago now. The Lacys came by to take me. They live a mile or so down the road, and on this Sunday I was dressed and waiting for them at the gate. The Lacys are wonderful neighbors, Mr. Hightower. She was a Sewall and her mother was a Flato — old settlers on her mother's side. Why, the town of Flatonia was named for them. Remind me to tell you about that later. Anyway, Mrs. Lacy's people all had money, and only a couple of years ago, what do you suppose? An aunt of hers she'd never seen died and left her a legacy. Mr. Lacy invested it for her in stocks and bonds and things, and they live very well from it. The income, you know."

There she was off the subject again, while the sun got lower and lower and here went another day we weren't on the way to Amarillo, but there wasn't any mannerly way for me to butt in.

"Mr. Lacy's people came to Texas much later," she continued, "from South Carolina, I believe; or it could have been North — Anyway, Mr. Lacy's people —"

I noticed Claudie through the window, and while he hadn't quit for the day, I could tell he might as well have. He was all tuckered out, and he looked like an alarm clock sounds when it's about run down. So I cut in on Miss Ernestine — strictly against my regular set of manners, too — "And did you lose the sunburst at church, Miss Myrtleblossom?" I was acting for all

the world like a man about to cave in with a broken
heart. Fact is, if I hadn't gone into so many other lines
in my time I expect I'd have been a fine actor. I may
yet, come to think of it.

"I really can't say where I lost it," she went on, gaz-
ing far away and looking like an old lady thinking
about something else. "But it was when I got home
from church Sunday that I first noticed I didn't have
it on. Right here in this room it was. I took off my
coat and walked over to that sideboard and looked in
that same little mirror you see above it now. My sunburst was gone. I took a cup of warm tea and then
walked and ran all the way to the Lacys in the driz-
zling rain. We looked everywhere in the Lacys' car for
it. Mr. Lacy went with me then to the church, and we
looked in the aisles and under my pew; then all over
the churchyard. Mr. Lacy was so thoughtful, you'd
have supposed it was something that had happened to
a member of his own family. But that's the way Mr.
Lacy has always been. Why, would you believe it, several years ago Mr. Lacy — It must have been the year
of the Labor Day hurricane, or the one after that —"

"Did you go then and look in the jewel case?" I
asked, still very bothered-like, but fast, just as any
good detective would.

"Oh, heavens, no," she answered. "It's bad luck to
open an empty jewel case. Everybody knows that. I
haven't opened it since that Sunday. Now back to Mr.
Lacy. As I was saying —"

Here the whole case struck me like forked lightning. This nice, forgetful old lady had simply gone off to church without her sunburst. Then she forgot she hadn't worn it.

I looked outside and saw Claudie drop his hoe and start toward the house — about as wrong a time as he could have picked if he'd been trying. So I ran to the back door and yelled at him. "Hurry, Claudie," I said; "go to Irving and get me another tablet. I've had an awful busy day and this one's all used up. Get two this time."

He didn't seem to want to leave, and he was fussing about not having any money, but I knew the iron was hot and I couldn't strike with Claudie wandering in and out of the room. "Charge it," I yelled and he left.

I went back inside to close in on the case and wind it up, but Miss Ernestine was pretty firm; she said she didn't want even me to know where the secret hiding place was; also, she wasn't sure she could ever bring herself to let me open up the jewel case.

I told her I wasn't at all superstitious about such things. After all, I explained, if I was going to write her and Five Pillars up, maybe into a whole book, who had a better right to know things like that than I did? I even rung in some scripture to back me up, the part that says, "Muzzle not the ox that treadeth out the corn." Oh, I was really in the groove all right.

But young women and old women are a lot alike in one way, I always say. Even when you are as right as I was in the fine arguments I made to Miss Ernestine, women sometimes will not agree to what they plainly should. Miss Ernestine balked on me, and she stayed balked, so that it fairly put me into a fever to be so near to the end of the case and still so far. Still, that's the way matters stood when Claudie came back without any tablet.

"We haven't got no credit in Irving," he said as he walked in.

After supper I and Claudie and Miss Ernestine sat on the front porch and talked a while. There was a nice cool breeze from the south, and for some reason the mosquitoes left us alone for a while that night. Miss Ernestine still had the sunburst on her mind.

"The very next day after I missed it," she went on, "I walked out on the highway and caught the bus to Dallas. I went up to the insurance office in the Kirby Building where I'd been paying premiums for so many years, and I told the men there about it. They made me fill out heavens knows how many forms, affidavits and certificates galore; then a little man named Gissel started coming here asking me all sorts of pesky questions. He's a detective. I found that out from the telephone book. But he quit coming when Ginger, my little Spitz, nearly chewed his pants off." At this Miss Ernestine let out a little giggle that was almost gay, and Ginger, who had been dozing under the rocking chair, barked when his name was mentioned.

"After a few weeks the insurance check came," Miss

Ernestine continued. "It was for twenty thousand dollars. I went straight to Mr. Lacy with the money, and he helped me invest it in some of the same kind of stocks and bonds and things the Lacys have. Now I get almost a hundred dollars a month in dividends, and I've had enough to live on for the first time since Mama died. I can buy groceries at the store now to go with my butter and eggs and what I can grow in the garden. I've gained over five pounds this past year. I sleep better nights, and my neuralgia is about gone. Really, my whole life has changed since I lost the sunburst."

Then the wind shifted, bringing the mosquitoes, and Miss Ernestine told us good night. Before I turned in, though, I told Claudie I'd solved the case, and how I had. "The sunburst is right here in the house," I explained. "All I've got to do is find it." But he seemed to be too sleepy to appreciate what I'd done. "Uh-huh," was all he said.

Next morning Claudie just about finished clearing the back yard, but I'll admit I never got Miss Ernestine's mind back on the sunburst at all. She put the whole morning in on the branch of her father's family that settled in Washington County on the Brazos and went Baptist.

Claudie came into the parlor at noon with his hands and face washed, looking hungrier than usual; and Miss Ernestine hopped right up and went into the next room to fix us some sandwiches. Claudie, I could see, had lost some weight on this work and light fare, and he complained of being dizzy.

"Sit down, then, Claudie, on the sofa," I told him. "A few vittles will pull you together."

But he didn't; he leaned against the mantel and seemed almost to have to hang on to the carved wood there to keep from falling right down on the hearth. Poor Claudie, I thought, he may not hold up long enough on this diet for me to solve the case.

"Wup!" Claudie grunted, and seemed to reel like a pussy willow in a high wind. Then I noticed a piece of the carved wood had broken off in his hand.

"See," I said, "didn't I tell you to sit down?"

But I saw that a little panel had slid back near the place Claudie's hand was, and I went over to look. I reached in the opening there, and I found what I had already figured was there — a little square box covered with purple plush. There was a gold fastener on the outside, and it was latched tight.

"Look, Claudie," I whispered, so Miss Ernestine couldn't hear. "This is the jewel case that's got the sunburst in it. I'll show you."

And I was about to unlatch it when Claudie put his big hairy, ham-type hand on mine and said, "I wouldn't right now, Clint."

"Why?" I said, while Claudie held on and kept me from opening the jewel case. Big as he was, though, I dern near jerked it free so I could open it up.

"Just because," he said.

"Listen, Claudie," I told him, "I and you've had a pretty lean winter. Of all the pie there is in Dallas, we've had dern little, and none of it a la mode. There's two hundred and fifty dollars for us in this deal — enough to take us to Amarillo in style. All we've got to do is to open up the jewel case and take out the sunburst. Miss Ernestine just forgot she'd left it in here; that's all. Miss Ernestine —"

I looked Claudie right in the eye as I spoke, but he didn't look down the way he usually does. I saw something in his face I wasn't used to at all. Then I found I wasn't pulling and tugging any more. I just quit; that's all.

I handed the little lavender-covered case to Claudie and said, "O. K., Claudie; you win. Put it back where it was."

But he never had a chance to do it.

Things that take place faster than greased lightning are sometimes hard to remember exactly, and what happened at this point was so fast I've never been at all sure just how it all came about. But no hawk ever swooped down on little turkey poults quicker than Miss Ernestine swooped down on us from the door she came in. All seventy-five pounds of her, and her eyes flashing pale blue fire. The next thing I could tell, she had the jewel case, holding it there to her thin little flat chest, clutching it with bony fingers that were like claws, almost.

First she was breathing hard; then as she saw she had things so well in hand — and she did — she got real calm.

"It has been almost nice having you men around," she said. "Ginger is getting old, and he isn't as much company as he once was. So I've let you stay because a lonesome old woman can't be too particular — especially one who despises weeds as I do. Now the weeds are all cut and the time has come for you to leave."

I and Claudie only stood there.

She held up the jewel case in front of us. In fact, she almost held it right under our noses as she spoke — sweetly now, I thought. "You don't know whether the sunburst is in here or not. You couldn't. It's locked so hard you couldn't open it with a sledge hammer. But I think you ought to know one more thing. About a year ago I made out my will. In fact it was the very day that I got my check. I willed the box and its contents to the insurance company. Now you go tell that to Mr. Gissel if you like."

"Mr. Gissel?" I asked, looking hard at Claudie so he wouldn't give any secrets away.

"Mr. Gissel," she answered. "I've known from the first day what you were up to. Now go tell him if you want to."

"Oh, no, ma'am," I said, as I picked up my tablet and pencil, and I and Claudie started for the door, "I'm sure we'll not be seeing Mr. Gissel any more."

X I
Jules Rabinowitz Was Close

I WISH the people that make the maps of Texas would take a little closer look on how far it is from Dallas to Amarillo. It's farther than they think.

We had to raffle off Claudie's blue serge suit at a Missionary Society bazaar in Wichita Falls, and that only got us enough flat-tire and gasoline money to make Vernon. In Childress it took a week of very manual labor on Claudie's part — chopping cotton to be exact — and a lot of scrimping on mine to get a broken axle fixed on the trailer house. But we pulled into Amarillo late at night, broke and happy, about the middle of June. I remember one thing I said to sort of fit in with everything and make Claudie feel good. The way I put it was about the end of the rainbow with a pot of gold and all that we were coming to.

I remember also there was a hell of a sandstorm blowing at the time, the street lights looked like lemons on fire, and after we found a parking place I went to sleep in the trailer with grit in my teeth.

The next morning the sandstorm had about blown itself out, and we had enough gasoline to get out of town. So we did, since there wasn't any way to miss the headlines on the *Amarillo Globe,* "Weathers Hughes Leaves on World Tour." I didn't read it all, but mainly it told how Claudie's magnate cousin was going to be gone a year to talk to a lot of foreigners about peace.

We went out the road we'd come in on, and I drove so Claudie could study the headline and the picture on the front page showing his cousin, Weathers Hughes, climbing on a train.

"That's Stink Foot all right," was the only thing Claudie said in the first ten miles — he was so stunned; and I swear, none of the things I thought seemed worth saying.

The next ten miles produced the kind of a remark that often makes me sorry Claudie's so much bigger than I am. He put the paper down on the seat between us, like a man that has figured everything out, including the last detail; then he said, "We must've went to Amarillo too late."

About thirty miles out on the road that leads east from Amarillo there's a place where you can get up on a big rock by the roadside and look a long long ways. You can look farther and see less right there, I do believe, than you can anywhere else in the whole world — at least anywhere else in the State of Texas. I and Claudie agreed it might do us both good, the way we felt by now, to climb up on the rock and look a while. There wasn't enough room for both of us, so I let him go first. When he finally came down, he said, "They's a little old white cloud way off out there to the west, Clint."

Clouds don't do well in the Panhandle during the summer, and by the time I'd got up on the rock and spotted this one the sun had about burnt it off. So I watched a whirlwind start close by, with only a few dry thistles and stickers stirring at first in the yellow dust; I watched it twist and weave and grow until it was a mile or more high and the bottom bouncing along like a bull whip against the rocky ground. Then it sagged and petered out.

I was about ready to climb down when I saw a sight that you will not believe, and I'll admit that I didn't either, at first. It was a buffalo — a real live shaggy buffalo, standing in a rocky red gully not over a hundred yards away, and he was looking right back at me. He pawed his front feet a couple of times, then started loping toward us with his big fuzzy head lowered and swaying from side to side in front of a big plume of dust he kicked up as he ran.

"Get on back to the road, Claudie," I hollered. "Hurry. There's a buffalo after us."

I climbed down from the rock and passed Claudie before it soaked in on him what I'd said. Then, instead of running for our car so he could drive us off, Claudie pushed his way into our trailer house right after me.

"Just how," I asked him, "are we going to get away from any buffalo with both of us in this trailer house?"

Claudie could see his mistake by this time, and he started out to get in the car, but it was too late. The buffalo was standing just outside the trailer house door, staring in at us through the isinglass. He was a pretty mangy buffalo, with curved horns grown way long and sort of rusty-looking. When he moved his head his eyes stayed right on us, and I could see the milky white around the edges of his big mud-colored eyeballs. Also, there was a little yellow foam along both sides of his mouth.

"Claudie," I said, "that old booger don't look so mean to me now. Maybe he's only thirsty. Reckon we'd better give him a drink of water?"

"How?" he asked. "Where's any water?" and I remembered we didn't have a drop in the trailer house.

"Claudie," I said, "tell you what you do. Get that little stewer — you know, the one that don't leak — and drain some water out of the auto radiator for this buffalo."

"I can't get out; I'm skeered of him," he said.

"But no," I explained. "You can get out under the trailer right through this hole in the floor. You can crawl under the car to the place where we drain the radiator, and the buffalo can't get at you. Also, I will keep him busy back here looking at me."

Claudie was covered with dust and grease when he came back, but he had the stewer full of brown water, and I passed it to the buffalo without stepping outside the trailer house myself. And, of course, I was right.

He was awful thirsty, and after he'd drunk the water he bawled for more, so I spoke to Claudie and said, "We've got us a pretty valuable animal here, and I believe you'd better get him one more stewer full of that water."

Well, it turned out that we had found a fine friendly buffalo. We gave him some apples and part of a loaf of bread that we ate the rest of ourselves — along with some sardines. Claudie said he wondered how the buffalo would act if we got outside, so I said, "Why don't you try?" He did, and sure enough, the buffalo acted like a pet.

By noon we'd got used to him, and he was used to us. Claudie even got on his back and rode him all around the trailer house. "All we need now," I said, "besides some water for ourselves, is a way to get this buffalo to Amarillo. He's probably worth a lot of money to a zoo or a circus."

Claudie was rolling a cigarette at the time, and before he could answer me or put his sack of Bull Durham back in his pocket, that fool buffalo grabbed it and ate it. That little round yellow tag on the string was the last thing I saw as he stood there chewing up Claudie's smoking tobacco.

"Was it a full sack, Claudie?" I asked him.

"Nearly full," he said, and then the buffalo snorted, bellowed, pawed up a lot of dust from the ground, and started bucking. He made for us with his head lowered, and we barely got indoors in time. He ran and butted the trailer house so hard I knew something had to give, and it was tin that gave, not that buffalo's horns. Then he settled down and so did the dust, and pretty soon he was his same old gentle self again. I and Claudie both got out and rode him some more just to prove it.

I declare, I don't know how we'd have fared if the two sheriffs hadn't come along about the middle of the afternoon. "Sheriff's Department, Potter County," it said around a big white star on the side of their car.

"Here's your buffalo, Chuck," the fellow that got out of the car said. Chuck got out too, and they came over to the trailer house, both wearing pearl-handled pistols and silver sheriffs' badges.

"What are you doing with this buffalo?" they both seemed to be asking all at once.

"We found him here," I said, "and we've been taking good care of him, too."

"Well, he belongs to Quagmyer's Dog and Pony Show," one of the sheriffs said — the biggest one of the two. "He got away after the show last night. We're going to take him back and collect the reward."

"How?" I asked, and Chuck, the little sheriff, looked at the other one without saying anything.

"Maybe you fellows can watch him until we can send a truck for him," the big sheriff said.

"And maybe you can give us about five hundred dollars of the reward," I said. "If we don't keep him, he's liable to go out there," and I pointed west where there was enough country for a buffalo to go and hide in forever.

"The reward ain't but twenty-five dollars," the big sheriff stated.

We settled for ten dollars out of the reward if we still had the buffalo when they came back for him, and we had him all right. The sheriffs came along about sundown in a truck and brought along some water I'd told them we needed for our radiator.

2

The next morning, with the ten dollars in my pocket, I and Claudie went all over Amarillo looking for Quagmyer's Dog and Pony Show, since during the night I'd turned up with such a fine idea about the buffalo and Claudie that it fairly dazzled me. But I found the show was not of the size to do as big a town as Amarillo. It played in small towns only, and I learned at the newspaper office that it would go on that night at Canyon, Texas.

Claudie drove us the seventeen miles down to Canyon, and I kept him quiet all the way so I could think my whole idea out. We got there before noon, and the first thing I did was to study the poster about the show pasted up on the side of a feed store. I wanted to see what the buffalo did in the show. The poster had a lot about Celeste Booker, the daring lady bareback rider, and it showed her picture in black tights and red hair; it had some colored pictures of trained lions and tigers sitting up on stools while a guy in bright green clothes cracked a whip at them, and clowns; but I liked to have never found anything about the buffalo. Way down in one corner where they'd run low on glue and the edge of the picture was flapping in the wind, it mentioned several wild animals, and along with Gila monsters, anteaters, two elks, and a boa constrictor, it sort of admitted they had a buffalo, too. No picture of him at all.

"What a shame! What a waste of talent!" I told Claudie.

"Howzat?" Claudie asked, but I didn't go into it any further since I hadn't yet told him anything about my idea. I only set about to find the head man in the show.

"Mr. Quagmyer," I went up to the man and said where they had pointed him out to me in a little green diner across the street from the show tent. It was a diner made out of an old streecar, with the wheels off, and this guy was eating fried chicken at a table about where the motorman would have used to sit.

"Colonel Quagmyer, please," he answered without looking up. "Colonel A. Frisbie Quagmyer."

"Hightower is the name," I said, and I found I could hardly keep my eyes on the Colonel because the lady that was eating there at the table with him looked so familiar and pretty at the same time. I noticed, too, that she was eating with nice dainty manners and daubing around her mouth with the blue calico napkin every time she took a bite.

"Where have I seen that pretty face before?" I was wondering when the Colonel said — stern-like — "I'll see you outside later. Right now I'm eating lunch with my little niece here."

"Your niece? Please to meet you, ma'am," I said, taking off my hat, but she didn't look up also.

"Outside!" The Colonel seemed almost peevish.

"Yes, sir," I said, catching one more glance at the Colonel's niece that he was eating chicken with.

3

Well, this niece came out of the diner first, and in the bright sunlight her hair wasn't really red. It was the color of new corn silk, but fine enough to make corn silk look like old rusty baling wire.

"Please, ma'am," I said, tipping my hat, "is the Colonel about through eating? We wish to talk some business with him — I and my associate. Hightower is the name, and —"

"Tell it to him," she said and walked across the street to the show tent. I noticed her plum-purple dress was very tight in the waist.

"A man might like it at the time," I told Claudie, "but I could never really care for a lady that would be too friendly right at first." Then I saw the big billboard, and it all came to me where I'd seen that pretty face before. She was Celeste Booker, the lady bareback rider, but the picture didn't begin to do her justice.

"I b'lieve I've saw her before, too," Claudie said. "Like I thought when I first seen the picture."

"Oh, no, Claudie," I told him. "You're full of prunes. You never saw Celeste before."

"Yes, I have," he looked worried like he always does when he tries to think. "A long time ago."

"All right, men, what is it?" the Colonel was saying. He'd come out of the diner when we weren't looking, and I saw that he was a lot taller than he'd seemed sitting at the table. He was picking his teeth with a gold toothpick and holding his broad-brimmed straw hat in his hand. When he put it on, a lot of his hair, the color of a palomino's mane, still showed behind like senators' hair.

"It's about the buffalo," I began. "We're the ones that found him."

The Colonel said, "But, dammit, I've already paid the reward." Then he looked across the street toward the show tent. He had little eyes, and the skin under them was pink and puffy like persimmons after a hard freeze.

"What," I asked him, "does the buffalo do in the show?"

"Old Woodrow?" he asked. "What the hell can any buffalo do besides be?"

"Be what?"

"A buffalo. He's an animal that's almost extinct. That's the reason old Woodrow is with us."

"But Woodrow may not be so near to extinct as you'd think, Mister — I mean Colonel," I said. "He can act."

By this time some more people from the diner were hanging around, and the Colonel sized them up before he said out loud, "Well, I've played to overflow crowds in Madison Square Garden; I've given command performances before the crowned heads of Europe; I've been impresario to talent in the sparkling sawdust of the greatest shows on the globe; yet I have to be told in Canyon, Texas, that I have overlooked latent virtuosity in a tame buffalo. I bid you good day, gentlemen." And while everybody around laughed, the Colonel bowed and walked across the street to the show tent.

Trouble was, the Colonel didn't know me; a haughty spirit like that has always been just my dish. I walked right across the street with him, and at the main entrance to the tent I spoke. "Colonel, in Woodrow you have a feature attraction and don't know it. You have a bucking buffalo."

The Colonel threw back his head and laughed, "Why Woodrow is gentle as a pussy cat," he said. "The children all ride him. You're taking a lot of my time."

"Would you let us show you?"

"Now?" he said.

"Now," I told him. He was tough, but he saw he'd met his match. He agreed to let us put on our act inside the tent since the show didn't come off until that night, and by the time word went around among the show folks we had a pretty good crowd. Celeste, the Colonel's niece, came too, at the last minute, and one of the show flunkies marched old Woodrow out into the ring. He seemed to recognize me and Claudie; he mooed a little and came over to us, shaking his shaggy head.

"Who's going to ride this ferocious bucking buffalo?" Colonel Quagmyer asked, laughing, and all the show people laughed. In fact, about everything the Colonel would say seemed funny to them.

"My associate, Claudie," I answered; "as long, that is, as he can stay on," and they all laughed again.

"Claudie Hughes!" someone said, and it was Celeste. "Where all have you been?" She almost squealed, she was so glad to see him.

"Effie," Claudie said, and they kissed. "Effie Wiggins," he turned to me. "She's my cousin from Flomaton, Alabama."

Celeste was red in the face, and so was the Colonel by now. "Celeste Booker is only my stage name," she went on to tell him. And all this time I was trying to figure out what kin Claudie was to the Colonel.

"Come on, the show must go on," Colonel Quagmyer said out loud.

"But, first," I spoke up, "I and Claudie need a few minutes alone with Woodrow."

The buffalo followed us out, and we took him into a little side-show tent. I looked everywhere to see that nobody was around, and then I whispered, "All right, Claudie, slip Woodrow another sack of Bull Durham."

"But I ain't gunna ride him after he's et it," Claudie argued.

"Oh, yes, you are; we're in the money, Claudie. This is no time to be unreasonable."

Claudie didn't get the point until the show people started yelling for us to come out, but after I'd given him the ten dollars reward money, he agreed. He gave Woodrow the sack of tobacco, and damned if he didn't seem to like it even more than he had the day before. Then, with Claudie on him, I led Woodrow into the big tent.

"Ladieeees and gennntlemen," Colonel Quagmyer announced, "Woodrow, the bucking buffalo." He was laughing fit to kill, and all the show people laughed and laughed. Then it happened.

Woodrow snorted a couple of times and made for Colonel Quagmyer. The Colonel got behind a tent pole just in the nick; then Woodrow started to buck, and for a lot longer than you'd think, Claudie stayed on him. But about the fourth or fifth buck was a lollapalouza, and it sent Claudie sailing off through the air like a big old water bird of some kind. He landed in the steam calliope and then tumbled off limp onto the ground. Celeste ran over to see how dead he was, but before she got there Claudie got up and dusted himself off, and while he still looked a mite dazed and ruffled, he was coming around fast. And there stood Woodrow, licking the seat of Claudie's pants as friendly as ever again.

"Now, Colonel, I hope you see what I mean," I told him, loud enough for Celeste to hear. By this time all the show folks were cheering, and I figured like this: If people in the show itself take on like this over our act — people that are used to the best in entertainment and have been all their lives — what would the public do?

The Colonel tried to run down the act some, but when I said, "O.K. then; let's just drop the idea," he followed me to the tent door.

"How did you make Woodrow buck?" was the way he put it.

"Colonel Quagmyer," I said as all the show people stood around, and Celeste too, with her eyes very bright, "Woodrow comes from a long line of fierce and proud ancestors. His ancestors were here, kicking up dust, bucking and enjoying themselves long before our ancestors got up the *Mayflower* trip. All the time you've kept Woodrow in the cellar, using him for no act except to be, he's been building up the ginger that was born right in him from his ancestors. I and Claudie have simply brought it out. That's all."

"But how . . ."

"You couldn't be expecting to learn that and then use some other bronco buster, could you, Colonel?" I cut in. Oh, I had him right where the wool was short.

"Certainly not," he said, acting like a Colonel with his feelings hurt.

"Another thing, Colonel," I pointed out. "Just imagine the billing 'WOODROW AND CLAUDIE, THE ONLY SHOW IN THE WORLD FEATURING A WILD BUCKING BUFFALO.' The act will put you in big towns like Amarillo and Lubbock. You're through with skirting the edges. You are in the big time."

You can see how, standing on such firm ground as this, I and Claudie made our deal to get on the Quagmyer pay roll and for our board, too.

Sure enough, our feature got us into bigger towns right away. At Lubbock the following week Colonel Quagmyer threw away all the old billboard signs and had some new ones made. Woodrow took some of the space away from Celeste, and after she saw the new billing she would not even look at Woodrow, she was so furious. It seemed to turn her against Claudie, too — her own cousin — but not against me.

4

With being featured and all, Claudie soon let it go to his head. He wanted to wear a green uniform in his act, one with brass buttons and gold braid like the lion tamer's, so only to humor him I made Quagmyer buy him one. Also Claudie wore a big ten-gallon hat in the act with a little blue feather in it, and pretty soon he was putting on all sorts of airs. When Woodrow would throw him, he'd lie there on the ground where he'd hit; he'd wiggle and squirm like a worm in hot ashes, all so as to scare the crowd; then he'd get up and bow, grinning like a jackass eating briers to make the people cheer more. Claudie went to putting on all kinds of airs, and started claiming kin with Colonel Quagmyer himself, but the Colonel didn't. It was almost disgusting, but I did notice that he began to look better and happier than I'd ever seen him before. So did Woodrow.

I told Claudie the day we played Brownwood, "We must be about the finest influence that ever came into Woodrow's life. They're feeding him better, his mange is improving, and he's getting some exercise these days. Just to be is no life even for a buffalo. It's right next to being plumb extinct."

"Let's give Woodrow a better brand of tobacco," Claudie urged. "He must be tard of that Bull Durham."

"The best," I told him, "is none too good for Woodrow." So the next day we took him out behind the tent and offered him his choice of several other kinds of tobacco. But he wouldn't touch a one of them. He had only the Bull Durham habit.

Celeste came around the corner of the tent about

this time, and I asked Claudie to kindly take Woodrow away so I could talk to her some. This was something I was doing more and more of, since my part in Woodrow's act left me with plenty of leisure time every day. I was finding out by this time that she was about the finest company in the whole show, with a nice personality and all, as well as the prettiest, whitest set of teeth I'd ever seen growing out of gums. How she could be so neat and little and pretty and still be Claudie's own cousin was beyond me, but I was liking her so much I didn't give a damn whose cousin she was. Celeste had been showing in several ways that she could care for me too. That was the day she said why didn't I come by her dressing room some night and talk to her after her act, and that was the night I went. Her act was over, and it wasn't near time for Woodrow to go on, since he was always last so nobody would leave and stop buying popcorn and stuff until the very end. And that was the night Celeste really lifted the scales from my eyes about Quagmyer. "Clint," she said, as she rolled a cigarette, "I'm afraid Colonel Quagmyer doesn't like you very much."

"Why?" I asked.

"He's jealous of you."

"How can that be, Celeste? He's your uncle."

"Well, confidentially, he ain't any uncle of mine. We only claim kin so the show people won't talk."

This really flabbergasted me. Just why Celeste would

be telling me this I couldn't tell. I said, "Celeste, I haven't figured Quagmyer was all he was cracking himself up to be for some time now."

"He ain't," she admitted; then she started speaking in a very confidential way and said, "Colonel Quagmyer is sort of new to the show. He's been the owner for less than a year."

"How'd he get aholt of the show, anyway?" I asked.

"Well, he went to see the show last spring when it was playing in Tuscaloosa, Alabama. He was running a pool hall there at the time. The show had an elephant then — a little old flea-bitten elephant, a she. Quagmyer managed some way to get stepped on by the elephant — she stepped on his foot, I believe — and he fell down with a sprained back. So he sued 'em for fifty thousand dollars and tied up the whole kit and caboodle with liens and things. Quagmyer stayed sort of paralyzed until the case was tried and the jury in Tuscaloosa gave him forty thousand dollars. The whole show wasn't worth that much, so Quagmyer took it over."

"Are you pretty sweet on Quagmyer, Celeste?" I had to know by then, with her showing this way how much she cared for me and all.

"I haven't exactly quit him — yet . . ." I remember she was holding my hand at the time she said this; then she went on, "Now, Clint, there's something I want you to tell me."

"Oh no, Celeste; you're a fine girl, and I'm getting fonder of you every way, but I'm not about to tell you that." I stood up and let her hand go.

"What?"

"How we make Woodrow buck. That's what you wanted to know, wasn't it, Celeste?"

"Oh heavens, no," she laughed. "I know how you make Woodrow buck." She was teasing me; I could tell from the look out of her pretty blue eyes. I know women. Then Celeste got very serious and said, "I only wanted to see whether you really trusted me."

"It isn't that I don't trust you, Celeste. I do, but I can't tell you that," and she looked so hurt I thought she'd cry. If you want to know the truth right here, some tears did come into her eyes.

"Don't worry, Clint," she said, and her lips were damp and pouty. "I would never tell Quagmyer."

The only thing I wanted to do right then was to kiss Celeste to make her feel better, but she pushed me away and said, "No, Clint, you don't trust me."

By the time we got to Waco, Colonel Quagmyer was beginning to show that he liked me less and less, but he was getting nicer to Claudie all the time; so I had to speak to Claudie about it, and he admitted that the Colonel had been working on him. First the Colonel had agreed that they were really relatives on account of both being kin to Celeste — a thing I knew better than, but I didn't let on to Claudie; then the

Colonel had offered him his pay and mine too if he'd tell how we made Woodrow buck.

"I have been tempted, too, Claudie," I said, "but you know what the Bible says about temptation. A man is not supposed to yield to it; specially if it might mean his job."

"But I'm the one this here buffalo bucks off every night. My joints is getting loose."

"Don't you see it's a trick, Claudie? Once the Colonel learned our trade secret, he'd fire you, too, and use Hung How, that little old Chinaman that cooks for the show. Hung How has been eying your job for weeks. He wants to wear that green suit."

"He'll never get it." Claudie looked his stubborn best when he said that, and I knew this fire was put out for a while.

It wasn't long after this that the telegram came from Houston asking us to go to the rodeo there and take Woodrow's act. After all, it was bound to happen; anything in Texas that is as good as Woodrow — and there is nothing else like it in the whole damned state — is bound to wind up in Houston. It's the way the state is set up.

The Colonel wired back that he'd go if they'd take Celeste's bareback act too, and they agreed. Matter of fact, they'd have taken a temperance lecture if they'd had to, they were so anxious to get Woodrow.

I explained to Colonel Quagmyer that I and Claudie

wanted just exactly one half of all he got paid in Houston, and he finally had to take us up on this, since I stood pat. But when he agreed, he was reddish-purple in the face, like a west-of-Amarillo sunset during a dust storm.

5

We wound up the regular circuit in Sweetwater a week before we were due in Houston, and by this time we had Woodrow famous. Even a little spell of indigestion he had in Laredo made the front page in the San Antonio paper. All this made Claudie more temperamental by the day — he got to where he wore his green suit all the time. Myself, I had to worry more and more about our trade secret, and not even telling Celeste, but it was breaking my heart not to, and hers also because I didn't trust her enough to tell her.

From Sweetwater we all went to Houston by train, except that I rode ahead with Celeste and Quagmyer on the fast train that had sleepers and diners and everything, while Claudie rode on a much slower train that brought Woodrow also. "Be sure nothing happens to Woodrow on the trip," I told Claudie just before we left Sweetwater.

All the way to Houston, Celeste teased me — the way people don't do, I figured, if they don't really like you — and right before Colonel Quagmyer too. She teased me in the club car, in the diner, and other places, too, on the train. The Colonel would listen to all of this he could stand; I mean until his face would twitch all over and the blue veins in his temples would stand out and quiver; then he'd get up and walk in the train aisles to cool himself off. What Celeste was teasing me about was still claiming she knew how we made Woodrow buck. She kept saying she'd spied on me and Claudie.

When we got to Houston we found we were all over town — on posters, that is. The big billing was our act, of course, with pictures of Woodrow all blown up, his eyes blazing and blue smoke coming out of both nostrils.

While we waited for Woodrow and Claudie to get there, I found I was seeing less and less of the Colonel and more and more of Celeste. I found, too, that this was slap-dab exactly the way I wanted it. And long before Woodrow and Claudie came, I knew I had fallen for Celeste about as hard as a man has any business falling for anybody, except for one thing: why did she keep pestering me to tell her how we made Woodrow buck?

"You can prove to me that you love me," she said one day out at Hermann Park Zoo. "Just tell me about Woodrow." Her arm was around my waist as we walked along looking at all the wild animals, and what I was thinking, to tell the truth, was that Jules Rabinowitz's crystal had been right after all. Jules had misread it a little, but he was close enough to suit me.

What he'd thought was money flaring up the crystal that way out close to Amarillo wasn't money at all; it was another kind of riches. It was beauty and love and a pretty girl like Celeste that I was crazy about by now. Enough, if you ask me, to set a man on fire inside, so I began to understand about what had happened to Jules's crystal ball. Maybe the time had come, I thought, to tell Celeste about Woodrow and the Bull Durham.

I watched a slippery old hippopotamus climb up out of his wallowing place, and while the red and yellow parrots squawked outside in the sun I sat there and thought and thought — like about Samson that was so taken, and then taken in, by the Gaza woman, Delilah; also about Joseph that, according to the Bible, walked right off, leaving Potiphar's wife talking to herself there by the couch — and I said, "Celeste, I do love you all right, but Houston is a hell of a long ways from that trailer house in El Paso for a man to be telling a trade secret — even to somebody he loves."

Well, with all the rest we did in Houston, this was about where we left things until Woodrow's and Claudie's train finally got there. And by the time it did, the Houston people had decided to change the place where we were to go on. The Coliseum wouldn't hold our crowd, so they had it out at the big First National Bank Stadium near Rice Institute. And what a crowd! They were still gathering when Celeste got into the black tights she filled out so nice and went on first with her bareback riding act. Matter of fact, it was a sort of a preliminary they made out of Celeste, and I didn't like it a bit.

I went around to Celeste's dressing room after her act to cheer her up for being done wrong by in the program; also to hold her hand, if you want me to be frank about it. We had nearly an hour to wait while some other small-time calf roping and steer bulldogging acts were run off. Naturally, Woodrow wasn't to go on until last.

I sat there by Celeste watching her comb out her pretty red hair and talking to her until all of a sudden it was later than I thought. What really brought the time up was that Claudie stuck his ugly face inside Celeste's dressing room.

He was all dressed up in his green suit with braid and brass buttons, but he had the same baffled look on his face as the guy I saw in a fine picture once, the guy with a hoe in his hand — except of course Claudie didn't have any hoe in his hand. Claudie's mouth was working, but he wasn't saying anything, he was so wrought up.

"Take it easy, Claudie," I said. "What's the trouble?"

"I haven't got it," he managed to say. "Have you?"

"You mean —" I said, and I knew what he meant. He'd forgotten Woodrow's tobacco.

"Hell, no!" I told him. "You're the one that's supposed to have it."

"But I forgot."

"Then we can't go on —"

"What's the trouble, fellows?" Celeste asked.

"Oh, nothing; nothing at all," I told her. Then I turned back to Claudie. "Where's the closest store?" I found I was yelling at him.

"I've already asked about that," Claudie said. "The stores are a mile or more away, and they're all closed up this time of night."

"How long before we go on?" I asked him, and Colonel Quagmyer answered me as he walked into Celeste's dressing room. "Five minutes," he said, "but don't hurry. It may be six or seven. Woodrow is waiting for you in the little tent out there."

Outside there was the hum and the buzz of all that big crowd ready for our act, and the whole thing seemed to be pressing down on my insides like a sack of wet oats. I noticed that Claudie's color was awful bad and getting worse by the minute. The green suit only brought it out more.

"What's the matter, Claudie?" Quagmyer asked. "Stage fright?" But Claudie didn't have any answer. He was all froze up, and so was I.

Things got so quiet then that when Celeste spoke up I felt myself flinch. What she said was "I feel like a smoke."

Quagmyer offered her a ready-roll, but she said, "No, I'll just make my own, thanks."

She opened her purse, but what she took out wasn't

the tin can of Prince Albert, the kind Celeste always rolled hers with; it was a brand-new sack of Bull Durham. When Claudie saw what I saw, his mouth flew open and his front teeth showed more than ever. Claudie's teeth never were very close together, and this time he looked like a man fixing to eat a pumpkin through a picket fence.

Celeste rolled, then fired up her new cigarette and laid the sack there on the dressing table so that the little tag at the end of the string was hanging down over the edge. When she got up, she left the Bull Durham sack right where it was. She flashed a sweet cozy wink at me; then took Quagmyer by the arm. "Come on, Uncle Frisbie," she said, "let's go get ourselves settled in our seats so we can see the best part of this show."

And as they walked out I thought no knights in tin suits or heroes in Hollywood ever loved their women any more than I loved Claudie's cousin Celeste.

1/69

Date Due

JUN 2 4 '55			
SEP 4 '56			
JUN 9 '57			
MAY 1974			
JUL 1974			
SEP 1974			
FEB 1975			
MAR 12 1977			
MAY 1978			
MAY 1978			
JUL 1978			

169693

Anderson, Dillon
Claudie's kinfolks

2c